MRS KECKLY SENDS HER REGARDS:
THE LAST DAYS OF ABRAHAM LINCOLN

By Tim Jorgenson

xulon
PRESS

MRS KECKLY SENDS HER REGARDS:
THE LAST DAYS OF ABRAHAM LINCOLN
by Tim Jorgenson

Printed in the United States of America

ISBN 978-1-60266-788-4

Unless otherwise indicated, Bible quotations are taken from the King James Version.

www.xulonpress.com

With warm regards to my family and friends.

PROLOGUE

—◊◊◊—

In the late 1890s I first visited Sister Elizabeth Keckly. She said she wanted me to hear her out about people close to her heart. A good number of visits, she said, would be necessary to accomplish this. Would I consent to visiting her? How could I say 'No'? She was a member of our parish. And she had been the closest family friend of our dear President Lincoln and his wife, Mary Todd. I have never regretted those visits.

Elizabeth Keckly was a remarkable person in so many ways. She knew many people on both sides of our nation's great civil conflict. She was on intimate terms with the elite of Washington and Richmond. This intimacy was a testament to her discretion, her business acumen, and not least the creative skills that placed her in such demand. With her gifts she was blessed and she was a blessing. But she was also burdened. To her dying day she agonized over her dearest friendship, the one she lost. In so far as possible she wanted the coming generation to know she never meant harm to any of the Lincolns.

I listened and have tried to remember all she had to say about the President and Mary Todd and about the others in her remembrance. What I have written mixes many voices: hers, others, and not least my own. I do not apologize for this. A blessed recollection is a gathering in love. I do however apologize for not presenting the reader with even the image of Elizabeth's quilt, the forever-silent testament of her love for the Lincolns. That quilt (lost to me) was hers, these words are mine, but love and beauty and truth were, are, and will always be of the Lord. In His grace, by His grace, and for His grace, Sister Elizabeth lived and lives. May she be so remembered.

> Dr Francis Grimké, Pastor
> Fifteenth Street Presbyterian Church
> District of Columbia
> February 12, 1909

CHAPTER 1

—⁓—

Mrs Keckly, baptized Elizabeth, on March 4th, 1865, resolved to a task that would come and go and come again. She resolved she must make a quilt for Abraham and Mary Todd Lincoln. The quilt, she hoped, would reaffirm for the two a love taxed by the Civil War, perhaps taxed even before the war.

None can doubt that Elizabeth was a gifted woman. None can doubt the President was a gifted man and, after all, March 4th marked the beginning of his second term as President. As for Mary Todd, debate about her gifts may never end. The three lived in a difficult time, a time that could cause thoughtful men and women to wonder about God. The trials of the time were more than momentous, more than momentary. They would mark many for death. And the living would often be marked with wounds that never healed.

Where was God in all of this? Had He kept faith with the faithful? Had He given hope when hope was needed amidst the slaughter? Or, was hope, like the slaughter, pointless? Where was God's love? It seemed, still seems, that only God's love can redeem the death, the savagery, the hurt, the lives so desperately in need of His fulfillment. In this Civil War had He sent His light and love as He once had in Jesus? Had He?

Some, some few, the always few (we can hope), have answered and will answer with a resounding 'No'. War is but savage butchery, they say, a pointless enterprise in a futile existence. Wars *can* be that way. Who can deny the bloodiness of war? War and rumors of war will always abound in a sinful world. The world cannot deny war. But need we deny God for that? The President and Elizabeth Keckly (God be praised) believed in God's redeeming presence even in every pain, even in war. Their story warrants telling. As Elizabeth was wont to say, the finger — or was it the hand — of God touched her that March 4th, prodding her to do something for the Lincolns. In the name of God's love, she owed something to the Lincolns.

She had performed many a civic duty. Elizabeth was a mover in the community. For her work in founding aid societies for so-called 'contrabands' she surely deserves remembrance. Yet how many former slaves liberated by Northern armies, in other words how many contrabands, had heard of Mrs Elizabeth Keckly? Her beneficiaries were almost countless; the benefactress is almost unknown. Benefaction is its own reward, to be sure, but benefaction is not enough. To do good is good; to free up to do good is greater. The Lincoln marriage for four years had been in bondage to war. The Lincolns needed to be freed up, freed up from the burdens of war. The hand of God could and would bring the war to an end. In the meantime He would, as He always had, provide signs of hope — to the nation and to the Lincolns.

That March 4th began what Elizabeth was wont to call the Forty Days, until April 14, 1865, when the President was assassinated. March 4th to April 14th wasn't exactly forty days, as Elizabeth knew, but the interval was close enough to 40 to recall the work of God. God's work, she'd say, needs recalling. Moreover, she'd say some things could be close and other things had to be right on the mark. Close enough can have more meaning than right on the mark. Elizabeth knew that from an early age. To get anywhere in this world you had to know what to do on the mark and whatever else you needed to 'let easy' as she'd say, taking after the man she called 'papa'.

Elizabeth said she'd never been one to memorize speeches. But her mama taught and her papa prodded her to learn and to appreciate learning. Besides sewing, her mama had taught her from two books kept in secret, a Bible and a Webster's dictionary. There was no telling when either might be discovered. So memorizing Bible verses and Webster's definitions came as early as the sewing lessons.

Her mama called the Bible the 'Power o' the Word and World,' the dictionary the 'Power o' the Mouth and Mind.' 'Use 'em wisely,' said her mama. And little Lizzy did. 'Mo' important than the sewing,' said her mama, and 'the sewin's right important. Could be your ticket,' she'd say to Lizzy, 'ticket to freedom.' *Could be* became *was*, said Elizabeth. And *was* eventually led to the White House.

March 4, 1865, was better for ducks than people. The driving rain had driven the vice presidential inauguration indoors to the Senate chamber. 'A good thing, too,' said Mary Todd, because Andrew Johnson (the new Vice President) was as 'drunk as a skunk and no better than a Tennessee jackass.' The crowd was spared his 'drivel', said Mary Todd, but the rain didn't let up until her Abraham was to speak. If it hadn't stopped, the President would have spoken under the Capitol dome. The work on the dome had just been completed. Mr Lincoln chose to come outside. Little did he know what everyone later learned, that his assassin was among the men assembled on the east Capitol steps to see him inaugurated.

While everyone agrees the sun came shining through during the ceremony, recollections diverge from that point. Mary Todd remembered the sun first shone through the moment she kissed the Bible upon which her Abraham had sworn the oath of office. She'd just been handed the Bible by Chief Justice Chase. Most other folks remember the sun breaking through as the President delivered the inaugural address, which preceded the swearing in. Elizabeth wouldn't want to deny the sun showered rays on Mary Todd, but the fact of the matter is Mary Todd was often at odds with just about everyone else. Often enough she was wrong, way off the mark.

How ever could Mr Lincoln have been attracted to someone like that? 'Mary Todd had her charms and her ways,' said Elizabeth. Of the two, Mr Lincoln was more than charming. He was more than a politician. He was a prophet just short of prophecy. Funny thing: he never really had a good speaking voice. His voice was high pitched, almost piercing. It didn't sound deep but the ideas he voiced carried well and far. Maybe because people always knew he meant every word he said, they listened. At the beginning of his second inaugural Mr Lincoln talked about his speech four years earlier. Then he got into 'the meat and potatoes', said Elizabeth. As he spoke the umbrellas came down. Shafts of sunlight crisscrossed the President's speech.

> *On the occasion corresponding to this four years ago, all thoughts were anxiously directed to an impending civil war. All dreaded it — all sought to avert it. While the inaugural address was being delivered from this place, devoted altogether to saving the Union without war, insurgent agents were in the city seeking to destroy it without war — seeking to dissolve the Union, and divide effects, by negotiation. Both parties deprecated war; but one of them would make war rather than let the nation survive; and the other would accept war rather than let it perish. And the war came.*

Some may have nodded a Yes to those words but the crowd stood all ears. The President continued.

> *One eighth of the whole population were colored slaves, not distributed generally over the Union, but localized in the Southern part of it. These slaves constituted a peculiar and powerful interest. All knew that this interest was, somehow, the cause of the war. To strengthen, perpetuate, and extend this interest was the object for which the insurgents would rend the Union, even by war; while the government claimed no right to do more than to restrict the territorial enlargement of it. Neither party expected for the war, the magnitude or the duration, which it has already attained. Neither anticipated that the cause of the conflict might cease with, or even before, the conflict itself would cease. Each looked for an easier triumph, and a result less fundamental and astounding. Both read the same Bible and pray to the same God; and each invokes His aid against the other. It may seem strange that any men should dare to ask a just God's assistance in wringing their bread from the sweat of other men's faces, but let us judge not that we be not judged.*

There was a smattering of applause in the crowd.

The prayers of both could not be answered; that of neither has been answered fully. The Almighty has His own purposes. 'Woe unto the world because of offenses! For it must needs be that offenses come; but woe to that man by whom the offense cometh!'

A hearty applause met that statement.

If we shall suppose that American slavery is one of those offenses which, in the providence of God, must needs come, but which, having continued through His appointed time, He now wills to remove, and that He gives to both North and South, this terrible war, as the woe due to those by whom the offense came, shall we discern therein any departure from those divine attributes which the believers in a Living God always ascribe to Him? Fondly do we hope — fervently do we pray — that the mighty scourge of war may speedily pass away.

There was applause accompanied by cheers.

Yet, if God wills that it continue, until all the wealth piled by the bond-man's two hundred and fifty years of unrequited toil shall be sunk, and until every drop of blood drawn with the lash, shall be paid by another drawn with the sword, as was said three thousand years ago, so still it must be said 'the judgments of the Lord are true and righteous altogether.'

With malice toward none; with charity for all; with firmness in the right, as God gives us to see the right, let us strive on to finish the work we are in; to bind up the nation's wounds; to care for him who shall have borne the battle, and for his widow, and his orphan — to do all which may achieve and cherish a just and a lasting peace among ourselves and with all nations.

The President had finished in sunlight but the breath of the audience seemed taken away. Then came a sustained roar of applause. As the applause receded a band struck up 'The Battle Hymn of the Republic' or at least that's how Elizabeth remembered the occasion. The hymn seemed like a benediction to the President's own words. What else could follow?

The war would continue for a time. Who could expect otherwise? But, God willing, Elizabeth hoped the war wouldn't last past summer's end. General Lee and his forces were hemmed in around Richmond, Virginia, and her old hometown, Petersburg. Encirclement was almost inevitable. The Southern Fox was no longer dealing with Northern generals who were all shadow and little substance. General Grant was like the day's rain, unrelenting but with a soft spot when the occasion demanded it. The only occasion would be Southern surrender. Grant was doing everything to run the South out of men, out of land, and out of time.

As for Mr Lincoln, he just seemed to be plumb running out. Elizabeth had seen enough men who had been taxed and lashed to the limit, but never one so exhausted as the President. Almost everyone wanted peace, it seemed, but few *needed* it as much as the President. He was the picture of exhaustion. So peace, it seemed, would be a personal blessing for him. But would it be? The North and South could have all the peace a man might want, but what if there were no peace in a man's own household? Peace was more than an end of hostilities. Mr Lincoln knew that. That's why he was so concerned about 'malice toward none' and 'charity for all'. Peace meant goodwill, not indifference and separation.

But being apart was the sand in the jam at the White House. Elizabeth loved them both, but how could she help bring the President and First Lady together again? Not that they were disloyal to one another. No. And not that they didn't care about one another. No. Nor were there any displays of disaffection. But the two were so different, so apart. Elizabeth had always puzzled how they could stick together in the first place. Yet they were husband and wife. And Elizabeth loved them.

She adored 'Mr Abe', as she called him. After Willie died Mr Lincoln had encouraged Elizabeth to address him other than as

'Mr President'. Said he, she'd practically become a member of the family. She had prepared Willie's body for burial. She had been with Mary and the President in their private grieving over Willie. Calling him 'Mr President' would no longer do. Elizabeth was pleased to respond to this recognition. She decided to call the President 'Mr Abe', a casserole name that mixed the formal and the familiar. Perhaps Mr Lincoln would have been satisfied with merely 'Abe' but Elizabeth would only be satisfied if 'Abe' were preceded by 'Mister'. That was *his* due as President. Anyway, he liked the casserole. He called Elizabeth 'Madame Keckly' or 'Mrs Keckly' and occasionally 'Madame Elizabeth'. She liked those names. She cherished the friendship and the respect the names implied.

There were no questions about address when Mary Todd Lincoln and Elizabeth first met. Elizabeth had been summoned to Willard's Hotel, where the Lincolns were staying in the days before the 1861 inauguration. Madame Keckly had been summoned there along with other candidate dressmakers to afford Mary Todd the opportunity to pick her first dressmaker (or 'mantua-maker' as a dressmaker was called then). Elizabeth thought she had little chance of winning the right to make Mrs Lincoln's inaugural gown, the one she'd wear to the inaugural reception and ball. Elizabeth was the last candidate given admittance to talk with the imminent First Lady. Without pretense or ploy Mrs Lincoln told Elizabeth she wanted *her* to make the inaugural dress. A rose-colored moiré antique fabric had already been purchased. All it needed now was someone of stellar reputation to make it into a stunning dress. Mary Todd knew of Elizabeth's reputation as a top dressmaker in St Louis. She'd heard about her through Springfield friends.

Making that inaugural dress proved a successful trial for Elizabeth, not only because her rates were so low. She was more than good; she was truly 'stellar' in Mary Todd's opinion. Elizabeth or Elizabeth's shop would make Mary Todd another 15 dresses over the next five months. Mary Todd called her new dressmaker 'Lizzy' or 'Lizbeth' and soon insisted she be called 'Mary'. Elizabeth would call the First Lady more often 'Mary Todd' or 'Mary T'. After all, Southern custom preferred the use of middle names.

From the outset Elizabeth would hear, see, and participate in things at the White House as few others could. By late 1861 and early 1862 she saw, as few could, that Mary Todd was grievously disappointed with her life in the White House. This disappointment was grounded in several things, not least a Washington society still wedded to the Southern elite and a free press wedded to slime. Mary Todd could outshine the 'capital snobs', as she called them. She as First Lady had more resources than they. As for the press, they might hurl slime at her, but they hurled 'manure' at her husband. The least she could do, must do, would be to stand by her man and toss the papers into the fire. 'Fire and forget' was her rule of press. But there was no forgetting what she lived with. What she lived with was an all-too-frequent loneliness. Elizabeth began to appreciate this when draping Mary Todd for a low-cut, off-the-shoulder white satin gown with black accents to be worn at a reception and ball of February 1862. The white and black theme was in honor of the recently widowed Queen Victoria.

'You know, Lizzy, my man has become a polygamist," said Mary Todd.

Elizabeth looked up at Mary Todd, dumbstruck. She saw a twinkle in the First Lady's eye. "You're joshing me, Mary T."

Mary Todd replied, "I want to say things to you I wouldn't say to anyone else. Can't say to anyone else, really. But I need to say them, if I'm not to go crazy."

"Yes," said Elizabeth. She reached for a scissors and sheared off excess at the bottom of the gown-in-the-making. "Mr Abe don't have time to be a polygamist, Mary T. He don't have time for anything hardly but this war."

"That's what I mean, Lizzy. Legally, he's married to me. But in every other way he's married to the war."

Elizabeth kept on working, not knowing what to say. Then Mary Todd, taking hold of Elizabeth's shearing arm, spoke again, "Don't say a word of this to anyone. I need a friend I can trust."

"I will be that friend," said Elizabeth. And she was. From that moment she was not only Mary Todd's primary mantua-maker. She was a member of the household, almost, and certainly a friend.

Elizabeth continued to reside at the Lewis household, in a brick row house at 388 Twelfth Street. Walker and Virginia Lewis provided her room and board and 'extra', said Elizabeth. Virginia, or Ginny as she was remembered, was a mother and a seamstress. Ginny would never even think of comparing her skills to those of Elizabeth but Elizabeth used her from time to time, especially when she got in a pinch. The Lewises had five children in their household during the Civil War. Walker was employed in government service, at first as a messenger, then later as a steward. His work and Elizabeth's boarding provided most of the family's income. The family was anchored in the Fifteenth Street Church, where Brother Walker served as an elder (Praise the Lord).

If Mary Todd needed a friend to be candid with, so did Elizabeth. As Walker would often say, 'The Lord provides.' The Lewis home became Elizabeth's place of candor, even before she became a close companion of the First Lady. Not that Elizabeth was a torrent of disclosure and disaffection. She was proud to have the White House as one of her many customers. She was delighted that Mary Todd would place so much trust in her. But she was disturbed by the sadness and strain that seemed to hold the White House in its grip. The stress caused by the war was understandable and impossible to alleviate short of the war's coming to an end. Or so Elizabeth thought early on. As the war progressed and as she grew in knowledge of the President and the First Lady, she began to realize she might play an indispensable role, perhaps even a God-given role, in bridging the chasm that had grown between husband and wife. She suspected it had been growing even before the Lincolns came to Washington.

As she would tell the Lewises the evening of March 4th, "I've had no idea how to help Mr Abe and Mary Todd, but for some time I've known they needed help. That's why I've decided to make them a quilt." Elizabeth talked a bit about the quilt and then she resumed talking about the Lincolns. "No one's closer to Mary than me, no one, not even any of her sisters. As for Mr Abe, he has friends, sure, and plenty o' people workin' for him. But who can he turn to to talk about how Mary Todd is…is…

"Going crazy?" said Ginny.

"Well, I don't know if I'd ever go that far, Ginny. She's got some peculiar habits, spending money and so forth…"

"Seeing spiritualists," Walker interjected.

"Well, you and I don't see eye to eye on that, Walker, but she's maybe over usin' the spiritualists, just like she overdoes a lotta things. But it's all to make up for what she lacks, so she feels: a husband. She's married, for sure, but in ways they're still strangers to one another. He's a man of God…"

"Amen," said Walker.

"And she's so individualistic, you know what I mean?"

"Peculiar," said Ginny.

"You like those dictionary words, Lizbeth," said Walker.

"Find a better word than 'individualistic' or don't blame me," said Elizabeth.

"I don't, not at all. You should be a teacher in one of our schools."

Ginny spoke up, "She's got more than enough to do, Walker. She's heard that before. She's just tryin' to see whether we think this idea of making a quilt for the Lincolns is a good idea."

"I know," said Walker.

"I think it's a good idea, 'Lizbeth," said Ginny. "When would you be givin' it away to them?"

"I don't know. Maybe their wedding anniversary."

"When's that?" asked Ginny.

"You know, I have to find out the exact date. It's sometime in the fall."

"That should give you enough time," said Walker.

Coaxing the anniversary date from Mary Todd didn't prove difficult. Mary Todd liked talking about herself. The Lincolns, she said, were married November 4, 1842. She would tell Elizabeth other things, not necessarily easy to hear, even if revelations were more 'let easy' than on the mark in the telling. There would be much to hear and bear in the days ahead.

CHAPTER 2

By late afternoon Inauguration Day the rain had resumed, though more lightly than in the morning. As Elizabeth walked up the White House driveway, she could see the sentinel standing guard at the front door. From her purse she'd have to retrieve a pass card to gain admittance.

The sentinel was a wounded campaigner assigned White House duty. From the earliest days of the war, soldiers had been posted about the Presidential mansion. But the pass card was a recent innovation. The card bore the signature of Ward Lamon. Mr Lamon was a Virginian who had moved to Illinois and become a friend of Mr Lincoln. He had made the protective arrangements for Mr Lincoln's travel to Washington back in '61. He had overseen those arrangements ever since. Despite the dangers of the time, access to the President, Elizabeth observed, had hardly been different than going to market, at least until recently. Anyone who wanted to, it seemed, could 'skidaddle' to the second floor corridor outside Mr Abe's office. Every day except Sunday the corridor was crowded with petitioners seeking office, seeking a pardon for someone, seeking something or other from the President. The new passes helped stem the tide of petitioners but there seemed more to it than that. As the prospect of the war's end came near, everyone seemed more anxious.

Anyway, Elizabeth had her pass or thought she did. When she came under the White House portico she put down her umbrella and the box she'd been carrying with its load of garlands for Mary

Todd. As she began to scrounge through her purse the mustachioed sentinel drawled, "I rec'nize you, ma'am. You can com'in."

Elizabeth just then found the pass and flashed it.

The sentinel nodded. "Thank ye, ma'am."

Elizabeth surmised the man was from southern Indiana or Illinois, perhaps even Missouri. Elizabeth bit her lip and nodded at him. She didn't want to think about her son George just now.

She must deliver the garland of flowers Mary Todd would wear at tomorrow's inaugural ball. At one time Elizabeth had made such garlands for Mary Todd, who had a fondness for flowers and for wearing them in her hair. At that February reception and ball in '62 Mary Todd had worn a headdress of black and white flowers to complement the white satin dress with black accents. Sometime later that year Ginny Lewis had introduced Elizabeth to a friend a few blocks over who had a touch for artful craft. The woman had proven so adept that ever after that Elizabeth paid her not only to fashion garlands but also to make dress appliqués.

Elizabeth handed her umbrella and coat to a genial attendant, a freeman, also from Virginia. He told Elizabeth that Mrs Lincoln hadn't returned home. The chief hostess might be absent but the White House bustled with caterers preparing for an evening reception. In the East Room, confectionary Union forts and confectionary ships bearing miniature flags and red, white, and blue ribbons dominated the center lengths of tables covered in white cloths around which the kitchen staff were placing sparkling glasses, china, and silverware. Two black-jacketed men from the greenhouse were arranging blue and white crocuses and yellow daffodils among the forts and ships. Others, men in the mulberry-colored outfits introduced by Mary Todd, were bringing in chairs to line the walls of this and other first-floor public rooms. There seemed little point in the chairs because people, as Mary Todd often said, would 'mill about like cattle', browsing over tables laden with the sumptuous edibles provided by the caterers.

Elizabeth didn't linger. She was always curious but always purposive. She had business to do. She went upstairs. Some of the clamor of the first floor rose to the second but otherwise the second floor seemed spookily quiet. It was so quiet Elizabeth paused to look around. She stood in the office vestibule that served as the anteroom to the anteroom to the nation's chief magistrate. As Elizabeth turned to leave the vestibule and walk the central corridor to Mary Todd's bedroom, she was startled to hear the President's voice.

"Madame Keckly, good afternoon to you. You didn't happen to see John Nicolay when you came through that business downstairs, did you?"

Mr Nicolay was Mr Lincoln's chief secretary, a young lawyer he'd brought from Springfield back in '61.

"No sir, Mr Abe."

"Here to see Molly?" Among family and friends, Mr Abe called Mary Todd 'Molly'.

Elizabeth held up the box in reply. "No, I'm just here to deliver this."

"For tomorrow night or tonight?" asked Mr Abe, looking over the top of his reading glasses, smiling and holding a fold of papers.

"For tomorrow night, Mr Abe," said Elizabeth trying to plumb his mood. She thought of Mr Abe's face as a landscape of leather folds, weather-beaten by time, history, and care. His eyes were liquid globes of light amidst the ravage. His smile now underscored the light.

"Well, I won't detain you from your business. I'm sure whatever you're deliverin' is goin' to make Molly look mighty good."

"Thank you, Mr Abe. I think she'll look good tomorrow night and tonight, too. And today, I want to say, what you said, well, it sounded good because it *was* good. I even got a copy of your speech. The papers are already circulatin' it."

"Good to hear. And thank you for your kind words. Kind words like this always mean a lot but, you know, it means a lot to me that the sun poked through the rain, if you hear what I'm sayin'?"

"Yes, Mr Abe, I think I do."

"God's hand is in history. Sometimes it's hard to see how, especially in times of trial. And we've all had our share in this war," he said, looking directly at Elizabeth. She thought that look was his way of acknowledging George.

"It's been four hard years for the country, Mr Abe."

"That's so. I've sometimes wondered if I ever should have been President. Don't tell Molly that…or anyone else." Mr Abe laughed. Elizabeth laughed, too.

"If I became President I think God had a hand in it. Mind you, I'm not above reproach, as you well know. But I'd like to think those rays of sunshine cutting through the clouds today were a sign, a sign of hope."

"I'd like to think so, too, Mr Abe."

"Not that we can become all afuss about ourselves if we think we're servants of God. God's ways are not our ways and, anyway, I've got feet of clay."

"The prophets ne'er had it easy," said Elizabeth.

"Ain't that the truth! They had to tend to the business God gav'em. But we can hope the end of *this* business is near. The sunshine helps but the business of war calls me," said the President, shaking the papers he was holding. Then he added, "You know it's a blessing that I can — we all can — begin to think about the business of peace."

"You been tendin' to business just right, Mr Abe. Your speech showed that."

"Thank you, Madame Elizabeth. I'd better let you go and excuse me, if you would. A good evenin' to you."

"And to you, Mr Abe."

"Thank you," he said, walking up a small flight of steps into the reception room outside Mr Nicolay's office.

When Elizabeth arrived in Mary Todd's bedroom the maid Annie was puttering about with an ostrich-feather dusting wand. She was a brunette Irish 'girl' in her early twenties. When she saw Elizabeth she nodded, Elizabeth nodded back, and then Annie left the room. Annie wasn't one to talk much when she was about work, but over a cup of coffee she could be quite talkative. Downstairs Annie and Elizabeth had often chatted in the White House kitchen. So far as Mary Todd was concerned, no such chatting could take place upstairs. Mary Todd had standing instructions that White House employees were not to loiter when family friends or guests were present, except to serve food and such-like tasks. Annie's departure was just another sign that Elizabeth was to be regarded as a friend.

Elizabeth set the box with the garlands on a side table next to the full-length oval mirror before which Mary Todd would dress. She took an envelope out of her purse and placed it on the box. It was addressed 'Mary T'. Inside was a note saying this was the last of the items Mary Todd had ordered in connection with inaugural activities. Everything else had been delivered except for an invoice. The note mentioned that an invoice would be delivered early next week. The note concluded with a thank-you for the business entrusted to Elizabeth and was signed, 'Your friend, Elizabeth'.

Friendship with Mary Todd had at least one business advantage. Elizabeth got paid in a timely fashion. Not that she entered this friendship with that in mind. On the contrary, after all Mary Todd had taken the initiative to welcome Elizabeth as someone more than a vendor. From the outset this had been so. Could Elizabeth help it if her business benefited from this friendship? More than a few had hardly been paid at all. Elizabeth was thankful to be among the fully paid.

The price of fulfillment was vigilance. Elizabeth shook her head as she looked at the envelope. With the war it was probably a blessing, she thought, that Mr Lincoln had not a clue to the staggering unpaid bills from jewelers, milliners, shoemakers, outfitters, and dealers in luxury goods in New York, Philadelphia, and Washington.

Elizabeth walked over to the shelving Mary Todd had had installed above a bureau of four drawers. The shelving had been built in the same walnut finish as the drawers, so artfully done as to appear to have been made as one piece. The four shelves and the drawers beneath were filled with pairs of gloves laid ready to wear. The top two shelves appeared to be rather too high for Mary Todd, who was five foot two barefooted. No matter. Mary had insisted the shelves be added so she could readily select gloves for all occasions. White House rumor had it that Mary Todd had purchased 300 pairs of gloves for the second inauguration. Annie had confirmed as much.

Once she had confirmed the matter with Annie, Elizabeth wouldn't talk and didn't want to talk about it with others, including the Lewises. Mary Todd's manic penchant for buying wasn't something Elizabeth wanted to think about. That penchant was one of those individualist or peculiar traits that made the First Lady unattractive to so many people. Indeed, much of official Washington seemed to despise her, though not over the gloves. Thankfully, none dared share this with the President. He had enough on his mind.

Elizabeth left Mary Todd's bedroom and went downstairs, retrieving her coat and umbrella from an attendant. As she walked along the White House driveway to Pennsylvania Avenue a brewery wagon entered the grounds with a load under its canvas tarp. Elizabeth tried peering under the shroud to see if the wagon was laden with beer. The beer was rather unlikely, of course. Mr Abe and Mary Todd were teetotalers. Elizabeth chuckled as she peered at the passing wagon. As her eyes followed the wagon to the White House portico her good humor vanished. She caught sight of a determined Ward Lamon eyeing her with more serious intent. Walking toward Elizabeth, Lamon shook his right hand aloft as soon their eyes met. Obviously he wanted to talk. What about? Elizabeth turned towards Lamon, a large man with a large forehead under cover of his black bowler hat.

The dapper Virginian doffed his hat. "Good day, Madame Lizzy." The Virginian was the only one in the White House to address her in a way that mixed the forms of address Mr and Mrs Lincoln had bestowed on Elizabeth. This casserole name neither favored her nor her opinion of her fellow Virginian.

"Good day to you, Mr Lamon. You wish to speak to me?"

"I do."

"Very well, here or back in the house?"

"Here's best."

Elizabeth opened her hand as a gesture for the man to continue.

"You are among the District's top mantua-makers, if I may say so," said Lamon.

You've noticed, she thought. She would never have ascended to the White House lawn if she hadn't long ago disciplined her tongue. She said, "Thank you."

"You're a *modiste* to many prominent women in the District."

Lamon is tongue-tied, too, in his way. "That too, sir."

"You make dresses even for Secessionist women, am I not right?"

He clambers around a difficult topic. What's he getting at? "I've always made it a policy to avoid discussions more likely to ruffle the feathers than ruffle the dresses."

The lower half of Lamon's face registered a smile but the eyes registered a heightened alertness. Elizabeth involuntarily looked over her shoulder to see what might have caught Lamon's eyes. There was nothing but the busy-ness of wagons, carriages, and pedestrians passing by. A couple of pigs nuzzled in the mud at the curb of Pennsylvania Avenue.

"Forgive me, Madame Lizzy. We're fellow Virginians, yet we fight the war from this side of the Potomac. I accuse you of nothing."

"I should hope not," said Elizabeth.

"I do not. But you've had a full career here in Washington these last four years, one that enables you to play all sides of the fiddle."

"Where I come from in Virginia they play only one side of a fiddle. What are you getting at, Mr Lamon?"

"You are shrewd, madam."

"Thank you. If you want my help in some way, say so."

"What kind of ties do you maintain with the Secessionists?" asked Lamon.

"I don't know because I don't keep count and, as I say, I don't talk about that stuff. My customers don't talk about it with me, either."

"I don't believe that. It's well known about town that Varina Davis asked you to join her and her husband as part of their household when they left town four years ago. Certainly, there must have been some discussion with you about the glories of Secession."

"Mrs Davis is a kind and sweet woman. She believes in the South and stands by her husband, I'm sure of that, but she never tried to turn me against the Union. She simply offered me a job…and was confident at the time she and her husband would soon be returning to this city in victory. The offer was for a job, a paying position in the household."

"And you considered it?" asked Lamon.

"I don't think that makes any difference now. I didn't take it. Just what are you gettin' at Mr Lamon?"

"I didn't mean to give offense."

"You been skirtin' it. Now, what are you're gettin' at?"

"Mr Lincoln is in danger," said Lamon.

"You think I don't know? What's different now from 40 days or 40 months past?"

"We've got wind that a capture or kill plot is afoot."

"Does Mr Lincoln know? What does he think?"

"He never seems to want to give much thought to this sort of thing. But then he brought me here four years ago to watch out for him — I mean his physical safety."

"You've tried to persuade him to be more careful, to allow…"

"I've tried to persuade, but I haven't made much progress."

"The sentinel knew to ask for my pass card, if that gives you comfort."

"That's not enough," said Lamon, flailing a hand in the direction of the White House. "We need additional precautions."

This conversation is takin' a whole different direction than it was a minute ago. "What is it you want from me?"

"I want you to keep your ears open to any talk any time that might help us locate these mal-factors intent on hurting the President and the Union."

"These mal-factors are men, not women, am I not right? It's not likely I'm going to run into these men. And the women I see — none's so stupid as to be plottin' against the President in my hearing.' Mr Lamon, you got one hard job, like finding a needle in a haystack… but I don't do any needlework under haystacks. Be assured, I'll keep my ears open wherever I go. That's my way anyway. But I doubt I'll see or hear anything you'd want to know."

"Thank you but could I be obliged to you for something else, too?"

"What's that?"

He hesitated. "I want you to ask Mr Lincoln to take more precautions."

"You're askin' *me* to do that? You must be desperate."

"Maybe I am. So what?"

He is one devoted man. "Why would Mr Lincoln listen to me and not to you? You're his watchman."

"He feels obliged to you."

"Stuff 'n nonsense. For what? That I help Mary Todd prepare his appearance, comb his hair, and such like?"

"It's more than that," said Lamon.

"I don't see how."

"Don't play blind on me now," said Lamon. "He values you on account of Mary."

Elizabeth didn't know what to say. She shook her head.

"I mean it," said Lamon. "More than once these last four years I've heard Abe say as much, startin' when Willie died. That's the first time he said to me, 'Ward, I thank God for sending Madame Keckly to be with Mary in this thing. I thank God,' he said."

"Whatever he says he means," said Elizabeth. "So we're talkin' about more than dressmakin'."

"Exactly," said Lamon.

"Enough said, that's enough." Elizabeth didn't want to hear any remarks that might even suggest disparagement of Mary Todd. No way. She looked at Lamon, now twiddling his right thumb and index finger.

"You want me to raise the topic of precautions in a general way? Or do you have specific things you want me to ask him to do?"

"Bring it up in a general way and let me know how it goes."

"I will," she paused. "But it might be a while. I ran into him just minutes ago. But you know I don't have cause to see him all that often one-on-one like that. When I see him it's with the family, with Mary Todd. I can't bring up this kind of thing in front of Mary Todd, no way."

"I know, but like today you might have a chance. If you can, make a chance," said Lamon.

"I'll see what I can do," said Elizabeth.

Lamon doffed his hat, Elizabeth nodded, and the two parted.

CHAPTER 3

—⟋⟍—

The next day, Sunday, Elizabeth attended Union Bethel Church. She was a member there throughout the war. Several times she'd been a guest of the Walkers at the Fifteenth Street Church, but she chose Bethel. Bethel, she would later say, seemed to show the hand of God. She needed that hand. But the feet, as she said, made a difference — her feet. Bethel was in easy walking distance of the Lewises. Elizabeth was less likely to mention that attending Bethel amounted to her declaration of independence. She had been raised Presbyterian but she wasn't going to stay Presbyterian through compulsion or inertia. Bethel, being Methodist Episcopal, offered a fresh opening from God. Moreover, Elizabeth once said, Fifteenth Street was too inclined to see the finger of God exercised in judgment against others and in favor of itself. And why not? Most Fifteenth Street folk, she said, were comfortable and successful. God had blessed them. Someone like Elizabeth, who wanted to get ahead, might discomfort Fifteenth Street, or so she believed then. So on most Sundays the Walkers went their way and she hers. There was no hard feeling.

At Union Bethel, of course, the Gospel was preached, hymns sung, prayers raised. There was an emphasis that the children of God had a God-given responsibility to use their gifts, to develop them in ways good for God's kingdom, for neighbors, family, friends, and self. The practical theology of Bethel emphasized the importance of building character, of raising the level of personal and community culture, and of striving to earn and save financial resources to strengthen the community, the family, and the individual believer. Union Bethel was a church, said Elizabeth, for people who wanted to achieve or attain. Elizabeth saw herself as a striver. Some might find that odd. For many, Elizabeth had already arrived, being a bosom friend of the First Lady and running a shop that would eventually employ as many as 17. So by the most obvious measures she had arrived, transcending boundaries that most could hardly approach. That wasn't enough for Elizabeth. She couldn't live on bread alone. She wanted more and perhaps all the more because by all appearances she'd already arrived.

That Sunday after the inauguration, when Elizabeth arrived at Bethel, she remained outside. She would wait for Tad, the youngest Lincoln, at a nearby street corner. Mary Todd had asked Elizabeth earlier in the week whether she'd consent to having Tad join her at church that Sunday. The Lincolns were expected at a service to be held under the new Capitol rotunda. It simply wouldn't do to have any distraction on such an occasion, or so Mary Todd said. If Tad were along he could easily make himself the center of attention.

Elizabeth was happy enough to accommodate Mary Todd. She had taken Tad to church a few times before. Taking Tad under wing would demand vigilance. Tad *could* behave as a growing young gentleman, especially when asked by his dad. But often enough Mr Abe was more than eager to engage in rough-and-tumble, at least on the home turf. And when Mr Abe wasn't near, Tad was a rebel and mischief-maker, always seeming to want to provoke attention, somewhat like his mother in that regard. Tad's mischief-making was often a blessing for his dad. He was able to deliver his dad — at least for a moment — from the relentless war. Tad couldn't get enough of his dad. Tad would play at Mr Abe's knees while his dad worked at his desk late into the night. Sometimes Mr Abe might be able to read Tad a bedtime story. More often he carried the boy to bed after the boy had fallen asleep at his feet.

Mary Todd in theory could have given Tad more time. While Willie was still alive, the two boys took care of themselves with Willie, two years older than his brother, being in charge. Neither Mary Todd nor Mr Abe set much in the way of limits. Mary Todd, after her mother died, had had a trial of a childhood with her step-mother. She'd said more than once to Elizabeth that her stepmother was 'smotherin'. She was determined she wouldn't set 'suffocatin' limits' with her boys. That determination worked well enough with Robert, the oldest son, who had entered Harvard the autumn before the Lincolns came to Washington. That may have worked with Willie. Willie was as sharp as his dad. But Tad wasn't an eager learner, not in school ways, at least. Mr Williamson, the Scottish tutor the Lincolns hired, was less a teacher and more a tender to Tad, at least judging by the results, as Elizabeth was to see.

Elizabeth missed Willie. Willie took to learning. He was like his dad in this and so many other respects. He was a charmer! Warm and tenderhearted, he sought to meet the needs and wishes of others. Tad was less attuned to others but that's not to say he was mean. His mischief *could* be charming. Collecting nickels from the office-seekers who descended on his dad was charming. Tad collected the nickels to help wounded soldiers. But often enough Tad just went too far. Willie had kept the boy from going too far. He had a sense of when enough was enough. Not Tad. Tad's charm got lost amidst the annoyance, as when he locked up Mr Williamson and refused to produce the key...except for his dad. His mama didn't want any annoying surprises this morning. Surely that's why he was being sent off to Union Bethel.

The boy was to be brought over from the White House by carriage, or so Elizabeth had been told. Elizabeth wondered whether the folks at the White House might be searching for the boy. Maybe he'd rebelled at being sent over and had hid out somewhere in the executive mansion. It would be easy enough to do. A recent remark of Mary Todd's came to mind. She'd told Elizabeth it was often easier finding Willie than it was Tad. And Willie had been dead three years. Of course, Mary Todd was alluding to finding Willie in the séances she frequented or seeing him at the foot of her bed. She'd gotten Mr Abe to attend at least one séance. Clearly she found more comfort in the séances than did he.

Elizabeth admitted to Mary Todd she'd sought and found her son George that way after he'd been killed. But you could only go so far, said Elizabeth, and then the séances became like 'spirit booze'. You could lose your way in séances, even *want* to lose your way. Mary Todd and Elizabeth had differing attitudes towards séances. Mary Todd wanted to become lost. Elizabeth didn't. The way Elizabeth saw things, there was too much to live for, too much to do. You had to get control of yourself.

Elizabeth looked up and down the streets for a sign of Tad. Elizabeth saw carriages in all directions, but none that looked like White House carriages. A foursome of chickens, three white and a Rhode Island Red, was crossing the street about a block away. The chickens were pecking among the mud and horse manure as they crossed the street. Despite their Sunday leisure they most likely had escaped from someone's backyard. Or had they been let out? That's something Tad might do.

When the first notes of 'Shall We Gather At The River' could be heard sounding on the church organ, Elizabeth looked towards the church door. She saw an unknown young man being whooshed inside by the usher, Tom Campbell. When the young man was inside, Mr Campbell looked at Elizabeth, seeking a clue as to her intentions. She had no intention of shouting. She held her hands out and up, shrugging her shoulders. Then she let her right hand droop and waved it back and forth. Was this the sign of a pendulum? She didn't know, but she hoped to convey the sense she'd continue to wait. Mr Campbell waved, smiled, and stepped inside the church, closing the door.

When the parishioners were well along into 'Let Thy Kingdom Come', a one-horse hansom cab came past Elizabeth and stopped before the church. Out stepped a blond-haired man, probably in his 30s. Elizabeth didn't recognize him. Then Tad jumped out of the cab, all in his Sunday best, dark blue knickers with a matching snug-fitting midshipman's jacket, a white shirt, and an unraveling black bowtie. The boy landed with a clatter on the wooden side walk, looked around, saw Elizabeth, and ran to embrace her, repeating over and over 'Lizzy' with great joy. He grabbed Elizabeth around the waist and she patted and kissed the boy's head. There was no denying the boy's enthusiasm nor his warm-heartedness, thought Elizabeth. He *could* be a charmer.

The boy's escort was less charming. He seemed to be giving Elizabeth the once over as she and Tad approached the church steps.

"Who are you, sir?" she asked.

"From the Treasury Department, ma'am," he said in reply, tipping his hat. "I'll wait outside."

Tad had never had an escort like this. Elizabeth surmised the fellow was employed by Ward Lamon as part of the enhanced precautions on behalf of the Lincolns.

"We better be along, Tad," said Elizabeth, taking the boy's right hand. The boy skipped even as the two ascended the church steps. He managed to open the church door for Elizabeth, the kind of thing Willie had been wont to do. *Perhaps*, she thought, *I've been too harsh in my judgment of the boy.*

Because Tad was no stranger to the church, Mr Campbell had reserved the same spot always reserved for Elizabeth when she had the boy in tow. The two were seated in the front left pew. As the congregation began lustily singing 'We Are All Brothers and Sisters in Thee', Tad handed Elizabeth the hymnal Mr Campbell had passed to the boy as he had seated the two. Elizabeth readily found the hymn. She let Tad hold the hymnal open with her. He sang with Elizabeth at times. Sadly, the boy, now well on 12, could neither read nor write to speak of. He'd had a big head at birth. That's why his dad had called him 'Tad', as in *tadpole*. The headiness was all promise and little to show for it now. As least the boy held up his side of the hymnal. He looked up at Elizabeth and smiled. Elizabeth smiled back. If the boy could only be made to realize how he'd squandered his years and his talents! Or had he no talents? If he'd been a black boy he might be considered an example of why those of African ancestry could supposedly never be educated. The thought rankled Elizabeth.

She resolved to give her full attention to the morning's Bible reading. John Grove, a Bethel deacon, after clearing his throat announced there would be two readings but one preacher, a *guest* preacher. Mr Grove pointed to the guest preacher, a man he introduced as a traveling freeman, one Clement Caldwell. As Mr Grove introduced him, the preacher stood up where he was sitting in the front right pew. He turned around to face the congregation, gave a modest bow, then sat down. Elizabeth was grieved that he had a body build so much like George's. They could have been cousins in that regard. All the more reason she'd give a careful listening to his sermon, which Mr Grove said Brother Caldwell was calling 'Two Feasts and God's Call'.

Mr Grove read first from the 5th chapter of the Book of Daniel. That chapter opens with King Belshazzar and his court having a feast at their court in Babylon. The king sees a finger write an inscription on a wall that none of his advisors or magi are able to interpret. The second reading seemed to bear no obvious relation to the reading from Daniel, except that as in Daniel a feast takes place. This reading was from the Gospel of Luke, a reading of Christ's parable about the prodigal son. Of course in that parable one son takes his inheritance, leaves his home, squanders the inheritance, and in desperation returns home to his father. The father joyously welcomes his errant son. The faithful son who'd never left home complains about the feast that his father orders to celebrate the return of the errant son. The father chastises his faithful son, but reminds him that he, too, is loved.

Following these readings Brother Caldwell arose from his pew and walked up to the lectern carrying what appeared to be a red leather Bible. Brother Caldwell placed the Bible on the lectern, then gripped both sides of the lectern with his mighty hands. Elizabeth wondered whether he'd been a field laborer before he'd been freed. A field laborer he may have been, but his tongue was well cultivated. Following a brief prayer thanking God for His word and invoking His spirit in his preaching, he began to talk about the two feast stories that revealed the one true God.

King Belshazzar, said Brother Clement, had it all or so it seemed. He was King of Babylon and could summon a thousand lords to tables laden with the best food and the best wine. But all that he had wasn't enough. He couldn't accept that the Lord God might set boundaries. Belshazzar thought that he was above God, the One who had revealed Himself to Daniel, to Daniel's people, to Abraham, Isaac, Jacob, and their descendants. The king overstepped the boundaries of God. He neglected to show love for God, even though God had granted Babylon the empire Babylon had acquired. Babylon had taken the gold and silver from the temple in Jerusalem to make the goblets and dinner finery used at this very feast.

And so a finger of God or from God, we don't know which, appeared at King Balshazzar's feast and wrote something on the wall. When God's finger shows up it's a time of judgment or reckoning, a time when God will reveal His mercy or His wrath! And no one, brother or sister, can stop God's judgment. To his credit, the king wanted light, wanted to know what the finger of God had proclaimed. He called in the enchanters, he called in the Chaldeans, he called in the astrologers, he called in his wise men, but none could read what had been written on that wall. His queen suggested he summon Daniel, who had been brought from Jerusalem when the Babylonians had captured and plundered the city.

Daniel could read what the finger of God had inscribed on the festal wall. The finger inscribed those fearful words: MENE, MENE, TEKEL, PARSIN, which Daniel interpreted. Those words meant God had numbered the days of Belshazzar's kingdom and the kingdom was now at an end. The king had been weighed in the balance and found wanting. He had taken vessels from God's temple in Jerusalem, used them in this feast, and praised gods made of mere gold and silver. Belshazzar's kingdom would be divided and given to the Medes and Persians. That very night the king was slain. Woe to the wicked who see the finger of God!

But blessed are those embraced by the full hand of God. The very hand that bears the finger of judgment also bears God's mercy. That hand is shown in Jesus Christ's parable so wrongly called the Parable of the Prodigal Son. This wasn't a story, said Brother Clement, just about a son. Anyway, there were two sons, both sinful, one wining and dining beyond the law, the other whining and complaining within it. The father was the prodigal, prodigious with his love. There is only one father prodigious in love in all places and times and that is our heavenly father, Almighty God. To Him all thanks, praise, and glory are due, Amen, said Brother Clement. 'Amen' resounded around the room.

Brother Clement continued, saying we must live lives worthy of the God who made us. God had sent His son, the Shepherd, whose hand, heart, and word was to redeem us all. 'Amen!' shouted the room. To redeem the world! 'Hallelujah!' We must renounce lives spent chasing false gods. 'Amen!' We must be selfless and self-sacrificing so that God's Spirit can grow in us and we in His Kingdom. 'Amen! Hallelujah! Glory be! Amen,' replied the assembled. Brother Clement nodded and resumed his seat among the congregation.

A deacon stood up, faced the people, raised his hands, and proceeded to pray aloud. He prayed for the congregation, city, and nation, for peace and reconciliation, for the sick and lame, for sons in the Army and Navy, for those yet in the chains of slavery, for freedom under God for all — all to the accompaniment of 'Amen' and 'Hallelujah' from the people. When the praying had begun Tad placed his left hand in Elizabeth's right, as he had done on previous occasions. She wondered whether the vociferous praying frightened the boy. She gently squeezed his hand from time to time. What did God intend for this boy? Had He intended more for George? Or did the results of sin — death and disease and war and such like — at times overcome God's will? Not permanently, of course. There was more to life than this life. But there was no denying death and sin. She missed George, missed what God might have intended for him. Tears came to her eyes, but none would notice. The packed church had become hot. The same handkerchief that would wipe the sweat from her brow would wipe away her tears.

There would be more prayers and hymns that morning, but Elizabeth found in them only the most transient of reassurance. As comforting as they might have been and *should have been*, she found herself wrestling with God. Brother Clement had unwittingly set off this match. The distinction between the finger and hand of God was enlightening but also frightening. The distinction gave new form to an old question. Was George *saved* when he died? Had he been faithful to the true God of faith? Or had he gone even more astray in the Army? Once he'd reached a certain age, his commitment to a life of Christian faith had become rather weak. He attended church, it seemed, more to please his mother than to please God. He gave no more attention to God's word than he might give to a newspaper. He was interested in the Word but seemingly without passion. His passion had been to fight against those who had denied the dignity and freedom of others. Elizabeth shared that passion, too, but hoped the passion had been fed by the deeper waters of a daily baptism in Christ's name.

At death's door had George seen the awful finger of God or known the welcoming embrace of the living God? Without the embrace George would be condemned for eternity to travel as a darkened spirit, never to know rest in God and love in His light. Elizabeth shuddered at the thought. She would often think of George, often wondering where he'd gone in the Beyond once his spirit left this world behind.

CHAPTER 4

—w—

After the closing hymn and the benediction, the parishioners arose, many flapping themselves with fans they'd brought this morning. Elizabeth hadn't thought to bring one. It hadn't been especially warm outdoors, but the church had become quite warm. She was ready to head for the door. That wouldn't be easy. The parishioners between her and the church door were now surging towards Brother Clement or to Tad. Elizabeth would have liked to introduce herself to the preacher. His distinction between the finger and hand of God would reside on her heart and mind for a good many years. Right now she could give little thought to what Brother Clement had said. Tad was her first responsibility. As Elizabeth had looked on those chattering around Brother Clement, Tad had begun to work the crowd toward the doorway. He seemed more politician than child. Elizabeth smiled. She knew she must catch up with the boy.

As she worked her way towards Tad, shaking hands and offering a quick 'hello' to everyone on her way, she wondered whether the boy truly would have been a distraction at the Capitol. He could rise to an occasion, especially in his dad's presence or when summoned by his dad. Right now Tad seemed more thrilled than his dad to be shaking hands with so many strangers. Tad was a magnet to the crowd. Was it *this* kind of attention that Mary Todd wanted to avoid this morning?

No matter. Eventually, Elizabeth and Tad exited the church. As they did so Mr Campbell congratulated the boy saying 'Good job, good job.' A small crowd waited at the bottom of the church steps, looking up at Tad. Apparently, more people wished to shake Tad's hand. The Treasury operative waited at the curb, his hands in his coat pockets and his mouth shut tight. Elizabeth wondered whether the operative had a gun. He kept looking up and down the avenue, alert to anyone or anything that might approach. Behind him a White House carriage waited, its steps down and door open, beckoning passengers to board. Sitting in the driver's seat was a coachman in mulberry livery. Before him were two chestnut mares one flicking her tail and the other shaking her head. A flick of the whip would hardly be necessary to get these two ladies on the go. As Tad and Elizabeth reached the bottom of the steps the operative approached, perhaps hoping to clear a way through the crowd. In good humor, the church people ignored him.

While this was happening, Elizabeth saw a stranger cross the street from the next block. He was a way off but quite notable. He was of African descent but unlike those in this neighborhood he was unkempt in appearance. If you gave him the benefit of the doubt, perhaps you'd say he was prophetic. His hair pointed in all directions. His clothes were apparent castoffs or perhaps he was a former veteran gone awry. He wore the sky blue jacket once issued to men of the US Army Invalid Corps. The Invalid Corps took in wounded soldiers and placed them in light guard duty. The stranger didn't appear to be carrying firearms. Affixed to the cross-buckled leather straps encircling his huge chest were two glass jars, one on each strap. The glass jars bore a golden liquid. One of the jars was almost half empty. The liquid therein churned around like honey. In his right hand the stranger carried a gnarled pole almost six feet long that came up to the level of his eye. Except for Mr Abe, Elizabeth hadn't seen a taller man in Washington.

The man shouted, "Repent and be baptized! The Ides are coming, the Ides of March is next! Repent and be baptized in the name of the Lord!"

By now the Treasury op had taken his own measure of the man and decided to hustle Tad and Elizabeth to the carriage. One of the Bethel parishoners, a formidable man, shouted, "We're already baptized here, brother."

"So you say," replied the stranger-who-would-be-prophet. "But have you really turned to the Lord?"

"Who are you to ask?" asked a church lady. "Just because you in some wild get-up John-the-be-Baptist costume don't make you holier than all get-out."

"You should head on down to the river, man," said a man of the church. "There's plenty o' folks down there boozin' and gamblin' that needs to hear what you're sayin'."

"So you say," replied John-the-be-Baptist. "But the Lord say the end is near. The Ides is at hand. You needs to ask whether you truly been saved. If you not saved, you need to repent right now."

"Go on down to the Potomac, Mister Baptist," shouted someone.

Someone else started humming 'Shall We Gather at the River' and soon several were humming the tune. Two men approached the prophet-to-be, seeming to take him on. By now Tad was at the open carriage door. The Treasury op helped Tad into the carriage, then Elizabeth, then slammed the door shut. He hopped on a small platform that had been built behind the forward facing seats. Partly standing by steadying himself against the passenger seat, Tad was transfixed by the baptist-to-be. The op shouted to the driver to get going. The driver whistled the mares right off to a steady trot. As the carriage came past, the two men who'd approached the baptist-to-be held their arms aloft and shouted, 'We'll go help you baptize, brother.'

"Glory, hallelujah!" shouted some in the crowd, which now began singing the words of the hymn they'd been humming.

As long as he could see the baptist-to-be, Tad kept his eyes glued on the man. When the carriage turned a corner so he could see no more, Tad sat down and asked, "Lizabeth, what's the Ides?"

Elizabeth knew it had something to do with a month's middle, but one thing she knew for sure. "Julius Caesar was killed on the Ides of March, but Ides is more than that."

"Who's Julius Caesar?"

Willie would have known. "He was a general and dictator in ancient Rome. Shakespeare wrote a play called *Julius Caesar*. Perhaps your dad can tell you about him sometime. Your dad has read parts of the play to your mama and me."

41

"I'll ask," said the boy. He was quiet for a while as the horses clopped along. Then he asked, "How do we know we're saved?"

"God does the savin', Tad. He does the choosin'. No use worrin' 'bout it. Read the Bible, praise God, try to love others, then let easy. If God's word lives in you, then you know you're saved."

"Saved from what?" asked Tad.

"You got a mighty load of questions, Tad. I don't know quite how to answer."

"You must. Mama says you're wise."

"I guess your mama and I appreciate each other," laughed Elizabeth.

"Do you have an answer, Lizbeth?"

"I think God saves us from eternal death for Himself. That's what all this 'savin' language is about."

"Is God selfish?"

"It may seem so, at times, but I think like the preacher-man says this morning, I think he's the reverse of selfish. There's no end to His love if you turn to Him. But if you turn away and worship worldly things, like King Balshazzar, then there's God's wrath. No gettin' round that. But God's love is big. It's one of those odd things of life — like those sons, we don't want to accept God's love, it seems, until we know we have to put ourselves under his mercy. Kinda odd, ain't it?"

"Yes'm," said Tad.

"Praise be to God He makes us recognize we need Him and His love," Elizabeth added.

"Yes, ma'am," said Tad, looking off into the distance. For the rest of the trip back to the White House, the two were quiet.

Once they were inside the White House and upstairs, Elizabeth and Tad came upon two white-jacketed stewards setting up a table and chairs in the library, an oval-shaped room overlooking the White House South Lawn and the Potomac. Now that the boy was on home territory, the awe he'd shown earlier was erased. He began running around the perimeter of the room, like a racehorse let loose. Elizabeth decided to let him run off steam. She walked to a window. While she stood there, the stewards proceeded with their business. From a nearby trolley cart they retrieved place settings, a sugar bowl, and the like, and set them out on a crisp, white tablecloth. One of the stewards told Elizabeth they would return with lunch as soon as they were summoned. The White House had a system of bell pulls connecting various rooms with the servants' quarters and kitchen, thereby enabling dispatch of a meal. Elizabeth wasn't sure whether she was to be included. Mary Todd hadn't mentioned anything about lunch. With all the inaugural activities, Elizabeth was rather surprised any table was being set for four.

She thought perhaps she ought to stop Tad, who had run again and again around the room. The boy wasn't inclined to accept limits set by outsiders and right now Elizabeth didn't want to test whether she was in or out of the envelope. She wondered if Mary Todd's attitude towards limit setting would have been different with a girl. No matter. Hopefully, Tad would soon run out of steam.

Elizabeth left the library to find Mary Todd. Mary Todd was in her bedroom, primping her hair, which was adorned with rose-colored silk flowers. When she saw Elizabeth in the mirror, she swirled around as if to model the wine-red, crinoline dress she wore. Elizabeth had made the dress about a year earlier and had added a flower appliqué two weeks ago.

"How do you like my flowers?" asked Mary Todd.

"In your hair or on the dress?"

"Both."

"You look fine, real fine. Did you get any help with the flowers in your hair?" asked Elizabeth.

"Annie helped."

"Tad's in the library. He's lettin' off steam now but he was well behaved this mornin'.."

Mary Todd looked surprised. She said, "That's good to hear. Will you stay for lunch?"

Elizabeth was happy to accept the invitation. Mary Todd grabbed then released Elizabeth's hand. The two walked to the library talking of one thing or another. When they arrived Tad was still running around. When he saw his mother he ran to her and gave her a squeeze around the waist. Mary Todd patted him on the head, then told him to go find his dad and bring him back. Tad ran off.

The boy returned in minutes with his father. The two were portraits in opposites: the boy rather short for his age, his father rather tall; the boy brimming with energy, his father haggard; the boy of roseate cheeks, his father ashen. They were united in hand and Tad's puckish smile echoed in the pucker of a smile on his dad's face. The father had the boy ring for dinner. Shortly two stewards appeared with trays of food, which they set on a library table. The two positioned themselves behind the end chairs, awaiting the opportunity to seat the Lincolns.

When the couple was seated, the stewards proceeded to seat Elizabeth and Tad. Elizabeth sat to Mr Lincoln's right. The President asked Mary to offer up a prayer. After she finished saying the Lord's Prayer, Tad underscored her 'Amen' with his own.

The stewards filled the soup plate set before each person. They ladled out a French onion soup. The boy rapidly consumed his portion. When Mary Todd and Elizabeth had finished their soups, Mr Lincoln was still supping with some indifference. When the stewards hesitated whether to serve more food, he gave them a gentle wave to serve the others.

"This will be enough for me, gentlemen, as long as I get a cuppa coffee," said Mr Abe.

"Yes, sir," said one steward, who went to the library table to retrieve a pot of coffee.

As everyone else ate the main course of plaice and potatoes fried French style, the President languidly consumed his soup and coffee. Elizabeth was happy enough to be eating with the family, a privilege accorded to few. Except for the coffee, which was just right, the other hot food was tepid, if tasty. Mary Todd was doing much of the talking, talking about the previous evening's inaugural reception. She had been going on at length about Senator A's increasing girth and about Madame B's insidious giggle, when she abruptly said, "You know, Father, you should be eating more. People are noticing you're losing weight. So I'm not the only one…"

"Mother, Tad can do the eating for me. Want some more, boy?"

"Yessir. More taters, please."

"Some extra for the boy, gentlemen."

"Tad can't do it for you, Abe," said Mary Todd. "It won't help your mood if you're always goin' round hungry."

"At every public function these days there's plenty of food," said Lincoln.

"But you don't hardly eat there either."

"No, I guess I don't. It'll help when the war's over. It's hard for me to think what's goin' on south of the river and ever where else and abide in a lot of food."

"Doesn't do 'em any good if you don't eat, Father," said Mary Todd.

"Mama's right, Dad," said Tad.

"And Madame Keckly, do you have any advice?"

"My only advice," she replied, "is what to put on the body, not what to put on the bones."

The President laughed. He looked at Tad and said, "I guess you and your mama are right." Eyeing a steward he said, "I'll have some of the fish and taters, please."

As he was served, Elizabeth noticed that Mary Todd's face was becoming flushed. Mary Todd blurted out, "Excuse me for a minute." She shoved back her chair, stood, and proceeded to leave the room.

"Mother, are you all right?" asked Mr Abe.

Mary Todd shook her head and then rushed from the room to her bedroom, adjacent to the library. She firmly closed the door between the two rooms.

"I think I said the wrong thing, Madame Keckly, if you'll excuse me."

"Mr Abe, that's all right. I'll go. You need to eat your meal."

He hesitated, then sighed. "Thank you, ma'am. I'll be right along, but perhaps you can help smooth the waters ahead of me. Would you?"

She couldn't say 'No'. Elizabeth entered Mary's bedroom. Mary Todd was standing at the window looking over the South Lawn, the marshes, and the Potomac beyond. Mary Todd was sniffling into a handkerchief. Elizabeth shut the door. In her opinion the stewards had seen quite enough, though nothing new.

Said Mary Todd, "He listens to his boy but not to me. He just don't listen to me like when we lived in Springfield."

"He wasn't President of these United States when you lived in Springfield," said Elizabeth. "And there weren't no war, Mary Todd. Anyways he listens to you. He's eatin' a meal, which he probably wouldn't have done if you hadn't brought it up. He's listenin'."

"Why isn't he here now?" asked Mary.

"He's goin' to come. I told him to finish his meal."

"He's just not takin' care of himself, Lizzy."

"It's the war, Mary Todd. This slaughter can't be over soon enough."

"The war, yes, but I sometimes think it's more than the war, Lizzy."

"Whattya mean, Mary Todd?"

"I sometimes wonder…I sometimes wonder…"

"Yes."

"I sometimes wonder…"

Then Mr Abe opened the door. He spread his arms out and smiled. Without another word, Mary Todd ran to him. He clasped her tightly round him. She hugged him for dear life it seemed. Elizabeth bowed her head but caught them both eyeing her as she left the room. They were both smiling as she shut the door behind her.

Just like that — the storm was over. Tad wasn't in the library. He'd been sent on his way. Elizabeth decided not to linger. Some weeks past she'd delivered the two dresses that Mary Todd would wear at this evening's and tomorrow's inauguration balls. Ah, but she hadn't gotten in a word with Mr Abe about precautions, as she had promised Lamon. It was too late for that today. Anyway, her mind was astir with speculation about what Mary Todd might have said if Mr Abe hadn't come through the door.

Elizabeth prayed that God would bring some peace and joy to the White House. She must begin work on that quilt.

CHAPTER 5

—⚏—

Elizabeth awoke the next morning to the sound of tramping feet and beating drums. Troops must be moving through the city. In the early months of the war that had happened often. But the sounds of marching men had become less frequent in the last year or so, except when Confederate General Early had threatened the city the preceding July, in 1864. Since then the District's tumult had reverted to the occasional bar fight and the clamor and crowds associated with political events like the inauguration.

Walker Lewis made it a practice to purchase a newspaper most mornings. This morning's paper, already on the big oak kitchen table, made no mention of troop movements in the city. There was coverage of the military campaign around Richmond and Petersburg, where generals Grant and Lee oversaw the opposing forces. General Sherman's drive into the Carolinas towards Virginia, anyone could see, was designed to entrap General Lee's forces between the hammer that was Sherman and the anvil that was Grant. *How much longer, oh Lord? How much longer?* Elizabeth asked.

The tramping beyond the walls of the Lewis home continued. Elizabeth sipped coffee as she leafed through the Washington *Daily Chronicle.* An inside article made mention of Frederick Douglass' appearance at the White House reception on Saturday evening. The paper touted this as the first White House visit by the prominent Negro American. First *public* visit, thought Elizabeth, but if she'd had the time and patience she would have informed the editor that

Mr Douglass had already paid a visit to Mr Abe. He was one of several prominent leaders of African descent for whom she'd opened a White House door.

Ginny Lewis, who'd gone upstairs to roust the children from their sleep, came back into the kitchen just when a loud thumping was heard at the front door. "Who'd that be?" she asked, not expecting an answer.

"I don't know," said Elizabeth, "but I'll answer the door." Thumping was heard again. "You gotta 'nough to do with the children."

Elizabeth set the paper down and went to the front door. When she opened it she saw a bespectacled black soldier bereft of a right leg standing tall with the help of crutches. The soldier looked to be in his late 20s. The soldier touched the brim of his kepi cap to acknowledge Elizabeth. "Mor', ma'am."

"Morning. Can I help?"

"Thizbee Lewis hum?"

"What? Is Thisbe Lewis home?"

"No, ma'am. Thiz da Lewis hum?"

"It is."

"Goo."

Elizabeth was becoming a bit unsettled. The soldier's way of talking might work on the plantation but she knew it didn't work well elsewhere. She was convinced the slaveholders encouraged this sort of talk. She hated it. That a man such as this could even enlist, she was sure, was a measure of the Army's desperation. Yet, she took pity on him.

"How may I help you?" she asked.

"Tol dat Ma'am Keckleee lib here."

"I am she."

"Goo mee you," said the man tipping his cap again. "Maname Caleb."

"Caleb?"

"Yessum."

"What brings you here, this morning? Are you with those troops going through the neighborhood?'

Caleb looked alarmed. "Nommum. Loo fa worg."

Elizabeth would have been at a loss if she hadn't been raised in Virginia and heard this kind of 'stone talk', as her mama used to call it. Her mama would say you're never gonna get anywhere in life if you talk like your mouth's full of stones. Only the slave-masters like that kinda talk. Keepin' people ignorant and down was a part of their business.

"So you're looking for work?" said Elizabeth.

"Sarge say mut fin somtin. Army help so long, then ober."

"Why'd you come to me?"

"You run countaband si'ety?"

"I started and help run the contraband society here in Washington. We help people that's escaped from slavery in the South. But it looks to me if you're in the Army you're not someone we'd ordinarily help."

"Sarge sa I nee read."

"I can see you could use some help reading and talking, Caleb."

"Yessum."

Elizabeth gave Caleb directions to a church nearby, which ran a school not only for black children but also for recently freed blacks who wanted to be taught to read and write. Caleb offered up a 'Thangee, thangee, thangee' then swiveled around to go down the stoop on his own. Elizabeth had offered to help but he had resisted. She had helped enough, he said. He headed toward the church. Elizabeth would remember his *thangees* in days to come. But of course she never expected to hear of him again.

When Elizabeth returned to the kitchen, she found three younger Lewis children eating breakfast at the kitchen table. Milk, biscuits, and scrambled eggs were their breakfast. Ginny offered eggs, biscuits, and coffee to Elizabeth. Ginny joined Elizabeth for breakfast at a small side table. They watched over the children and talked about events just beyond the front door. Elizabeth told Ginny about the stone-mouthed young soldier. Ginny vowed her children would never talk that way.

"This soldier can count his blessings. He's still alive to do something about hisself," said Elizabeth.

After Ginny poured another helping of milk into the tin cup held by her oldest boy, she looked at Elizabeth and said, "It goes by frightfully fast, don't it?"

"It does, it mighty does," replied Elizabeth, knowing Ginny referred to life. She took her last sip of coffee, then stood up. She must be off.

She didn't have far to go. Her shop was across the street and down the block, over a grocery store. Crossing the street wouldn't be pleasant this morning. It had rained overnight and the wind was picking up. The marching units now visible at the far end of the street had stirred up the street into a thick mud soup. Elizabeth raised her dress and inner skirt as she carefully negotiated a passage across, hoping that no on-coming carriage would force her to hurry up without regard to the cleanliness of her dress. No carriage came, though the sidewalks were busy enough with pedestrians. Once across Elizabeth scraped her laced boots against the wooden side-walk. She would remove as much mud as possible in this fashion, then remove the remainder with damp rags from a bucket just outside the entrance to her dress shop. Her shop was at the top of a flight of covered stairs hugging one side of the corner store where the Lewises and neighbors purchased milk and other groceries.

Once Elizabeth had wiped off her boots she entered the shop through a door with a large glass pane. Even before entering she'd seen there were no customers waiting. She saw none being fitted for dresses. Customers at this hour would have been unusual. Six young Irish seamstresses and two older black women from Virginia were at work at tables near the windows. Elizabeth's other seamstresses had been given this Monday off. Many of her seamstresses worked out of their homes in any event. Her crew of seamstresses had worked extra long hours preparing dresses for the ladies attending inauguration events.

The dress business was a business of fits and starts in more than one way, mused Elizabeth. Only one of the six wooden torsos, used to drape in-the-making dresses, sported a dress this morning. It was a summer dress of light blue silk being made for the daughter of the Chief Justice, the former Kate Chase, married since 1863 to Rhode Island's Senator Sprague. Whether as Kate Chase or Kate Sprague, Kate was regarded as a stunning beauty and compelling hostess in the capital. Was anyone surprised that Mary Todd had declined to attend Kate's wedding? For four years she had vied with Mary Todd to be the leader of Washington society, at least that society with roots in the North. Because of that challenge, Elizabeth would never even think of telling Mary Todd that Kate was one of her customers. Not that Mary Todd would ask. She made few inquiries about Elizabeth's business. The business of interest to Mary Todd Lincoln was the fit to the T that was Mary Todd.

Elizabeth walked to a small office with a glass window offering a view of the workroom. Thomas Oliver was at work at the office desk reserved for his visits. He was a self-taught accountant, a born freeman from Boston. Elizabeth had sent a messenger to him early in the previous week asking him to come by early this Monday. She wanted him to prepare invoices for all her inauguration-season customers. As always, his paramount standing instruction was that any bill for Mary Todd should be the first prepared.

As Elizabeth came into the office, Mr Oliver held up an envelope, no doubt holding an invoice.

"It's ready," he said.

Elizabeth took the envelope, turned it over, and saw that it was addressed in Mr Oliver's hand: 'Mrs Lincoln'.

"Thank you, Mr Oliver," said Elizabeth. She opened the envelope, brought the invoice closer to a gas lamp and satisfied herself that it was correct and inclusive. She returned the invoice to the envelope, placing it in her purse.

As she was doing so, her accountant asked, "Did the Lincolns see a man who tried to force himself into their presence at the Capitol Saturday before the inauguration?"

"Don't know. That's the first I've heard of this. What happened?" asked Elizabeth.

"I don't know more than what I just said. I was outside and this man was on the inside, in the Capitol building. I heard about it later, heard he was arrested, then let go."

"Don't know a thing about it. It don't sound good," said Elizabeth.

Could Ward Lamon have known of this incident? She couldn't imagine Lamon so quickly releasing a man whose actions would have invited many questions. Elizabeth mulled over the incident as she pawed through a basket of dress scraps. She was looking for pieces of the white inaugural ball gown she'd recently made for Mary Todd. She wanted pieces of it for use in the quilt. She found pieces and asked one of the seamstresses to cut four squares of roughly equal size, which she would use.

She put away the pieces in a camel-colored hatbox she'd set aside for scraps of Mary Todd's dresses. Elizabeth had purchased the box four years earlier, when she had arrived in Washington from St Louis. Shortly thereafter, after she'd made Mary Todd's first inaugural ball dress, she'd put the scraps of that dress in the box. Ever since it had become a repository for scraps, but only from Mary Todd's dresses. She hadn't kept scraps for other clients but then there was only one First Lady, well, almost. There was Varina Davis. As warm as Mrs Davis was, working for the Davis household could not be. So Mary Todd was *the* First Lady and her scraps got a home.

She placed the hatbox back atop a cherry wardrobe in her office. That done she turned her attention to business matters. She provided direction to the seamstresses. They were all preparing spring dresses. She discussed the February business results with Mr Oliver. He told her, as he had on many occasions, that she had the lowest proportion of receivables of any of his clients in the city. Elizabeth couldn't afford any other way of doing business. She liked to say she'd started her business on a dime and was even now too small-time to be a banker to her customers. With that in mind she headed for the White House to present her latest invoice to Mary Todd.

The White House that noon was receiving members of the city's diplomatic corps. The ambassadors and resident counsels had come to offer the newly installed President the best wishes of the governments they represented. Their carriages and those of other invitees clogged the White House driveway. Elizabeth saw the visitors and cabinet secretaries and their assistants and a few Army and Navy officers bantering back and forth in high spirits, quite unlike the situation four years earlier. The favored suit color among the foreign diplomats was black, the better to offset the jewel encrusted orders and silken red, blue, or green sashes they wore across their chests. The cabinet officers, of course, merely wore black. Mary Todd had more than once spoken of her desire to wear a jeweled order or two. None had so far been given her by crown, prince, or a grateful people.

Elizabeth found Mary Todd in her bedroom. A hairdresser, Mademoiselle Lafante, was in the last stages of preparing Mary Todd's hair for the evening's ball. The mademoiselle touted herself as a native of New Orleans who had fled the city when South Carolina declared secession from the Union. She had spent the Civil War in Washington attending to the fashionable ladies of the city. Like Elizabeth she had access to virtually all the prestigious homes of the city and of all political stripes.

Elizabeth wasn't sure she trusted Mademoiselle Lafante. Was it professional jealousy? No, the lady from New Orleans didn't begin to have the business Elizabeth had. If anything, the mademoiselle had too little business to sustain her enterprise in the city. Even in Washington hairdressers weren't in great demand. The ladies of fashion relied on their own efforts assisted by their household help. Even for all her love of extravagance, Mary Todd only rarely used Mademoiselle Lafante. She was present today, no doubt, to help Mary, at least in her mind, mark the onset of her second tenure as First Lady.

As Elizabeth watched the mademoiselle finish her work, she wondered if Ward Lamon had ever inquired about how this lady was able to make a living. Elizabeth could easily imagine that Mademoiselle Lafante's activities might be subsidized by the Confederate government. The Secessionists would be quite happy to use her ears to obtain useful information. Elizabeth resolved she would say nothing to Lamon. After all, she was indulging in speculation. She didn't want to appear vicious or petty.

While the hairdresser was still present, Mary Todd and Elizabeth exchanged chatter about who would be at the ball. After the hairdresser's departure, a steward was summoned to deliver tea and sandwiches. Before he appeared, Madame Keckly tendered to Mary Todd the invoice for the new dresses that Elizabeth had made for the season of inaugural balls and receptions. Mary Todd began to air out the dirty linen she couldn't display at these public affairs. She went on at length how she anticipated that Senator A's wife would come soused and that Senator B's wife would arrive as if she'd just come from the barnyard. Chief Justice Chase's daughter, Kate, would of course look stunning — she always did — but couldn't people understand that a stone thrown at the head could also be stunning? Did people want that? Did they really want this striver to be the queen of Washington, when she — Mary Todd Lincoln — was by rights the queen of the city? She was married to the nation's chief magistrate. The good press that Kate inevitably received was simply unfair, remarked Mary Todd, as she tore into her ham sandwich.

"Lizzy, you know the Copperhead press [the anti-war press] will fault me however I appear this evening. They think because I'm a Kentuckian I've betrayed my Southern roots by having married the man who leads the Union."

"Yes, we all know what they'll say. You presume to be queen, Mary Todd. Presume," repeated Elizabeth, liking the sound of the word.

"And you know, Lizbeth, I say, 'What of it?' The people want a queen. And shouldn't they have one smart enough some 25 years ago to see they'd one day elect Abraham Lincoln their king, not Stephen Douglas, who everyone thought had the silver tongue with the quicksilver mind."

Mary Todd had often repeated the tale that she'd chosen Mr Abe over his chief political rival from the state of Illinois. Elizabeth didn't want to remove the comfort this tale brought Mary Todd but she knew this talk of kings and queens irritated Mr Abe. He always told Mary Todd it was out of place and should be put out of mind. Mary Todd was nothing if not irrepressible. For Mr Abe's sake Elizabeth would try to put a cap on the royal talk.

"Mary T, you will look like a queen tonight but let's just keep that a secret between you and me. If the papers got wind of that kinda talk, you know what they'd do to Mr Abe."

"Isn't it the truth! Even some of the Republican papers seem too ready to question my loyalty just because I have 'Southern airs', as they put it, and a 'Southern accent'. The papers are populated with hack writers, telling the same stories over and over again, hoping eventually some will stick. The papers need them to stick as a way of confirming their righteousness. Stickiness is the one sure form of truth for weak minds. The papers are populated with idiots, imbeciles, insects. The hacks may sting but it's a comfort to know they're creatures beneath human contempt."

"Let's not think about 'em," said Elizabeth.

"You've always got practical advice," said Mary Todd.

"It's the only advice worth giving," said Elizabeth.

The two ladies laughed. That didn't stop Mary Todd from resuming her general-issue lambasting of the ladies of Washington. Even the sweet-tempered Mary Jane Welles, wife of the Secretary of the Navy, got rained on in today's bad weather report, albeit with only a few spatters.

After the sandwiches, Mary Todd tried on her inaugural gown for what was the third time. She had said she wanted to try it on with a full stomach, since she would be attending this evening's ball in that condition. Elizabeth couldn't deny the wisdom of such a trial. Both the ladies were pleased the dress proved up to the pressure.

Mary Todd's maid, Annie, was present for the latter part of the test fitting. Elizabeth provided some tips for the dressing that would take place later in the evening. Mary Todd asked Elizabeth to return in the evening in any event. Annie would be able to handle the dress, yes, but someone would need to help her man be presentable. She couldn't be sure Mr Lincoln's valet, Will Slade, would be up to the task. She knew her friend would be. Elizabeth promised to return to the White House by 6 o'clock. As she left, Mary Todd handed her the pair of gloves Mr Abe had used at the inauguration ceremony. Elizabeth had previously asked for these as a memento of the occasion. Said Mary Todd, "I don't ever want to see them again. They're loaded with filth." With that admonition, Elizabeth quickly placed the miscreant gloves in her handbag. The two ladies hugged one another and then Elizabeth departed.

As she walked along the White House driveway to Pennsylvania Avenue, Elizabeth was accosted by Ward Lamon once again. Neither was satisfied with the encounter. Elizabeth had no insights, no rumors, and no news, other than the story from Mr Oliver about the thwarted man temporarily held by the city police. Lamon, too, had only heard of the accoster — assailant, exuberant, whoever he was. The police were unable to provide a consistent and adequate description of the man. Lamon asked whether Elizabeth had had a chance to caution the President, but she replied she had not. She promised to caution him at the earliest possible time.

Elizabeth spent the afternoon at her business. Mr Oliver was gone, no doubt helping other clients manage their accounts. The seamstresses were still working on the projects they'd been working at earlier in the morning. Elizabeth resumed work on the dress for Kate Sprague. She'd taken measurements right here in the shop about two weeks earlier. Kate and Mary Todd were alike in that both were willing, even eager, to come to the shop to be measured and fitted. Many of Elizabeth's clients demanded that she come to their homes for measurements and fittings. Elizabeth was glad that unlike Mademoiselle Lafante she had a shop she could call home. The thought of Mademoiselle Lafante caused Elizabeth to wonder whether she should have said something about her to Mr Lamon. But what could she have said?

CHAPTER 6

—〜〜—

When Elizabeth returned to the White House, the gaslights were just being turned up. Mary Todd informed her friend that Senator Sumner had acceded to her husband's invitation to accompany the Lincolns to this evening's inaugural ball. Mr Lincoln and the senator from Massachusetts had recently been at odds over what was already being termed the Reconstruction of the South. As he made evident yet once again in his inaugural address, the President favored methods and policies that would, as he put it, 'heal the wounds'. Senator Sumner, on the other hand, wasn't too eager for the healing of wounds. In 1856 he had been caned and beaten in the Senate chamber by one aggravated and provoked South Carolina congressman. The senator's recovery took three years. Perhaps his own 'reconstruction' left Sumner unmoved and unmovable by a spirit of brotherly love. In the senator's estimation, rigor was called for throughout the South, proscribing the liberties that Southerners had been so eager to deny the colored people in their midst. As for Southern leaders, their heads must fall. The South had been led by traitors. Traitors must be executed.

The President, said Mary Todd, would fight that sort of attitude and win, but on another day. Today, she said, the occasion of inauguration demanded a show of unanimity. After all, the war wasn't over yet. Who knew when it would end? Anyway, Mary Todd liked Senator Sumner. He was handsome, single, and a man who had always behaved in the most courtly fashion to her. She would do her part this evening to help him see the wisdom of her husband's course of action.

Mary Todd was delighted to see Elizabeth. How many times had Elizabeth helped Mary Todd see to the correct appearance of her husband? Elizabeth always said 'Yes' and she always lived up to the 'Yes'. Yet, Mary Todd always looked relieved when Elizabeth arrived to help. The First Lady was always a bit anxious. From a wardrobe she retrieved a soft canvas kit bag she and Elizabeth had put together about two years back. The two called it the 'Presidential Preparation Kit' or the 'Kit'. The Kit contained brush, comb, thread, needle, scissors, and other 'handies' to prepare Mr Abe for public appearances.

Mr Abe was in the Presidential bedroom. His valet Will Slade, as pleasant as he was, was altogether too deferential to the man he served or so Mary Todd claimed. The President would look manageably neat but nowhere as splendid as he should. Elizabeth was to make up the difference between what Will could achieve and that to which she, Mary Todd, aspired.

Mr Abe sat in an armchair next to a table covered with folded maps and dossiers. He was already dressed in his evening outfit, a black suit with tails set off by a crisp, highly starched white shirt with winged collars. The black tie he wore appeared a little loose. Not that that would matter to Mr Abe. He was thoroughly absorbed in the black leather-bound book Elizabeth recognized as his personal Bible. A kerosene lamp cast a yellow glow over the President. There was sufficient light from the wall gas fixtures to enable Elizabeth to readily see a slight showing of skin above the tops of his boots and below the hem of his trousers. He probably wasn't wearing socks. Mr Abe would go about barefoot if he could but he knew that would be unseemly in a President.

Will wasn't immediately evident. Mr Abe appeared to be alone. Elizabeth peered over the President's bed and saw the valet rummaging through the bottom drawer of a wardrobe. How should she start reforming what Will was too shy to address?

Mr Abe looked up from his reading, his glasses perched on the end of his nose. "Good evening, Madame Elizabeth."

"Good evening, Mr Abe...and Will."

Will looked over his shoulder at Elizabeth. "Evenin', Madame Elizabeth," said he before turning back to his work. He had a butter-scotch color that always reminded her of George, but unlike George he was short and compact and persistent, as he was now. If anyone could find something in the White House it would be Will. After all, among other things, he was the keeper of the White House keys.

"I got Will looking for a patriotic pin I got several years back at the Illinois State Fair. After seeing all those ambassadors earlier today and looking at this black suit, I thought it might be nice to have a touch of color that would make up for what I won't be able to say tonight. It's an old brass pin that says 'Union Now & Forever'. Dangling from it are red, white, and blue silk ribbons. So far Will's not been able to find it.

"Maybe it's somewhere else, Will."

"Yessir," he replied.

"Kind a ya to drop by, Madame Keckly."

"Mary Todd asked me to. I'm happy to oblige."

"She sent you over here?"

"Yes...she did."

"I figured. Well, let's get to the business that needs to be done."

Will turned around and held aloft the pin Mr Abe had wanted. "I found it, sir."

"Thank you, Will. Just lay it on the table here 'cause I got another favor to ask ka ya."

Elizabeth saw that the ribbons bore creases from the crumpling they'd been subjected to in the drawer. Something would have to be done about that.

Mr Abe plucked something from the further side of his chair and handed it to Elizabeth. "Take a looka that, will ya? Ain't it beautiful?"

It was a polished copper flask, roughly six by four inches, with a chrysanthemum blossom etched on one side and an eagle on the other. The eagle had raised wings, but the design of the eagle echoed the blossom on the other side. The neck of the flask had a brass cap tied to the flask by a fine brass chain. The flask was cool to the touch and warm to the eye. Elizabeth couldn't but admire the elegant beauty of the flask.

"This was a gift from the Japanese ambassador earlier today. He told me it was specially made for me. In Japan they make 'em for plum wine but he said he was sure I would put it to other use. And I will. May I?" asked Mr Abe.

Elizabeth handed the flask back to Mr Abe, who gave it to Will. "Fill it from the spring water, not the city water, Will, if you would please. I'll want it this evening."

"Yessir." Will took the flask and left.

Elizabeth went to a dresser bureau whose top drawer she knew held a dozen pairs of black socks, including ones that covered the calves. She plucked a rather large balled up pair and returned to Mr Abe. Without a word said, he knew what Elizabeth required. He put the Bible aside and began taking off his shoes.

"Watcha readin', Mr Abe?"

"The Gospel of Mark, his account of the baptism of Jesus in the Jordan. I thought Mark would be on the mark tonight. I tol' myself I needed to read that before going off to any celebration. A lotta people tonight will see the ball as a celebration of my being invested with another four years of power. Jesus was someone sent by God, invested with power, and yet he humbled himself to be baptized. Can ya see him at the Jordan, waiting his turn to be baptized by his cousin, standing there with all those sinners who came to repent? What a humble and powerful love that was, *that is*."

As Mr Abe pulled on the second sock, he continued, "But we all have feet of clay. The power of this world don't last. God's love does. That's what's powerful and because God loves He has expectations. I tell ya, Madame Keckly, if our hopes aren't in His expectations we're lost. It never hurts to remember that from one day to the next but especially on this kind of occasion. One can never be too humble, unless one makes a fuss about it."

Elizabeth joined Mr Abe in laughing then she shook her head, saying, "Mr Abe I often wonder how those folks down South see you as a power-hungry tyrant. I think most people up here see you for whatcher are, Mr Abe, a man tryin' to do right."

"Thank you. I try, I try...but doin' good is somethin' ya can hardly ever do alone."

"Oh, yeh. You've got lots of people in on this..."

"Hard to call a war good," said he, "but it can be necessary. There's worse things than war."

"Ain't that the truth," said Elizabeth. She took a brush from the Presidential Preparation Kit and walked over to a dresser bureau. On the dresser was a large crockery bowl and pitcher. She poured water over the brush into the bowl. The brush became thoroughly wet. It needed to be if she was going to tame Mr Abe's hair. "I got enough water here to baptize you, Mr Abe."

"You can only be baptized once," replied Mr Abe.

"Mr Abe, you been baptized?" Elizabeth asked. She held the brush aside awaiting an answer as she stood hovering over the President's right side. Much rode on Elizabeth's question. Many a time the President's opponents had tarred him with being an ungodly man. Mr Abe had no public record of being baptized. And Mary Todd had several times confided to Elizabeth her desire that her husband be baptized. Baptism would be politically useful, said Mary Todd.

Up till then there'd been joy, even merriment, in Mr Abe's eyes. Now he looked alarmed. Had she been out of line in asking the question?

"You are always straightforward, Madame Elizabeth. I regret I can't give you a straightforward reply. I will be deeply indebted to yeh if you never mention we've ever had this conversation. Not to anyone, not even Mary Todd," said Mr Abe, looking up at Elizabeth.

Without hesitation Elizabeth knew she would keep this secret. She had a hunch the President had been baptized. She loved him too much not to keep this promise. She said, "You have my word. I won't mention this to anyone, Mr Abe. I better brush your hair."

"Thank you," said he.

Mr Abe was very sensitive about this matter, so sensitive he didn't want the conversation even reported, not even within the household. Why could that be? He didn't even want Mary Todd told of the conversation. Why? The Lincolns were such a mystery. She felt relieved to be able to address the tangible.

Elizabeth managed to get Mr Abe's hair sufficiently wet to tame it. All the while she was taming and combing his hair, Mr Abe closed his eyes. The combing seemed to bring a measure of peace. When she had finished with the hair, Mr Abe thanked her and resumed reading Mark. Elizabeth placed the brush on a towel to dry out then took the Union Now & Forever pin, promising to bring it back pressed. She would take it down to the laundry room, where hot irons were always available, kept on an oven dedicated to that very purpose.

When Elizabeth returned, Mary Todd was with her husband. Mr Abe was still seated, but he was half engulfed in the cream-colored crinoline dress that Elizabeth had made for this evening. Mary was straightening her husband's tie.

"Lizzy, let's see this pin that Abe's been talkin' about," said Mary Todd, turning away from her husband.

Elizabeth handed the pin to Mary Todd, who immediately shook her head. "This is more toy than decoration, my dear. The sentiment is fine, but the pin isn't the sort of magnificence the ambassadors will be wearing this evening."

"It reflects a magnificent sentiment," said Mr Abe, "because if a free people can remain united despite their differences, there's hope for democracy. Isn't that magnificent enough for our republic?"

Said Mary Todd, "It looks the sorta thing you'd get at a state fair, not anything better an' that. We shouldn't look like some rubes just come in off the street."

Mr Abe laughed. "Well, the tall an' the short of it is we don't look like rubes, I'd say. We're a magnificent pair, don't you think, Madame Elizabeth?"

"I think so, you both look mighty good tonight."

"Thank you, Lizzy, but I think we'll look better if we leave the pin behind."

Will entered the room with the copper flask in hand. "Here you are, sir," he said, handing it to the President.

"Good. Thank you," said Mr Abe.

"What's that?" asked Mary Todd, taking it from Mr Abe.

When Mr Abe explained where the gift came from and how he proposed to use it, Mary Todd's face reddened

"You can't do that. This will be a disgrace! People will think you're drinking some kind of liquor. If you get thirsty, I would think someone could bring the President of these United States a glass of water. Abe, you will have to leave this flask here."

"As you say," said Mr Abe, "but I *will* wear the pin."

Mary Todd accepted the compromise. The two went off to dinner, which would be followed by the inaugural ball held in the Patent Office. The newspaper accounts of the evening pretty much fell along party lines, the Democratic papers excoriating Mary Todd's regal airs, the Republican papers praising the significance of an election and inauguration carried off in the midst of a civil war. Political baptisms are fraught with contention, thought Elizabeth, so the different take on the same stream of events was inevitable. Real baptisms were, on the other hand, so much simpler, so much more open to a shared interpretation. Or were they? In the days following the inauguration ball, she asked again and again, *Did Mr Abe really get baptized or had she read too much into his reaction?* And, *If he were really baptized, as his reaction suggested, why would he want to keep his baptism secret, even from Mary Todd? And where was the hand of God in all this? Or, had Mr Abe invited the finger of God to tear away the façade of his secret?*

There were so many questions and she still hadn't mentioned a thing to the President about his personal safety.

CHAPTER 7

—⚏—

Elizabeth next returned to the White House the Saturday following the inaugural reception and ball. While she was overseeing the creation of a new round of spring and summer dresses, the President was overseeing the appointment of a new round of officials for this his second administration. Dressing a government was obviously more taxing than dressing the ladies of the capital. But Elizabeth believed the dressing of government was as nothing compared to the pall of war, which hourly fell on Mr Abe's shoulders. The dressage of war was exacting and the toll heavy on the President.

Elizabeth caught a glimpse of him as she delivered a personal note of thanks from Frederick Douglass. When Mr Douglass had been invited to the White House reception held a week earlier, certain gatekeepers had attempted to keep Mr Douglass from entering. These gatekeepers hadn't yet adjusted to the fact that black Americans were quite able to be citizens of the Republic. Black Americans had already taken on the duty of citizenship. Some 180,000 had enlisted in the Army or Navy. They were willing and eager to play all the roles of citizenship, including participation in the workings and decorum of the Republic. Walker Lewis, Elizabeth recalled, had termed Mr Abe's reception of Mr Douglass 'an act of decency and respect due a leading American citizen'. It was, Elizabeth agreed, but given everything that had or hadn't happened before, she knew Mr Abe's act was also courageous and deserving of thanks.

Others might call him 'Ole Abe', but if Elizabeth thought of him as old anything it was as Old Warrior in an age-old, time-told battle never ending in this life. This morning Mr Abe very much looked like the incarnate, unrelenting warrior for justice. Often enough she'd seen Mr Abe sitting at his desk with his head bent over whatever he happened to be reading, sometimes with his right arm propped against his face. This morning both arms were propped up against his face. If she hadn't known better, she would have thought he was grieving. Grieving no doubt he was. He'd had cause for that every day he'd served as the nation's chief magistrate. No, he was more than merely grieving this morning. Elizabeth guessed Mr Abe was exhausted. And to think his second term was only beginning!

Mary Todd that Saturday morning was effervescent with elation. "Good mornin', good mornin', good mornin', Lizzy, have I got news for you!"

"What news, Mary T?"

"Montgomery Blair's going to be sent off to Spain or Austria as ambassador. The Blairs are nothing but Southern opportunists. They have always set the so-called 'better set' of this town against me. With the Blairs out of town there's real hope Washington can become a better place!"

That meant, thought Elizabeth, *a better place for one Mary Todd.* Until 1864 Montgomery Blair had served as Postmaster General in the Lincoln administration.

"The only better place for the Blairs would be some desert," said Mary Todd. "And have you heard about the Jaundice Twins?"

Mary Todd was alluding to John Nicolay and John Hay, the first and second secretaries to the President. Neither was yellow looking but Mary Todd liked to think of them as yellow. Mr Abe had brought these two young lawyers with him when he came from Springfield four years ago. Mary Todd hated them both, but that wasn't widely known, though Hay's penchant for calling Mary's behavior 'hellcatical' was. In any event there had been nothing about the two Johns in the morning's *Daily Chornicle.*

"Haven't heard a thing, Mary T."

"They're both being sent out of the country. Both!" As she spoke, Mary Todd fluttered about her bedroom, straightening a pillow, adjusting a curtain, flitting from one to another thing like a bird in frantic search for a branch on which to sing its song.

"Exiled like Napoleon?" asked Elizabeth, with a touch of mischief.

"Exiled enough, I'd like to say, but at least sent away. I'll make merry any day those two are sent away." Mary Todd assumed a stern visage. "Nicolay is to be sent to Paris, Hay to Berlin or Vienna or somewhere. No matter, he'll be gone. They'll both be gone! Good riddance to them both."

"Nice, real nice for them," said Elizabeth realizing the Twins wouldn't be jaundiced in these European capitals. She added, "Their departure will be good for you."

"And Abe," added Mary Todd. "I've had to suffer their presence for four years and Abe has been poorly served. For four years, Lizzy, for four miserable years." Her brief moment of delight was now over. The sting of those four years of sufferance had transformed her. Mary Todd slumped into an armchair facing a window over-looking the White House south lawn.

"Lizzy, only you can see the truth about me. Everyone thinks of me as the First Lady and too many resent the fact that I, I, a Southern woman am in such a position of power. Ah, yes, and with a brother and six half brothers or brothers-in-law in the Confederate army. How could I be allowed near the White House! Would that I had a thousandth of the power attributed to me. Not one ounce of the bitterness I've drunk has been deserved. I am the scapegoat for every sin committed under Abraham's name.

"For four years those two men have thwarted, obstructed, contained my every effort to bring some dignity to this feeble excuse for a national mansion. For four years I've been cut off from guiding my own husband in making political decisions. Lizzy, you should have known us when we lived in Springfield. I had my husband's ear then…and I don't just mean in running the things in our home. The state of Illinois was a better place because I made Abraham a better politician than he would'a been on his own. If I hadn't been his wife what would'a he amounted to? After all these years he still doesn't know how to dress. And he still hangs out with the likes of the Jaundice Twins, telling yarns just as he did when he was on the judicial circuit in Illinois.

"Thank God he never took up chewin' tobacco or liquor. But I had to clean 'im and guide 'im in ever other way. And for all that, these transfers out of the White House came out of the blue, Lizzy, out of the blue. I feel almost as helpless as a child. But I've got hope, this morning more hope than I've had in some time. Lizzy, there's got to be hope in this world if you want to keep going."

"Oh, I know about hope, Mary Todd," said Elizabeth without rebuke.

"Yes, I guess you do," said Mary Todd, looking into the distance.

"As for Mr Abe, you can never forget the war. War not only ends lives, it changes those who live through it," said Elizabeth.

"I know, oh, I know. That's why I want to make every effort with peace on the horizon to make sure things turn back the way they were when we lived in Springfield. I want a say in things, in things that matter, Lizzy. Will you help me?"

"I don't know what I can do, Mary Todd. I got my hands full. I'm no politician."

"Maybe not, maybe so. You formed that contraband society to help the newly freed. You even got me to donate money." Mary Todd chuckled. "Which reminds me I have an envelope right here to pay you for the most recent dresses."

Mary Todd rose from the chair and walked to a dresser bureau. Opening a drawer, she removed a small cream-colored envelope, which she handed to Elizabeth. It was weighted with coins and greenbacks, mostly coins. Elizabeth wanted to put the envelope in her purse, but she'd left her purse on the vanity table at the other end of the room. Right now Elizabeth would give Mary Todd her undivided attention because Mary Todd wanted that.

"I want you to help me, Lizzy. If I'm ever to be First Lady of the Land, someone's got to help me be the first lady in my very own house. Abraham needs my attention. I need to spend more time with him talkin' politics, like in Springfield days. I need someone I can rely on to oversee running the household."

"You got people for that Mary Todd, all kinds of people."

"I know, I know. But those people aren't used to takin' orders from you."

"I don't think they ever would, Mary Todd. Oh, no, there'd be a mess of bad feelins' if I were to speak outta place. How 'bout if I listen, not speak. My mama said for every person that got in trouble 'cause of their ears, there were four hundred got in trouble 'cause of their tongues. If I listen that'd help."

"Maybe. But I need help in running the White House so I can spend more time helping Abraham politically, if you know what I mean."

"There's only so many things you can do, Mary Todd. Why not let the White House take care of itself. There's enough people to do that. You can pick china sets or curtains or carpets when it comes to that but let the day-to-day stuff take care of itself. As for Mr Abe, maybe you should make a point of not only suggestin' ways of being together, but just say you want to be with him more. Mr Abe needs a rest from all the things he does. He looks mighty tired. It won't do him or the country any good if he runs down like a watch not wound-up."

"There's plenty who'll wind up the White House, Lizzy, but only I can help Abe."

"He loves summer out at the Soldiers' Home," said Elizabeth. "It'll do him good again this year."

"I can't wait for summer. Now is the time to strike, before peace comes along. But you know, Lizzy, that's a great idea."

"What?" asked Elizabeth.

"Let's ride out to the Anderson Cottage at Soldiers' Home. It's sunny. It's warm today. We'll take Tad with us."

"But what about the reception that begins this afternoon?"

"Lizzy, you just said let the White House take care of itself. Anyway, we'll be back in plenty a time. I'll get Tad from his class. You go on down an' get a carriage for us — an open carriage. It's too nice a day to be cooped up in here."

"Shouldn't Master Tad stay in class? He's got so much to learn," said Elizabeth. *How can Mary Todd be so...so...indifferent seeming about her boy's education?*

"Tad needs fresh air, Lizzy. We all do."

There was no arguing. The carriage and Tad were fetched. With the carriage came an Army outrider, a sergeant. The outrider escorted and the boy sat with the two ladies as they rode out Vermont Avenue and Rhode Island Avenue to 7th Street Road and then along to Soldiers' Home. Soldiers' Home was an Army retirement home established in the 1850s for wounded soldiers. On the shaded grounds stood a modest house, the Anderson Cottage, built in the Gothic revival style so recently fashionable. The house had served as a retreat for the Lincoln family in the summers of 1862, '63, and '64. It insulated the Lincolns from the bustle of the White House and the trees insulated the house from the worst heat of the day.

There were numerous people walking along the avenues and even a few on the 7th Street Road. Because of the presence of an Army outrider, many pedestrians, equestrians, and carriage riders appeared to recognize Mary Todd as her carriage rolled past. The gentlemen tipped their hats and the ladies nodded. The cavalry sergeant riding just to the rear of the carriage provoked Mary Todd to complain about Ward Lamon's officious intrusion into her life. Elizabeth was all ears, as she remembered she'd yet to broach the matter of Presidential safety with Mr Abe.

It was quite one thing to protect the President, quite another to interfere in his family life, said Mary Todd. She wondered if the Jaundice Twins somehow had had a hand in this devilment, in this sudden show of interest in protecting the whole Lincoln family. What had they been doing the last four years? No, it wasn't too hard to see this protection business was a clever parting shot from the Jaundice Twins. The two were too clever by half. No, less than half, because neither one was even half witted. Mary Todd laughed at the accuracy of her character accounting.

Elizabeth half smiled. She knew that Mr Abe valued both John Nicolay and John Hay — for good reason. They were smart, they were shrewd, and they spoke and wrote well. She thought of them as the right and left wheels of Mr Abe's chariot. True, at times they wanted to ride over Mary Todd but she had a habit of wanting to stand in the way. It would do her and Mr Abe good, she thought, if Mary Todd would concern herself more with her husband as a husband and father and less as the country's chief political officer.

All things considered, Elizabeth was feeling good about the direction Mary Todd seemed to be taking.

As elsewhere in Washington the trees at the Soldiers' Home were just beginning to bud. Crocuses and daffodils basked in the unfiltered sunlight. As throughout the Civil War, white tents peppered the grounds of the Soldiers' Home. The tents were occupied by men of Company K of the 150th Regiment of Pennsylvania Volunteers, as they had been since the autumn of 1862. The men of Company K had become part of the extended Lincoln family. They saluted and shouted 'huzza' as the carriage entered the grounds. Tad was bouncing up and down in his seat as he saluted in return. Mary Todd beamed at the goodwill of these familiar soldiers.

When the carriage came to a halt at the Anderson place, Tad jumped down, shook the hands of the soldiers nearby, and ran intent on a campaign of hearty good cheer. Mary Todd was about to admonish him, then thought better of it. She watched her boy run off into a thicket of tents. She was put at ease by a kind sergeant of Company K who promised to keep an eye on the boy. Not that there was any danger. The boy would be among his summer friends.

As the Company K soldiers drifted towards their other companions in arms, the outrider and driver hitched their horses to a hitching post. Mary Todd and Elizabeth made three large circuits around the Anderson place, then headed back to the carriage. Mary Todd asked that Tad be retrieved. The outrider sergeant went off to find the boy. The driver assisted Mary Todd and Elizabeth in boarding the carriage. Elizabeth would long remember what Mary Todd said as they waited for the sergeant to appear with Tad. Mary Todd returned to the topic that had become a veritable obsession.

"Tad's an easy one to manage, Lizzy, but not my husband, not anymore. I've lost him in this war. If I'm goin' to get him back it's goin' to have to happen before General Lee surrenders, or I'll never get him back."

"You'll get him, Mary Todd. He's never left home. He's been preoccupied with this war." *How many times had she said this?*

"I'll have to fight to get him back. Fight. There's so many others that want to tear him from me."

"Oh, I don't think so." *Who could be fighting to tear Mr Abe from Mary Todd?*

"I know so," said Mary Todd.

There was nothing Elizabeth could say that would vanquish Mary Todd's fears that she was about to lose her husband once and for all. When the sergeant and Tad returned, Tad insisted on lifting himself aboard. As soon as the boy was aboard, the sergeant unhitched and mounted his horse and the carriage driver whistled up the horses to return to the White House.

That afternoon Mary Todd hosted her last Saturday reception of the social season. Most attendees were men, just as Mary Todd would have it. She had always looked upon her receptions as an opportunity to glad-hand and bring suasion on behalf of her husband. Men were the ones whose hands held the levers of power. Among those in attendance were senators and congressmen, clergymen, a smattering of Army officers, one admiral, several diplomats (though, of course, not in diplomatic dress), correspondents of all the important papers, and as Mary Todd termed them 'the usual hoard of office-seekers and free-loaders' come for coffee, tea, and cakes provided by the White House kitchen. Among the few women was Mary Jane Welles, wife of the Secretary of the Navy.

The surprise of the afternoon was the appearance of the President, who joined his wife in greeting guests. Mr Abe's appearance at the reception put Mary Todd in the best of temper all afternoon. The President was affable enough but looked more haggard than ever. As one congressman later put it, 'The President was pleasant but not present.' He seemed preoccupied. He was clearly not up to retailing the stories he was otherwise so wont to tell. Perhaps he'd been instructed by Mary Todd to avoid the off-color stories today. She never said and Elizabeth never asked whether the President had been given story-telling instructions. Elizabeth's curiosity about the President's quiescence was soon overridden by a more urgent concern.

Mr Abe took sick. That Saturday he went to bed early. Sunday he excused himself from accompanying Mary Todd and Tad to the service at the New York Avenue Presbyterian Church, Dr Phineas Gurley presiding. He later managed to get dressed and to confer with Congressman Arnold of Illinois. He offered the congressman a position as an auditor in the Treasury Department. All other official activities were cancelled for the day.

That evening Dr Anson Henry, the family doctor, paid a call to the White House. Will Slade had already helped Mr Abe get into his nightclothes. When the doctor came round, he found the President propped in bed. The President had no fever. He was able to drink and sup but was without appetite. His stomach and such wasn't acting up. He had a slight cough, a very slight cough. He might be coming down with something but the cough gave no clues. Dr Henry surmised what had long been evident: the President was plumb tired. He needed a month of good nights' rest, said Dr Henry, but he knew that was likely impossible. It would be enough, he suggested, if the world were told he was sick. Stick with that as long as you can, he told Mr Abe, and you'll feel a lot better. Stay in bed at least a few days, drink plenty of good water, and get plenty to eat.

The following day the press reported that the President was indisposed due to sickness. No official visitors were being received at the White House. Elizabeth came shortly before noon. Over lunch Mary Todd told her friend everything that came to mind concerning the Saturday reception and the subsequent 'collapse', as she termed it. Later in the day Annie and Will provided additional details. Mary Todd had long before told them to treat Elizabeth as family, so they could be counted on to be generous in their eyewitness accounts. Will, of course, had the most telling impressions of Mr Abe. He told Elizabeth the President was shaking when he helped him into his nightclothes, shaking not shivering. Had Will mentioned this to the doctor? No. To Mary Todd? No. Elizabeth chose to say nothing of it either.

Mary Todd was not one disposed to caring for others. When those she loved were in need, she became even more anxious and fretful, unable to adorn herself even for a moment with a measure of calm. She needed someone else now to hover over her sickly husband. That would have to be, could be none other than, her dear friend Lizzy. So for the next few nights Elizabeth would stay at the White House. A messenger was sent to the Lewis home to explain Elizabeth's absence and to fetch a few items that Elizabeth had requested.

Elizabeth was given a small, furnished room in the White House but she spent little time there. Rather, as consoler-in-chief she traveled among the rooms in which each of the Lincolns was held hostage to Mr Abe's collapse. In Elizabeth's eyes, Tad had a good excuse. He was anxious about his dad. He had visited him several times the first evening and would on subsequent evenings ask how his dad felt, always eager to bring a fresh pitcher of water to his father's bedroom and ready to help in other ways. In the evenings, when it was time for the boy to go to bed, Mary Todd would come in for 'tuck and kiss', as she called it. She'd pull the bedspread snug up under Tad's chin, then give him a kiss on his right cheek. Tad's arms would come out from under the sheets and latch on to his mom as he endeavored to bring her closer. The two would hug and then she'd tell Tad that Lizzy would read to him a bit. Then the lights must be out.

Elizabeth could select from a considerable number of books given to the boy, along with numerous toys, all intended to endear the giver with the boy's father. Tad was most taken with the toys, but of the books Tad's greatest affection seemed to be for an illustrated collection of the tales of the Brothers Grimm. The hand-colored illustrations would capture anyone's attention, so the boy's interest was almost inevitable. What Elizabeth found so striking was that the Grimm book was in German, a gift of the Prussian ambassador. Neither Elizabeth nor Tad could read German, at least not in easy fashion. But the Gothic script and the foreign wordage had the felicity of beckoning the boy to try. Tad's tutor, Mr Williamson had been teaching the boy to sound out letters. Tad was happy enough to let Elizabeth read the tales written in English, but he was the one who would point to a Grimm word now and then and try to pronounce it. When Elizabeth told Mary Todd of Tad's interest in German, Mary Todd replied she already knew of it. If the book had been in French, she could have helped. But first things first. He needed to learn to read English first, said Mary Todd.

Elizabeth and Mary Todd would talk late into the evenings, but other than helping Mary Todd stall the inevitable, she couldn't help put her friend to sleep. She found she was of more help to Mary Todd in the mornings. She would provide a report on Mr Abe's condition and Tad's too. And then she would listen to whatever Mary Todd might have to say. Mary Todd had something important to report each morning for, as it turned out each night during the President's 'collapse', Willie paid a visit to his mother, or so Mary Todd reported.

Had Willie said anything? No. Did he appear concerned? No, au contraire, he appeared happy. Should any of this be relayed to Mr Abe? Yes, of course. Willie had been dead three years and his spectral appearances at the foot of Mary Todd's bed had become much less frequent in the last year or so. Mary Todd took his reappearance as a good sign.

Elizabeth said nothing of this to Walker Lewis, but she had talked with him about it three years earlier, when she'd encouraged Mary Todd to attend séances to reassure herself that her Willie was happy in the Beyond. Walker became quite indignant. No one needs any other assurance than what's in the Bible, he said. Our Lord promises a life in His kingdom and there's no call to get involved in witchcraft trying to spook the dead back into this world. No call.

Elizabeth said nothing more of it. She didn't consider the séances as witchcraft. And who was she to deny Mary Todd the comfort of knowing about someone so dearly loved in the Beyond? Walker Lewis didn't have any dead children. Mary Todd did. She, Elizabeth, did too. She couldn't help attending at least a few séances right after George was killed. She knew calling up the dead was Bible wrong and life deadening. You couldn't get anywhere with the dead. If you thought you could, you were only fooling yourself and you'd pay. But surely just a few visits could be forgiven.

Mary Todd couldn't leave the dead in the Beyond. Whether seeing Willie at a séance or at home, Mary Todd would quietly share the visitations from Beyond with her husband. Mr Abe would pat his wife's hand as she'd talk about the specter of Willie. Tears would come to his eyes. Everyone knew that Mr Abe loved that boy so much. But otherwise he'd just listen.

CHAPTER 8

—〰—

While the President lay abed, Elizabeth brought him soup and Tad brought him sunshine. Mary Todd would usher in the boy and after a time usher him out. While with his papa, Tad would play act, being a knight in armor, a farmer, a soldier, a sailor, a clown in a circus. Sometimes his papa would read from one of the boy's storybooks. His papa might ask Tad how he was doing with his lessons. Tad wouldn't have much to say on that account. Neither of his parents pressed him to account for what he was or wasn't doing in school.

Mary Todd, of course, had Dr Henry come by mornings and evenings to check on her husband. But she chose to rely on her friend, Elizabeth, to bring her husband back to health. When Willie had taken sick in February 1862 she'd asked Elizabeth to come by her side. Neither Mary Todd nor Mr Abe could abide the boy's sickness. Elizabeth told Mary Todd then about the peppered chicken and onion soup her mama had made whenever she was sick. She'd been taught how to make that soup and still kept a bottle of the New Orleans pepper sauce the soup needed, just in case of sickness. Elizabeth had offered to make the soup for Willie back in '62 but Mary Todd had insisted then on placing total reliance on the attending physicians' advice. When she relented, the boy was only three days from death. This time Mary Todd insisted that Elizabeth's soup be included in the regimen of rest and recuperation prescribed for her husband. The

White House kitchen was instructed to follow Elizabeth's instructions to the 't' in preparing a healthy soup for the President.

The Tuesday following his collapse, Mr Abe held a cabinet session in his bedroom. Otherwise he either slept or tried to read reports that had been stacked on a table next to his bed. Mary Todd preferred to see her Abe at mealtimes, when they would eat together in the Presidential bedroom. Otherwise Mary Todd had decided to distract herself by reading three French novellas by turns. The thought of losing her husband was simply unbearable. Being forced to read and think in a foreign tongue was a good diversion.

Tuesday evening, following the cabinet meeting, Mary Todd wasn't up to having supper with her husband. She reported a severe headache and felt sick to her stomach. If it was 'catching' she didn't want to pass it on to her husband. So she asked Elizabeth if she would join the President at supper. When Elizabeth arrived in the Presidential bedroom Will was finishing placing chairs for Mr Abe and for Elizabeth at a small side table covered by a crisp white cloth. Mr Abe wore a dark green dressing gown over his night-clothes. Elizabeth certainly hadn't made it for him. She wondered if Mary Todd had purchased it on one of her shopping trips to New York. In any event the gown was quite different from the silk dressing gown she'd once made for Varina Davis to give as a Christmas gift to her husband.

Mr Abe looked weary, but he smiled as he caught sight of Elizabeth. "Good evening, Madame Elizabeth. Thank you for joining me. How is my Molly?"

"She's not feelin' rightly, but she'll come 'round, Mr Abe."

Will assisted the two in being seated, then positioned himself by a door at the other end of the room. A few minutes later a steward, white jacketed like Will, pushed a wooden trolley cart over the threshold into the room. On it sat a lidded silver tureen and a silver teapot. On its lower shelf were a plate with slices of bread and a plate of butter. While Will placed the plates on the table, the steward ladled out the soup and set it before Mr Abe and Elizabeth. The steward soon left, leaving the trolley nearby. Will waited at a nearby doorway against the possibility that someone would want more soup.

Mr Abe bowed his head slightly, kept silent, and Elizabeth followed suit, saying a silent prayer herself. Mr Abe ate his soup with gusto, finishing his bowl before Elizabeth half finished hers. Will ladled out another bowlful for Mr Abe, which was soon consumed in like speed.

"You like the soup, Mr Abe?"

"I do. The recipe's from your mama's kitchen, Molly tells me."

"It is."

"Is your mother still living?"

"No, she died in Vicksburg in '57."

"Ah, I'm sorry," said Mr Abe. "I expect your mother was dear to you. I can't remember much of my mother. She died when I was eight. But I know I have good feelin's to her and, this may sound strange, even more so to my stepma. Her name was Sarah. My father married her soon after my real mother died, yet she's very dear to me, too. She was loving and encouraging to me. My pa never was. I'm thankful to God for her. In fact she means far more to me than my father. That's not somethin' I often talk about.

"How was your father?" asked Mr Abe.

"Depends on what you mean by father," replied Elizabeth, "if you know what I mean."

Mr Abe looked down at his plate and said quietly, "I think I know what you're gettin' at."

"But the man I consider my real papa married my mama and treated me as his own. I never saw him much after the family was broken up, if you know what I mean."

"I know what you mean," said Mr Abe with an intense look.

"My papa would visit us at Christmas and Easter, when they would let visits like that. He loved my mama and me dearly. He always encouraged my learnin'."

"Yup, fathers can show the way, must show the way," said Mr Abe. "I coulda done a mite better in that department with Tad."

"He'll come along, I'm sure," said Elizabeth, but she wasn't so sure. While she finished her soup, Mr Abe took a piece of bread, then beckoned Will to come over and pour a cup of coffee.

"Thanks, Will. Would you like some, too, Madame Elizabeth?"

"Please," she replied.

Will poured a cup then stepped away. The President and Elizabeth ate and sipped silently for a minute or so. Then he spoke.

"Families are important to accomplishing what's good in life. But they can also be a source of the bad. I suppose that's not sayin' much," said Mr Abe with a twinkle in his eyes, "because you'd be hard put to prove me wrong.

"I guess what I'm gettin' at is that families are where we learn so many things, both good and bad, and one of the good things is loyalty. Another is obedience to authority. I'm all mindful of that just these days because I ask myself and our God how can we become one family again as Americans.

"The fighting in this war has been on a scale far exceeding what most would have imagined four years ago. There's been so much killing. So much destruction. So much bitterness. I've prayed to God asking how to restore the unity of a family. Not that a family is ever perfect. Not that people don't disagree, have spats. But we've got to be reconciled.

"And when I've prayed these days, what's come to mind is Luke. I've always been told that Luke wrote his gospel and the Acts of the Apostles. So I've been reading both. Forgiveness is writ all through Luke. And that hits my heart right in the center. But what about my head? Forgiveness without some kind of practical plan is like a horse tryin' to get traction in the spring mud. Ya ain't goin' ta get anywhere.

"As I have read the Acts, I see again and again how one man's actions can make a difference for a whole family, a whole household, even whole towns. So I've asked myself who in the South is that man, if there's any such man there."

"That you're askin' in that way," said Elizabeth, "tells me you don't think it's Mr Davis. He would seem the obvious one."

"He's too stubborn," said Mr Abe.

"But he was always kind to me and others," said Elizabeth.

"Now there's loyalty for you," said Mr Abe.

"But I didn't join 'em in Richmond," said Elizabeth.

"That was wise."

"I still love Virginia, now more than ever, Mr Abe. I so want to see this war over and the slaves all freed. Then people can get on with buildin' a new Virginia."

"You are one gracious lady, Madame Keckly."

"Thank you, Mr Abe. They teach it down there in the Good Book."

"You put yer finger on it. And I think the finger of God is pointin' to one of your fellow Virginians, General Lee."

"General Lee," repeated Elizabeth. "I've done work for his wife, too. He was very much the gentleman."

Mr Abe chuckled. "Yes, he's a very good man and a terribly good general. You know he was the first one I asked to head the Army when the Secession crisis started. The war might have ended three years ago if he'd taken me up on the offer. Not that I hold it against him. He did what he thought was right as a loyal son of Virginia."

"The people of Virginia — the South, too, from what I hear — love that man," said Elizabeth.

"All of which gives me hope. He's managed to keep his cause goin' so many times, when the flame was about to burn out. Now I'm hoping he can help, God willing, to bring this all to a merciful end."

Mr Abe sat back in his chair and closed his eyes. Elizabeth asked, "Are you all right?"

"I'm all right. I just got to get well."

"Do you want more soup, Mr Abe?"

"No, I think I've had enough. It's good as could be, a testament to your mama, Madame Keckly. Thank you for substitutin' for Mary. I don't like eatin' alone."

Elizabeth took that as a signal that Mr Abe was ready to be alone again. Just then she remembered her promise to Mr Lamon. The conversation with Mr Abe had taken such a pleasant turn she was unwilling to deflect it now to a potentially gruesome topic. Surely, she felt, she'd have another chance to be with Mr Abe without Mary Todd present. *Another opportunity for discreet conversation will present itself ... or perhaps not.*

Will scurried over to pull away the chair that might otherwise encumber Elizabeth's dress. That put a cap on Elizabeth's uncertainty. She resolved to talk with Mr Abe some other time. He began to rise from his chair to bid her good night. She motioned him to

81

remain seated and bid him good night. He weakly shook her hand, thanked her, and bid her a good night, too.

On the following afternoon, March 15th, Elizabeth again visited the White House. She learned the President was again receiving official visitors, but only on a very limited basis. He'd received the new Austrian ambassador, Count Wydenbruck, in the morning and conferred with certain cabinet officers. That evening he and Mary Todd attended a production of Mozart's *The Magic Flute* at Grover's Theatre. Count Wydenbruck was there, too, but not accompanying the Presidential party. Instead, Mary Todd had asked Clara Harris, daughter of New York's Senator Harris, to join them with her escort, General James Wilson. Miss Harris was an avid opera aficionado and relayed many a tale about Mozart and the opera. Among the tales was the story that Mozart may have been murdered by Masons angry that he had divulged and degraded Masonic rites in *The Magic Flute*.

Mr Abe was rather skeptical of this particular story. He knew too many Masons. While he could imagine a Mason being upset with Mozart, he found it hard to believe anyone would want to kill the composer over the imagined slight. Yet while he disbelieved the story, he brooded over the possibility, at least so Mary Todd reported to Elizabeth. Mary Todd thought she wouldn't be inviting Clara Harris again soon to the opera. Miss Harris was convivial enough, but these lurid stories were not good for the President. He must be made to remember the bright side of Mozart, whose music revealed a temperament the very opposite of her husband's. Mary Todd told Elizabeth she'd been struck by the charm of the bells and chimes heard throughout *The Magic Flute*. She had resolved to purchase a bevy of 'table bells', as she called them, that could be scattered about the house.

"How will you use them?" asked Elizabeth.

"They will be used to summon the servants," said Mary Todd.

"But don't most rooms here in the White House already have bell chords that can be yanked to summon the help from downstairs?"

"They do, Lizzy, but I'm thinking beyond that. We've got to think beyond the present. In four years we'll be leaving the White House. I'm not quite sure where we'll be going. Abe wants to return to Springfield, that I know. But who knows where we'll be. It won't be in any house as grand as this one, that's for sure. We'll need an arrangement for summoning servants. Table bells will set a tone of discreet cheeriness."

"Maybe you should buy the bells after you see how many are needed," said Elizabeth.

"The need is already clear. I'm thinking ahead."

So the two went off that afternoon on a shopping expedition, while Mr Abe and Tad took a brief carriage ride around the city. A plain clothed policeman escorted the ladies and Army outriders escorted the President.

There was no one who could police the First Lady's purchasing impulses. With Elizabeth in tow, she visited Galt's, where she purchased all eight table bells the jeweler had in stock. In the next block they visited Milliken's. There Mary Todd purchased another dozen pairs of gloves to add to the 300 pairs she had recently purchased. You could never have enough gloves as far as Mary Todd was concerned. They always got so filthy so fast.

Could you have enough time? Elizabeth begged off further shopping when the two left Milliken's. She had to return to her dress shop to attend to her business. Later she would learn that Mary Todd purchased a score of table bells elsewhere that afternoon. After showing them all to her friend, Mary Todd had them packed away in a trunk stored in the attic. The invoices for these purchases would come tumbling into the White House in ensuing days. There was no telling where the bills would land except for one certainty. On absolutely no account was the President to be informed of the invoices. He had enough on his mind and Mary Todd had long ago gotten word to the entire staff that anyone tendering an invoice to the President would lose his head over it.

While Mary Todd was securing arrangements for a home beyond the White House, as Elizabeth would later learn, Mr Abe began arranging to vacate the White House more immediately. General Grant had suggested a vacation after he'd read newspaper accounts of the President's illness. He invited the President to get away from Washington, to be a guest of his own Army staff. The President was pleased to accept the invitation in no small part because he wanted to talk with General Grant and others about ways to bring the fighting to an end that would make for the healing he had in mind. Only the Lord God knew Mr Abe had but a month to lead this healing campaign. And hardly anyone knew the President was to go on vacation until he was gone. Elizabeth wasn't in the know.

When she tried recollecting the days preceding Mr Abe's battlefield vacation, nothing particular came to mind, except for one evening just before Mr Abe and Mary Todd left town. On that evening the two Lincolns were about to go off to another opera. Going to plays and operas was one thing they truly enjoyed doing together. Elizabeth remembered the occasion and the dress made from a bolt of Italian silk cloth purchased by Mary Todd. The silk was colored sky blue imprinted with interlacing golden flowers. Mary Todd was easily pleased with a flowery dress. But she'd asked Lizzy to come by just after dinner to insure that she and Mr Abe got off in good appearance.

When Elizabeth entered Mary Todd's bedroom, Annie, the maid, was buttoning up the sky blue dress in the back as Mary Todd stood before a mirror primping her hair.

"How do I look, Lizzy?"

"So far so good, Mary T."

"But not good enough, is that what you're too nice to say?"

"Not at all, you look good just as you are."

"Lizzy, good enough isn't good enough. You've made this lovely dress for me and what do I have to show for it?"

"Everything you need to show. I wouldn't show any more," said Elizabeth. She thought back to 1862 when Mary Todd had worn the white dress with black accents made in honor of Queen Victoria. That dress, with a rather low cut front and a long train, had provoked Mr Abe to suggest the dress needed less tail and more head.

"I'm not thinking what you're thinking, Lizzy," as if she had read her friend's mind. "I need something in my hair."

Elizabeth replied knowing what Mary Todd had in mind. "You don't need lots o' flowers in your hair. You got plenty o' flowers on the dress. Do you have any silk florets that could match the colors in the dress?"

"You know I do, Lizzy."

Indeed, she knew. And she knew there was no stopping Mary Todd from putting florets in her hair. "You want some help?" she asked.

"Annie will help, Lizzy. You go make sure Abe is ready for the evening."

She walked to the President's bedroom next door. Will was there helping the President put on his shoes.

"Good evenin', Mr Abe. I hope you're wearing black socks this evenin'."

Mr Abe turned to Elizabeth with a smile and pulled up one pant just enough to expose the black sock underneath. "Good evenin', Madame Elizabeth."

"Looks like your hair's still a mess."

"I guess it is," said he. He sat down and she proceeded to brush his hair into a dignified mass. Will, meanwhile, sought and found the tickets for the opera.

Mr Abe asked, "Did Molly mention we'll soon be leaving town?"

"No, Mr Abe. Where you goin'?"

"To the front, to City Point, near Richmond."

Mary Todd entered the room just then, now with golden florets in her hair.

"How do I look?" she asked no one in particular.

"You look like you got caught in the flowery brambles," said Mr Abe. "You make that dress, Madame Elizabeth?"

"I did," said she.

"A beautiful bramblin' dress it be. You look just beautiful, Molly."

"Really?" she asked.

"Really," said he. "I've just informed Madame Elizabeth we're leaving town for a bit."

"Oh, yes, Lizzy, we're leaving town. I forgot to mention that to you. But now that Abraham has told you, please keep it quiet. The papers must not know."

"Is that all?" asked Mr Abe. Elizabeth could tell he'd been expecting Mary Todd to say more. But only later would Elizabeth learn what that more might have been. She sensed a disagreement between the Lincolns and knew best to keep quiet.

Two days later on Thursday, 23 March, Mr Abe, Mary Todd, and Tad embarked on the *River Queen* at the Washington Arsenal dock. Their destination would soon be known. Elizabeth would learn much in the coming days by what was reported in the press. She would learn even more from Annie and Will and eventually Mr Abe, but not before he'd got caught in the brambles. No, not before then.

CHAPTER 9

—∽m∼—

When the *River Queen* pulled away from the Arsenal dock there were no reporters around. The President's departure had been kept secret. The Marines brought a touch of dignity to the occasion. Dockside a platoon stood in two ranks, their rifles held rigidly in front as a salute to their departing commander-in-chief. Following an obligatory 'Hail to the Chief', the President's own Marine band played the gentle, popular airs of Stephen Foster, so recently deceased. As the *River Queen* pulled away and began to make way, the band offered up Foster's 'Swanee River' for an adieu.

President and Mrs Lincoln were observing the departure from the stern rail with Will standing nearby in attendance. Will heard Mrs Lincoln remark to the President that the Marines looked old-fashioned. Indeed, they did. The men in arms wore crisscrossing white bucklers, set against long military jackets. They were capped with tall military hats typical of 50 years earlier. Their commander-in-chief looked rather old-fashioned, too, with his stovepipe black hat. The President's response to the First Lady was to lift his hat right off his head and tip it in salute to the Marines. As the *River Queen* kicked up her heels in mid river, the musical airs became less clear. When they could no longer be heard, Mr Lincoln escorted Mrs Lincoln into the aft saloon. This was a comparatively large room appointed in plush red chairs and Belgian carpets. Windows, not portholes, gave a fine view aft of the boat's wake.

Mr William Crook, an operative from the Treasury Department or the Washington police, Will wasn't sure, had been waiting for the Lincolns in the saloon. He was a tall, well-built man, among a number who'd recently been assigned to protect Mr Lincoln. Will assumed Mr Crook carried a gun. The valet didn't think personal assaults were anywhere likely on this trip. If anything, impersonal assaults were likely. After all, the *River Queen* was entering a zone of war. The Navy had provided an escort for the paddleboat *River Queen*, which was an unarmored commercial vessel chartered for Mr Lincoln's trip to City Point. The Navy escort was a smaller, speedier gunboat, the *USS Bat*, commanded by Lieutenant Commander John Barnes. There were no soldiers aboard the *River Queen*. Will assumed there might be a small contingent of Marines or armed sailors aboard the *Bat*.

Tad hadn't stood with his parents as the *River Queen* pulled away. Nor had he stayed in the saloon. As soon as he'd come aboard, the lad had decided to explore the boat. Annie and Captain Penrose, of the US Army, had taken the boy up to the wheelhouse where the kindly boat captain allowed Tad to watch the riverboat get underway. Once the *River Queen* got underway the first mate acted as tour guide for Tad and his party. It would be a while before the boy's initial exploration came to an end. He readily endeared himself to the crew, who welcomed him (and his parents) to their quarters afloat.

All along the Potomac the trees were in bud and the crocuses and daffodils were in blossom. Birds along the shore were abundant, seen but largely unheard because of the *River Queen's* thumping steam engine and splashing paddles. Blue-jacketed soldiers were seen in abundance, too, on both sides of the river. Many were doing their laundry at the river's edge. Before a storm caught up with the *River Queen,* the smell of burning oak drifted from fires the soldiers kept to warm coffee pots and tubs of water. A spring gale stirred the boat about two hours out of Washington, but not one shot disturbed her passage.

As the afternoon wore on Will assisted the two-man galley crew in serving the evening meal, or 'mess', as the cook called it. Will was out of his element aboard the *River Queen,* but the galley crew took their work and the gale in stride. The cook was an old Navy hand, a Nor'easter, by the sounds of him, prone to frequent tasting of his preparations. His assistant was a man in his early 20s who worked in bursts. The work bursts were separated by pauses while the man held his arms akimbo and stood with his legs well apart, proving he 'couldn't be bowled over by work or water', as he said. Both cooks had pleasant dispositions but neither was able to satisfy Mrs Lincoln.

A baked chicken and mashed potato dinner had been prepared for the first evening's dinner. Sitting at the table with the Lincolns (Tad included) were Mr Crook and Captain Penrose. Tad sat to the right of his mother, who sat at the opposite end of the table from Mr Lincoln. When a plate of chicken and mashed potato was placed before Tad, she demanded that it be taken back. There simply wasn't enough potato on the plate. Mr Lincoln suggested the cooks would probably offer a second helping or, come to think of it, he'd exchange his plate with the boy. He wasn't all that hungry anyway. Mrs Lincoln insisted the boy's plate be returned to the galley for an additional dollop of mashed potato. Mr Lincoln told a few stories, but otherwise the table was silent. Except that before the meal was over Mrs Lincoln pointedly asked that henceforth Will and Will alone serve Tad and her.

During the night the *River Queen* and the *Bat* anchored in an embayment on the lower Potomac near Fortress Monroe. The next morning the two vessels called at Fortress Monroe. The President and party had become sick. Perhaps the gale was the cause. Speculations on the sickness came to rest on the *River Queen's* freshwater supply. The drinking water was discharged and a fresh supply taken on at the fort around noon. With fresh freshwater aboard, the *River Queen* and *Bat* proceeded to City Point, Virginia.

City Point was near the head of the navigable portion of the James River. The James like the Potomac fed an arm of Chesapeake Bay. City Point was an excellent location for supporting an army besieging Petersburg and Richmond. Petersburg was slightly to the southwest of City Point and Richmond slightly to the northwest. Grant's army had almost enveloped the two cities protected by Lee's army. General Lee's army was supplied over Confederate railway lines still open to the west and southwest not yet cut off by the Union army.

City Point was the site of General Grant's headquarters. Over some two years the Union army had developed the site into a city of war, populated with wharves, warehouses, hospitals, barracks, stables, and a huge assemblage of tents, housing the men and horses working in or passing through City Point. Amidst the wharves and stretching its tentacles to the fighting front was a railway constructed to somewhat crude standards by Army engineers. The railway network enabled the Union besieging forces to be efficiently provisioned with food, medical supplies, ammunition, and fresh men and horses. The railway also acted as a conduit for removing wounded men and prisoners of war. The dead rarely passed over the railway. Most often the dead were buried in graves near the places where they'd fallen.

The navigation from Fortress Monroe to City Point took about nine hours, a day that passed uneventfully and afforded the Lincolns time to recuperate from their little bout of intemperance. Just past 9 PM Captain Penrose was able to telegraph Secretary of War Stanton that the Lincoln party had arrived at City Point with both the President and his family entirely recovered from their earlier indisposition. Penrose had been personally assigned by Mr Stanton to escort the Lincolns on their City Point stay. When Penrose went ashore to telegraph Washington, the Lincolns remained aboard. The *River Queen* would act as their home away from home.

The following morning, Saturday 25 March, the President arose early but looked ill. He asked Will whether he could rustle up a cup of coffee and a biscuit but without gravy. He really wasn't very hungry, he said. While Mr Lincoln partook of his breakfast in the aft saloon, Captain Robert Lincoln, his son, reported aboard. Robert, the oldest of the Lincoln boys, was attached to the staff of General Grant. He had graduated from Harvard College in '64. His failure to join the Army then or even earlier had provoked a rumbling chorus of complaint across the North. Little did the citizenry appreciate that Robert Lincoln joined the Army only over the strenuous objections of his mother.

Will could see the President was pleased to see his son. Mr Lincoln stood to greet him. Robert brought not the best of news. That very morning early in the dark General Lee's forces had launched an attack against the Union forces in a sector of the Petersburg siege field known as Fort Stedman. Fighting was heavy. While Robert recounted the morning's developments with his father, Mr Barnes of the *Bat* joined them. Robert opened a map, pointing out where the morning's battle had begun. There was no telling whereto the fighting might now have spread. There were only so many places where General Lee could push at once.

Mr Lincoln was anxious to walk to General Grant's headquarters to obtain a direct report from the Union's general-in-chief. The President would not be detained by vague disease while the rumblings of war were so near. Robert, Barnes, and several other officers escorted the President to Grant's headquarters. The general and his aides were poring over maps when the President entered the log building that served as headquarters. After a round of handshakes and a summary briefing from Grant, Lincoln showed no mind to linger at headquarters. He asked to be taken to an area where fighting may have abated. General Grant wasn't eager to allow this but he also wasn't one to say 'No' to the commander-in-chief, especially with others present. He asked for a delay to insure that safe conditions would prevail wherever the President and his party traveled. The telegraph line along the military railway connecting City Point and General Meade's headquarters near Petersburg had been cut when the Confederates had begun their breakout assault. Grant wanted communication restored with Meade before Lincoln took to the fields of battle. General Meade was the commanding general of the Army of the Potomac, a position he'd held since three days before Gettysburg.

Mr Lincoln agreed to the delay. During this delay, General Grant's staff provided a briefing on the growing Union encirclement of Richmond and Petersburg. Before boarding a special train assembled for the journey to General Meade's headquarters, the President and his party sat down to lunch with Grant and his staff at the headquarters building. Beans, bread, and coffee were served with Army-issue tin-ware and flatware. While the men were having lunch, Will and Crook arrived with Mrs Lincoln. She wanted to be with her husband. She partook of the coffee but passed up the offer of beans and bread. In contrast to the evening before she was rather chipper and chatty, sustaining conversation with the officers around her. Julia Grant, the general's wife, joined the traveling party

After lunch the Lincolns, the Grants, and a large number of others including Barnes boarded the train for General Meade's headquarters. The ride to the headquarters was over a roadbed likened to corrugated washboard. Hence, the train was slow. As it approached the Fort Stedman sector, the travelers entered ground covered by the wounded, the dying, and the dead. The train slowed even further here, as stretcher-bearers crisscrossed the battlefield fetching the wounded. The wounded were being loaded into ambulance wagons and farm wagons. A railway work detail had cleared the track of bodies. Every 200 feet or so, it seemed, alternating stacks of blue jacketed soldiers and gray jacketed soldiers had been ordered like so much cordwood of the morning's work. Elsewhere the blue and gray dead lay intermingled where they had fought to the death as fighting brothers. Pools of blood had spread from their shared, final sacrifice.

When the special train arrived at what was called 'Meade's Station', the traveling party was greeted by an obviously preoccupied General Meade. While Grant was known for his self-control, the bespectacled General Meade was known for his short temper. Mr Lincoln appreciated the situation and suggested that no one need provide a briefing on the course of battle, still ongoing. Rather, he asked that he be taken to a part of the battlefield where fighting had ceased. General Meade provided a staff officer to escort Lincoln, Grant, and others to a now quiet sector of the day's battle. Meade also provided horses for the men and a field ambulance for Mrs Lincoln and Mrs Grant, who wished to travel with their husbands.

The group was first taken to a field hospital, where the Union wounded and occasional Confederates were being treated. Treatment often amounted to severing one or more limbs. In a nearby field squads of blue jackets were removing the Union and Confederate dead. Following the visit to the hospital, Lincoln and the others on horses were led to a nearby field that still smelled of gunpowder. The men dismounted, tethered their horses to trees, and began spreading out into what had been a battlefield just hours before. In the field a blue-jacketed sergeant and his assistant were searching and scrutinizing the Union dead. The sergeant was taking notes on a hand-held board, while an assistant searched the dead for rings, portraits, and other personal effects. These were placed in numbered kit bags, like those issued to sailors, to aid the subsequent confirmation of the dead. Under a flag of truce a Confederate sergeant and his assistant and a detail of gray-jacketed men would be permitted to identify and bury the Confederate dead later in the day. A Union corporal moved among the Confederate dead tabulating their bodies and identifying their unit affiliations.

President Lincoln escorted by Penrose came upon Barnes, who was exploring the battlefield on his own. At Barnes' feet lay a boy blue of face in gray uniform. Blood was seeping from the boy's head, besmirching his tawny hair. Mr Lincoln looked away, closed his eyes, and listened to Barnes relate how the boy had just died as he held his hand. The boy hadn't spoken a word. The drum next to the boy had apparently been his. As Barnes finished telling this, he arose from his crouched position. He took the boy's hands and folded them together on the boy's chest. He found the drumsticks and tucked them under the hands. Then he stood up facing the boy. He saluted and bowed his head. Lincoln touched the brim of his hat and Penrose did likewise. Penrose noted tears in the President's eyes. As the men walked away from the boy, Mr Lincoln asked for the boy's identity if that could be determined.

The President's battlefield tour was followed by a review of the Army of the Potomac's Fifth Corps. Troops of the corps passed in parade, accompanied by a regimental band standing opposite the President. Mr Lincoln reviewed the troops astride a horse. The ambulance bearing Mrs Lincoln and Mrs Grant arrived while the parade was underway. General Meade escorted Mrs Lincoln to a vantage point where she, too, could see the troops pass in review. Mrs Grant joined her husband a discreet distance from the First Lady.

The ambulance ride with Mrs Lincoln hadn't been a pleasant one. At least as the story would be retold to Elizabeth, the un-pleasantry of the ride hadn't stemmed from the dismal battleground. Rather, it stemmed from Mrs Lincoln's behavior — bordering on 'hysteria', as one person put it. General Grant had sent his aide de camp, one Colonel Badeau, along with his wife and the First Lady when they left Meade's Station. In the course of conversing with the ladies, the colonel had mentioned that the wives of the officers in this sector of the Petersburg siege field had earlier been ordered to the rear, a sign that fighting was then imminent. There had been only one exception to this order, for one Mrs Griffin, wife of General Charles Griffin. Badeau said she'd obtained a special permit from Mr Lincoln to remain with her husband. Why was that? Mrs Lincoln asked. Badeau didn't know. It was unusual, to be sure, but it had happened from time to time. And what might he mean by that? asked Mrs Lincoln. The colonel was stumped. He didn't know what to say. But Mrs Lincoln wasn't deterred. Was he suggesting that Mrs Griffin saw her husband alone? Was he? He replied that he hadn't given the matter much thought one way or the other. He had no idea when or where Mrs Griffin had seen Mr Lincoln, only that she'd received a special pass from him. That was an outrage, replied Mrs Lincoln. She never permitted Mr Lincoln to see a woman alone, particularly one such as Mrs Griffin. She found the suggestion from Colonel Badeau very, very offensive. The colonel and Mrs Grant tried to assuage Mrs Lincoln, to assure her the colonel could not have intended to offend Mrs Lincoln and that in any event any appearance by Mrs Griffin before the President was surely bereft of any impropriety. Mrs Lincoln was not mollified until the ambulance had arrived at the Fifth Corps review, when she dashed up to General Meade. Mrs Lincoln relayed the story she had heard and asked whether it was indeed true that the President had seen Mrs Griffin alone. The general was nothing if not sagacious. He told Mrs Lincoln that the Secretary of War, Mr Stanton, had issued Mrs Griffin the special permit by telegraph. Mrs Lincoln was immediately satisfied and made a point later of telling Colonel Badeau that General Meade was a gentleman.

Mrs Lincoln would eventually tell her side of the story to Elizabeth. She identified Badeau as just another example of the vicious people the war had placed in positions of responsibility, where they day by day undercut the authority and reputation of her husband. The entire cabinet deserved to be fired, with the possible exception of Navy Secretary Welles. The entire cabinet! Mrs Lincoln had suggested this before and was frustrated her husband wouldn't listen to her. Elizabeth always found the suggestion unnerving. She admired the President. But the tale of Mrs Griffin's special pass wasn't the only unnerving tale she would hear from the visit to the Petersburg front.

The next day, Sunday, March 26th, another review was conducted and yet again Mrs Lincoln and Mrs Grant were conveyed to the review by ambulance wagon. This time General Porter traveled with the ladies and Colonel Badeau. General Grant could have retrieved Badeau from the ardor of campaigning with Mrs Lincoln but Grant was nothing if not stubborn. Badeau would not be relieved but rather strengthened. Or so General Grant hoped. He and the President and General Ord would ride on to the review of General Ord's troops. Ord was honored and delighted that the President would be reviewing his troops. It would be a morale booster for his men.

As it was, Lincoln and the generals arrived at the reviewing ground later than they had been expected. The Navy had hosted a luncheon at City Point of palatial proportions, delaying the departure of Mr Lincoln to the review. When the President was told the troops had been waiting way past *their* lunch, he insisted the review begin immediately, even though his wife and Mrs Grant had yet to arrive. The President was escorted, of course, by generals Grant and Ord, but there were numerous others on horseback, mostly US Army officers. Among the cavalcade were two who would incur Mrs Lincoln's wrath. The first was Mr Barnes. Mr Lincoln had asked the Navy officer to accompany him that day. The second was Mary Ord, the general's wife, who rode alongside Barnes.

Once Mr Lincoln had given the go-ahead for the review, General Ord had ordered the bands to strike up an uninterrupted succession of martial airs and marches, starting with 'Hail to the Chief'. As Lincoln and the generals led a cavalcade of officers along the line of troops at 'present arms', Mrs Ord posed the question to Barnes of what she should do. Should she join the cavalcade? Or should she wait here at the roadside for the appearance of Mrs Lincoln's ambulance? Barnes confessed he wasn't familiar with Army protocol. He turned to a nearby Army staff officer on horseback, who promptly replied that by all means they both should feel welcome to join the cavalcade. So the two joined the Presidential reviewing party. Indeed, when the President saw Mrs Ord, he sent word he would be honored if she would join him and her husband and General Grant in reviewing the troops. So it was that as Mrs Lincoln approached, she received word that Mary Ord and the President rode side by side on horseback along the line of troops.

Elizabeth would hear about Mrs Lincoln's conduct at General Ord's review from many sources, some present, some not that day. But within 24 hours of the review, Mrs Lincoln's conduct was the story all over Washington. Elizabeth could never bring herself to ask Mary Todd what happened. And Mary Todd could never bring herself to discuss the matter. But the outlines were obvious enough. When Mary Todd learned of Mrs Ord's presence, she immediately lit into a tirade against Mrs Ord. At first Mary Todd labeled the woman unduly ambitious, then presumptuous, then unbridled, then seductive, and finally nothing but a strumpet! When she could do nothing to immediately displace Mrs Ord, Mary Todd turned on Julia Grant and shouted that she — Mrs Grant — would like nothing better than to be in the White House. Mrs Grant, like her husband, reportedly kept cool under fire. She said she and her husband were quite satisfied with his position, which was far greater than anything they had ever expected. She defended Mary Ord, who would never think of somehow furthering her husband's position by riding alongside the President. But Mary Todd would not hear of this.

When the ambulance arrived, the reviewing party was at a standstill. The troops were now marching past. Mrs Ord rode up to greet the First Lady, who was being assisted to the ground by Colonel Badeau. Mary Todd replied to the greeting by unleashing a string of invective that ended with her calling the general's wife an 'Army hell queen and strumpet'. The officers who stood by would have found such language more or less customary in certain Army settings, but this was not such a place. Nor had they ever imagined that barracks language would be pouring forth from the mouth of the wife of their commander-in-chief. Julia Grant continued to defend Mrs Ord, who burst into tears because of the verbal assault. Finally, Mr Lincoln got wind of what was happening. He left his reviewing position, dismounted, and took Mrs Lincoln in hand. In a calm voice and with hushed tones he called her again and again 'Mother' and suggested they walk away and talk things over. The officers and soldiers had never seen or expected anything quite like this. Elizabeth was sure that from that day forth every Army officer who knew anything about Mary Todd must hate her. And those who knew nothing soon learned they had every reason to avoid and despise her.

The Ord incident caused Elizabeth a good deal of unease. Mary Todd was a bomb ready to go off, more than she'd ever been prepared to admit. She was a bomb that almost surely would hurt those closest to her. The quilt project, so far nothing more than an idea and some scraps, seemed now a feeble effort to muffle the rage coursing through Mary Todd's heart. Mary Todd seemed beyond reason. There were only so many scraps of soothing words that Elizabeth could supply. If there weren't some kind of ordering of the soothing words, if there weren't some truth and some willingness to see the truth, whatever suasion she might apply would soon get lost in the tempest of emotion. Mary Todd had complained that her husband had become distant because of that other woman — the war. But hadn't he *had* to become distant to salvage his ability to do anything?

This thought was coupled with the distressing realization that Mary Todd hadn't been using that 'other woman' language as a mere figure of speech. She seemed to truly believe a flesh-and-blood woman — really almost any woman — could be and almost surely would attempt to attract her husband. There wasn't an ounce of truth in such imaginings. No, not an ounce. How convince Mary Todd of that? How give her and Mr Abe some peace? The poor man had enough war on hand without having a war at home, too. How bring peace into the household?

CHAPTER 10

—ᴍ—

The evening following the Ord episode and with Army guests present Mary Todd vehemently argued with the President that General Ord and his wife ought to be sacked immediately. When her vehemence was unavailing she left the company and became indisposed. For the several days following she remained indisposed, unable to receive visitors and unwilling to leave the *River Queen*. Mary Todd could hardly get out of bed. When she dressed she would curl up on a sofa and spend much of her time weeping. She seemed unable to respond to words of comfort from her husband, who in any event was taken up with events beyond the *River Queen* and was often enough in a state of semi-exhaustion because of them. Mr Lincoln was involved in extended discussions with generals Grant and Sherman and Admiral Porter about the campaign to capture Petersburg and Richmond and — hopefully — to secure the surrender of General Lee and his army. The President was resolute that terms of surrender should be generous and entirely bereft of a spirit of recrimination.

While his father weighed in matters of great moment, Tad had a lark of a time. When he wasn't on tours of City Point, guided by Army officers, he had the run of the boat. He enjoyed watching the comings and goings of the generals and admirals. He was befriended by these men of high rank. He was also befriended by the *River Queen's* crew, who took him to every nook and cranny, explaining the *River Queen's* workings. The boatswain taught Tad to tie several knots. The boy showed himself adept at learning such things. With relish crewmembers persuaded Tad to put his hands to painting a deck and to peeling potatoes. The President several times expressed his gratitude to the *River Queen's* captain for the attention the crew was giving his boy. Mary Todd told Annie this attention was the very least that was owed and said nothing more of it.

Secretary of State Seward visited from Washington to participate in war conferences on the *River Queen*. Mary Todd, as always, found Lincoln's chief foreign minister an almost unbearably conceited man, though he had his uses. When she got wind he would be returning to Washington on the river packet *Monahasset,* she let it be known she must travel with him. Mr Seward didn't object nor did the President. A messenger delivered a telegram from Mary Todd to Elizabeth at her shop mid-morning on Saturday, April 1st. The telegram reported Mary Todd would be arriving the following morning at the Navy Yard at 11 o'clock. Would Elizabeth be so kind as to meet her on arrival? Elizabeth replied she would.

That meant she would miss the Sunday morning church service at Union Bethel. In Elizabeth's mind Mary Todd's need for ministrations of comfort outweighed her own need for ministrations of the Lord's word and community. No one had said how she could enter the Navy Yard. Mary Todd wasn't one to give thought to practical matters. So when Elizabeth went to the yard she took Mary Todd's telegram and the White House pass issued by Ward Lamon. The Marine sentry didn't know what to make of the telegram and the pass. The duty sergeant happened to visit the sentry post while Elizabeth was presenting evidence of her bona fides. He looked over the pass, read the telegram, then looked in her face, seeming to appraise her.

"Walk with me please, ma'am," he said. She complied, not knowing where he would lead her. Past some warehouses and armories they came upon a dock facing the Potomac. Already two drivers, their horses, and their open carriages were there. Elizabeth recognized one driver, a man from the White House. He offered a "Good mornin'" to her and she replied in kind. She thought she heard a sigh of relief from the sergeant, who excused himself immediately. She had passed the Marine's test of recognition.

When the *Monahasset* tied up at the dock, Mary Todd was the first passenger down the gangway. Elizabeth thought the dress Mary Todd wore was too hooped out to be wearing on a boat. Ah, well, at least she was leaving the boat. Just behind Mary Todd were Annie and a burly deckhand bearing luggage. As soon as Mary Todd saw Elizabeth, she ran to embrace her.

"Oh, Lizzy, it was just awful, awful. Dante's Inferno was a picnic compared to what I've been through. The people were atrocious in their behavior. The thought that Abe must put up with this day after day just tears at me."

Elizabeth had read the morning's *Intelligencer* and half hoped Mary Todd would be, must be, referring to the battlefields. But as the carriage was being loaded, Elizabeth's lower intimations were confirmed when Mary Todd began expostulating on her encounters with generals' wives.

"You know, Julia Grant, when you first see her, you see her as pretty in a country kind of way. She's so quiet, like her husband, I guess. Like her husband she wields a knife. He's just a plain butcher, but she's got little knives, cutting this way and that trying to undermine the reputation of my husband at every little twist and turn. And then there's General Griffin's wife. Everyone remarks on her 'noble beauty', but there's nothin' beautiful in someone who models herself after Lady Macbeth. To top 'em all you can't beat Mary Ord. She shouldn't be allowed anywhere near the Army or near my husband. Abe is so naïve. He doesn't see how she's nothin' but an ambitious Army hell queen determined to seduce and destroy him if need be to gain advantages for her husband and herself."

Elizabeth didn't quite know what Mary Todd then meant, but she knew her Mr Abe was no idiot. She said, "Mary Todd, Mr Abe don't seem to take second place to no one in being able to size up people." *And yet he married Mary Todd*, she thought, adding, "Where's Tad?"

"Abe and I agreed Tad should stay with his dad. He seems to be having a good time down there at City Point. He loves the *River Queen* and all the things the crew and the Army people show him."

"Has he been to a battlefield?" asked Elizabeth.

"Not yet," replied Mary Todd, who looking toward the *Monahasset* offered a weak smile and wave toward Mr Seward, now coming down the gangway. The Secretary of State offered a dutiful wave in response.

"Driver, let's be off," said Mary Todd. "I've had my fill of battle-field antics. If I'm going to review any troops it's going to be from the comfort of Washington and the Army wives, thank you, can be in another reviewing stand miles away as far as I care."

Mary Todd continued in this vein the whole ride back to the White House. There was hardly a mention of the battlefields traversed. Elizabeth heard an exposition on the wretched ambulances endured, on the lying and persiflage heard, on the degradation suffered by Mary Todd. In all this Mary Todd said she'd hardly received the comfort or true understanding of her husband. He might lead a nation. But he succumbed to others whom he innocently trusted. For everyone's sake her counsels must once again be taken seriously by her own husband. The expedition to City Point had been a failure. But she hadn't given up. No, she hadn't given up.

That pluckiness, that feistiness, was something that Elizabeth admired and just then she'd almost been convinced by Mary Todd. But she knew Mary Todd was hardly a reliable source of information. How could Mary Todd visit battlefields and be blind to anything not having to do with her personally? How could she not be moved by what she had seen and heard? Couldn't she feel for others? It was if she were locked in her own closet and didn't want to get out. She seemed more alive *in there* with her own gallery of afflictions than she did anywhere else. Mary Todd's closet wasn't the world. Elizabeth knew too many women (and men) in this gallery and in the light of day they didn't appear to be the people Mary Todd was happy to castigate. Mary Todd's world was too often a world of demons, figments of her imagination. Yet there was no denying Mary Todd spoke with a conviction unsullied with doubt, at least not right now. *Thank heavens, the doubt will be expressed later. Otherwise, Mary Todd would be intolerable.*

Uneasy with Mary Todd's conviction, Elizabeth also felt uneasy about where the Lincoln household seemed headed. How could the wise and the foolish be yoked without things coming amiss? How could Mr Abe and Mary Todd continue in marriage without one or the other being hurt? The trip to City Point had to be a social disaster for Mary Todd. Mary Todd hadn't acknowledged the disaster, except by withdrawal. Elizabeth was confident Mr Abe wouldn't be tarnished by Mary Todd's behavior. He had done too much for the nation. His wife's behavior wouldn't detract from his account. But he still could be hurt. Sooner or later Mary Todd's unpaid bills would blow up like a torpedo underfoot. There was no way that making a quilt would patch over that.

For all that, Elizabeth had no desire to flee. Despite everything she knew, she knew too she would continue to be more than a friend to Mary Todd. Mary Todd needed her. Mr Abe, in his own way, needed her, too. That felt good. Thank God, she was a free woman. Nothing compelled her to give attendance on Mary Todd. But Elizabeth knew she wanted the attachment to the Lincolns. Her mother was dead. Her father, George, was dead. Her son, George, was dead. She had friends and acquaintances to be sure but she had no family — except the Lincolns. Being with the Lincolns had pulled Elizabeth from the waters of mourning and death. With the Lincolns she felt extra alive. With that extra life you had to endure the bad with the good. That was both alarming and comforting. What else was she to do? She chose the Lincolns because she seemed chosen for them. That was vital by God Almighty.

On the very Sunday Mary Todd arrived back in Washington, Petersburg fell. With Petersburg in the hands of Federal troops, Richmond's fate was sealed. Richmond fell the following day, Monday, 3 April 1865. Washington and the North could hardly believe the news that morning. Newspaper offices were crowded with people demanding confirmation of the news. The news was a fact. The goal 'On to Richmond' had been the prod of countless Northern newspapers early in the war. Year by year had gone by, battle after battle, yet Richmond had stood, the proud capital of the Confederacy. Now she had fallen. The war's end had to be near.

Washington could hardly contain its elation. Army batteries around the capital, only recently used to repel the assaults of Confederate General Early, were now put afire in a 300-gun salute to the fall of Petersburg and a 500-gun salute to the fall of Richmond.

The citizenry hung Union flags from windows at home and at work. Bands played, fireworks were sent aloft. Elizabeth, like so many employers, gave her workers Monday off with pay. The delirium in the streets and the spirits running in the bars were capped that evening by light shows on government buildings. Most prominent of all was the Capitol building. Over its western façade a large, gas-lit transparency had been erected, printed in bold letters: 'This is the Lord's doing; it is marvelous in our eyes.'

The evening of the fall of Richmond, Secretary of War Stanton received a telegram from the President saying he intended to visit Richmond the next day. As a courtesy Stanton sent a messenger to the White House to inform Mrs Lincoln of her husband's plans. Elizabeth was present with Mary Todd in her bedroom when Stanton's message arrived. Mary Todd read Stanton's note, then handed it to Elizabeth.

"I must return to City Point, Lizzy. Truly, Abraham should not enter Richmond without me by his side. We have endured so many defeats, so many setbacks. Shouldn't I be with him in this hour of victory?" Elizabeth could hardly disagree. Mary Todd summoned a messenger to whom she dictated the following:

To the President, City Point, Virginia. News of Richmond's fall received in Washington. Stop. Wonderful news. Stop. City elated. Stop. Will return to City Point to be with you. Stop. Wish to visit Richmond. Stop. Give Tad a kiss from me. Stop. Yours. Molly.

Once the messenger departed Mary Todd decided to select dresses for her return to Virginia. She asked Elizabeth for help. Selecting a dress for Mary Todd's appearance in Richmond consumed the most time. It came down to choosing between a royal blue dress or one that was maroon. Both dresses were high-necked and made of satin. Mary Todd said she thought she preferred the blue dress. Elizabeth reminded her that the newspapers would probably describe the dress as 'royal blue', the right description after all. Was that what Mary Todd wanted to appear in the newspapers?

"Lizzy, if I'd wanted the newspapers to decide what I ought to wear, would I have asked for your help?"

"No, but because you asked for my help, I'm tellin' ya the papers that don't like you or Mr Abe will have a hay day with 'royal blue', tossing it back and forth in front of their readers, making you out to be hoping to be the queen."

"*Hoping* to be the queen," said Mary Todd, laughing. "I *am* the queen, the Republican queen, so why not live up to my reputation?"

"Cause I think deep down you don't like the hurt that comes with that kinda name calling, Mary T."

Mary Todd had been holding the royal blue dress up against herself. Now she threw it down on the bed. "You're right, Lizzy, as always you're right. I'll take the maroon dress for Richmond."

The two sorted through additional dresses for another hour before another messenger appeared. He delivered a telegram from the President. Mary Todd dismissed the messenger, removed the message from its envelope, read it to herself, then read it aloud to Elizabeth.

To Mrs Lincoln, at the White House, Washington. I visit Richmond tomorrow. Stop. Do come to City Point. Stop. Tad and I miss you. Stop. Ask Senators Sumner and Harlan and family to come. Stop. Invite the Frenchman Chambrun and Madame Keckly. Stop. Admiral Porter will provide Monahasset for travel. Stop. Confirm who can come. Stop. Yours, Abraham.

Mary Todd kissed the telegram after reading it aloud. "Isn't it wonderful! Instead of all this dreadful war business and the tedium of managing generals, we'll be able to do as we could and should at peace."

"Who's the Frenchman?" asked Elizabeth.

"He's a marquis, a very charming fellow. He's here in Washington on his own. As far as I'm concerned, Abraham, too, he could represent all of France and several other countries besides. He came to one of my receptions. We spoke in French. Can you come along, Lizzy?"

"How could I say 'No'?" she replied. She would ask Mr Oliver to keep an eye on the shop in her absence.

The following day, Tuesday, April 4th, Mary Todd and others made preparations to travel to City Point. Mr Abe visited Richmond that day as planned. Elizabeth later learned from Penrose what happened. The *River Queen* got underway early, heading up the James River towards a rendezvous with Admiral Porter's flagship, the *Malvern*. The *River Queen* was escorted by the *Bat*, Mr Barnes commanding. When the *River Queen* met the *Malvern*, the Presidential party transferred by launch to the *Malvern*. The party included the President, Tad, Mr Crook, and Captain Penrose. The *Malvern* then traveled up river escorted by the *Bat* to a point at which the *Malvern* couldn't pass an obstruction constructed by Confederate engineers. The captain's gig from the *Malvern* was launched. The Presidential party came aboard the gig along with Admiral Porter. A crew of 12 sailors, armed with rifles, manned the gig. Admiral Porter commandeered a Navy tug, the *Glance*, to tow the *Malvern* gig. Aboard the *Glance* were 30 Marines who were to serve as guards for the travel party.

The James River was littered with the debris of war. Sunken warships, Confederate ironclads, and hulks of commercial vessels littered the channel. Burnt bridge timbers and bloated horses floated down the James towards Chesapeake Bay. One Navy gunboat, the *Commodore Perry*, had already run aground attempting to reach Richmond. Its captain was taking measures to get his converted ferry paddle steamer off the river mud. The *Perry's* gun crew was attempting to move cannon to the boat's high side, while other sailors were dumping coal overboard. These activities were part of an effort to lighten and shift the boat's load. Below decks the engineering crew kept reversing directions on the boat's paddles in an effort to rock the boat free of the mud.

The *Glance* couldn't possibly tow Porter's gig beyond the *Perry*. The gig was cut loose from the *Glance*. Porter ordered the sailors to man the oars. But when the gig endeavored to make the narrow passage between the rocking *Perry* and the shore, she was nearly swamped. Why that happened was a whole story on its own, but the Presidential gig managed to make it through the gap. Mr Barnes endeavored to follow in the *Bat's* much smaller gig. The *Malvern's* gig soon left the *Bat's* gig far behind.

The venture up the river had other hazards, not least the prospect of lingering Confederate troops, who would be more than happy to take potshots at Mr Lincoln. As always he was wearing his black stovepipe hat and his long black coat. He was also wearing his good humor. The frazzled Admiral Porter may not have been amused but everyone else was thanks to the President. Mr Lincoln said the trip reminded him of a time when a man came to Washington asking for a position abroad as an ambassador. When the President turned him down, the man asked to be appointed a consul abroad. When that was turned down, he asked to be appointed a customs officer. Mr Lincoln told him that wasn't a possibility either. In the end the man asked the President for an old pair of trousers, which was provided.

Porter got the gig beyond the 'trousers' to a landing about a 100 yards from Richmond's old Libby Prison, liberated only yesterday of its prisoners of war. Beyond the prison you could see the old Virginia statehouse high on a hill, where it had served as the Confederate capitol for nearly four years. It was still intact as were some of the city's residential districts. The business and commercial districts between the river and the capitol, however, were in flames or smoldering ruins.

At the landing several of the sailors jumped out to secure the gig to the shore, then assisted the President and Tad out of the boat. Several black men working in a nearby field noticed the arriving party. They came to observe the goings on and recognized the President for who he was and for what he had done for them. They were effusive in their praise. Some even threw themselves at Mr Lincoln's feet, calling the President 'Messiah'. Somehow the presence of the Emancipator was communicated throughout the neighborhood. The landing was soon crowded with hundreds of the emancipated.

Mr Lincoln appeared embarrassed and chagrined. He asked everyone to arise. There was no need to be on knees except to the one Lord God who truly was the one who had delivered them. He had done nothing but what God had wanted: to free them. 'Thank God, not me, in your prayers,' he repeated several times. The gathering of freemen responded in kind, breaking into the spiritual 'He's

Got the Whole World in His Hands'. When they had finished this song, some among them began asking, 'Are we free? Are we really free?' The question became a chorus.

The President put up his hand for silence. A hush spread over the crowd. He said, "You are all free men. No one can ever shackle you again unless you break the law. There can be no law against you being a colored man."

"Tha's right," shouted someone. The crowd hushed that man and the President continued.

"We all learn many things as we go through life. Now you must learn to be free men, to properly enjoy the liberties that God gives all of us. As free men we must be responsible for ourselves and acknowledge what we owe to others and to God. Others before you have taken the path to freedom, so take courage and learn from their examples. May God bless each and every one of you. And pray for the healing of our country. God bless you all."

The freemen cheered, then led by one of their number began singing 'I Thank God I'm Free at Las'. The President nodded to Admiral Porter, who understood that he wanted to be off to the capitol. The admiral couldn't wait for the Marines, who were still out of sight. He ordered the sailors to fix bayonets to their rifles. Once the bayonets were fixed, six sailors two abreast took positions in front of the President and Tad and six sailors similarly arrayed themselves behind. Crook and Admiral Porter walked alongside the President. Captain Penrose walked alongside Tad. A cipher clerk trailed the party, which now began its two-mile walk through a city clothed in smoke and bereft of government.

If there had been any dead or wounded in the streets of Richmond they were now gone. Instead, the streets were astir with common folk, white, black, mulatto, reconnoitering the districts they once knew, now oft but ruins of war. The curiosity that impelled the goings about that morning was heightened by the appearance of the tall man in the stovepipe hat with his escort of sailors. No one had expected the appearance of this man in Richmond this morning, but all the town soon was abuzz with the news that President Lincoln was in their midst. If Mr Lincoln could be curious, most of Richmond was merely curious in return. Richmond folk mostly stood in doorways or at windows watching the Presidential party pass. A few — in upper crust Richmond — slammed their shutters shut. One beautiful young girl ran up to the party and managed to pass to the President a bouquet of flowers. With the flowers was a card that read 'From Eva to the Liberator of the slaves'.

Along the entire walk from the James to the capitol the President and his party were preceded by a throng of freemen and freewomen, sustained by an uncontainable joy at the presence of the Liberator. Hats were thrown in the air. Coats were thrown before the President. Captain Penrose later remarked to Elizabeth that it was like a Palm Sunday, which truly was only a few days off. The President did nothing to encourage or discourage such a display, said Penrose. He seemed much determined to reach the capitol.

The day had become quite warm and the President was weary. On three occasions the walking party paused to allow the President to catch his breath. At the last such pause, about a half-mile from the capitol, a Federal cavalryman happened to appear around a street corner. He looked over the ecstatic crowd towards the stove-pipe man surrounded by bayonets. He didn't know what to make of it until Captain Penrose appeared before him and identified the man in the black hat. The cavalryman hoofed off to gather a troop of guards. From that point the President had an escort amplified by cavalry troopers.

Near the capitol the President was received by General Weitzel, who had captured Richmond and was in command of the troops now taking possession of the city. Nearby was the home of the President of the Confederacy, Jefferson Davis. When it was discovered that the Davis housekeeper was still present, she was asked whether she'd consent to the party's viewing the home. She consented, taking Lincoln, Weitzel, and others on a tour of the presidential mansion. Eventually a mid-afternoon Army lunch was served the Presidential party elsewhere. Afterwards the President toured the capitol building. The august building was abandoned except for roving looters and refugees.

When the Presidential party returned to the riverside, the *Malvern* was there awaiting the foot-weary. She was a welcome sight.

CHAPTER 11

—◦◦◦—

The President arrived back at City Point the morning of April 5th. He spent that morning meeting with former Supreme Court Justice Campbell, a native Virginian who had come to discuss how Virginia might be brought back into the Union. Several times during the day the President conferred by telegraph with Secretary of State Seward.

On April 5th Mary Todd and her travel companions left Washington for City Point on the *Monahasett*. Elizabeth easily surmised why Senator Sumner and the Harlans had been invited along. Senator Sumner accompanied Mary Todd for political reasons. The senator from Massachusetts was a leader of the radical wing of the Republicans, those determined to punish the South for its transgressions against the Union. Mr Abe had often enough said that honey was the best way to catch a bear. Mary Todd had often enough said she could defang the bear once caught. So she gladly invited Senator Sumner along. Besides he was always the consummate gentleman. Senator and Mrs Harlan and their daughter Mary accompanied Mary Todd for reasons political and domestic. Politically, the senator from Iowa headed the powerful Joint Congressional Committee on the Conduct of the War. Mr Abe wanted to include him in the circle of discussion that would bring the war to an end. And the President and First Lady were happy to facilitate a meeting between their son Robert and Mary Harlan. Now that the war seemed beginning to end the Lincolns would do what they could to encourage Robert to marry, although Mary Todd had at best mixed feelings about Mary Harlan.

More of a puzzle to Elizabeth at first was the invitation extended to the Marquis de Chambrun, only recently arrived from France. Elizabeth met him for the first time on the *Monahasett*. He seemed likeable, to be sure. His broken English with a heavy French accent was charming. Elizabeth surmised the marquis could not have been invited for any political reason. He wasn't even a member of the French embassy. In fact he was already known to be less than an enthusiastic supporter of the French monarchy. He came across as a very independent-minded man with an avid interest in all aspects of American life. An invitation must have been extended for personal reasons. Clearly, Mr Abe and Mary Todd liked the man, otherwise he wouldn't have been invited for an extended outing. But there had to be more than mere likes at work to invite this man to join the Lincolns on their vacation at the edge of battle. Mary Todd's last visit at the battlefront had ended in the Ord incident, a deep embarrassment all round. Elizabeth speculated that Mr Abe hoped the Frenchman's presence would help temper Mary Todd's behavior. The marquis and Mary Todd would speak in French, enough to cause Mary Todd to want to work away at the rusty edges of her French. And the two could engage in long conversations on French literature. Yes, the marquis must have been invited aboard because he was a truer friend of the Lincolns than he could have imagined. Mr Abe was shrewd.

Elizabeth couldn't stop this train of thought short of figuring out how she placed in the journey to City Point. Her presence must be for domestic reasons. She was a friend of the family. She was less exotic than the Frenchman but like him she was to temper Mary Todd. Or so Mr Abe must hope. Or was there something less...or more...in the invitation to City Point? Mr Abe had named her in the telegram as one to be invited. Was there something else, some other reason for her being asked to come along? If it had been left to Mary Todd, would she have been invited? Perhaps, but she hadn't been invited in Round One, perhaps to Mr Abe's disappointment.

Elizabeth, while flattered at being invited in Round Two, had misgivings. Like it or not, she found herself increasingly discomfited by Mary Todd. The stories coming back from Round One had been appalling. She could make all kinds of excuses for Mary Todd, but she didn't like making them. Especially when Mary Todd's behavior so directly hurt Mr Abe. There was no call for that behavior. Aside from the discomfit with Mary Todd, Elizabeth was vaguely miffed that somehow she was expected to placate Molly. Yet she was gratified that a man so great as Mr Abe had identified *her* as someone he could depend on. She liked that.

On the journey to City Point she saw the side of Mary Todd attractive to Mr Abe. After partaking of a meal of roast beef, potatoes, and carrots, Mary Todd and her guests adjourned to the aft saloon for dessert. The dinner conversation had amounted to an exchange of Washington gossip. Mary Todd and the senators did most of the talking, occasionally abetted by Mrs Harlan. The marquis and Elizabeth listened. As a steward cut up the vanilla cake, Mary Todd herself served round the pieces, while one of the cooks delivered the cups of coffee. Mary set the tone for the after-dinner conversation by asking if the senators had given thought to putting President Davis and his cabinet on trial following a cessation of fighting. Senator Sumner replied that there had been much Senate backroom talk about putting Davis on trial. Senator Harlan, agreed, having heard as much.

"But do you think that would be wise to put Mr Davis and his government on trial?" asked Mary Todd.

"I don't see how it can be avoided," said Sumner. "Davis was an elected senator from the State of Mississippi who violated his oath of office when he joined and then led a rebellion against the government he'd sworn to serve. He has committed what has always been recognized as high treason. There's no getting around the facts."

"But at some point we must leave the war behind," Mary Todd softly replied. "Given the strong feelings this conflict has reflected and stirred up, shouldn't we allow the Confederate leaders to resume private lives in their homes? I can tell you Southerners view this war as a war of liberty, just as we do in the North."

"Not quite as we do," interjected Senator Harlan.

"They want liberty from the North, not liberty for the Negro," said Sumner.

"Yet, I've read they're thinking of arming their Negroes and giving them freedom," said Mrs Harlan.

"That is a measure of their desperation," said Sumner. "Freedom for the Negro is not a first principle for them."

"No, it hasn't been," said Mary Todd. "But I think what they're doing in these desperate times shows what *is* important to them. For the sake of the South they're now willing to give up slavery."

"It's crazy," said Sumner, shaking his head. "If they'd only been willing to do this four years ago or forty years ago we wouldn't have gone to war."

"Well, they weren't willing then but they are now," said Mary Todd. "And we, too, need to think about changes in spirit that would have been unimaginable but months ago. Yes, I suppose, we should by rights hang Mr Davis and his likes."

The very suggestion made Elizabeth wince.

Mary Todd continued, "What would we accomplish in a bunch of hangings? The men of the South are now willing to discard slavery for the sake of the South. We should be willing to forsake revenge for the sake of restoring unity. We are all brothers and sisters in this America, are we not?"

Senator Sumner smiled at Mary Todd. "Mary, I compliment you on your generosity of spirit. You and your husband are preaching from the same sermon, I must say, and I promise I will take it to heart."

"And Senator Harlan?" asked Mary Todd.

"Well, you know, war has its costs and so does peace, at least a peace that's more than just a truce waiting to break into another fight. I think the President is leading us toward a way that will restore and conserve a brotherly peace. I'm willing to follow him on that path. You know that, Mary."

"That's music to my ears," she replied.

If only Mr Abe had been there to see his Mary Todd in action. She could be so smooth in her persuasions. Some in Washington might resent her politicking, but she was good at it. When she applied herself she was a great ally to her husband. Elizabeth felt a surge of pride in her friend. It helped that Mary Todd was wearing a green silk crinoline dress Elizabeth had made for her in '63. Elizabeth still had swatches of that material. She resolved to include it in the quilt, even if she wasn't sure how she would use the green. After all she hadn't yet formulated a design.

As the two senators and Mary Todd continued their discussion, the marquis turned to Elizabeth and softly asked, "And how zink you, Madame Keckly, in zee treatment of Monsieur Davis?"

Elizabeth was taken aback. But she had an opinion. "Mr Davis was always kind to me. Mrs Davis, too. They're both warm people. You always have to look at how people really behave as well as to how they talk. I hate slavery, always have, always will. There's no defending it in my opinion. I'm glad Mr Abe has always hated it and glad he came 'round to fightin' it, too. There's a time for fightin' but the fightin's almost over. Now it's time to forgive. Mr Abe and Mary Todd, they've got it right."

Mary Todd, who had become engaged in a one-on-one conversation with Senator Sumner, must have heard her name. Across the room she interjected, "Thank you, Lizzy."

The marquis added, "You are kind, Madame Keckly. I zink zee word is 'generous', oui, in English?"

"Thank you, monsieur. God has been generous with me, with all of us really."

"Zat is so," said the marquis.

"Love conquers all," chimed in Mrs Harlan, who'd been listening to the conversation between Elizabeth and the marquis. "Have you seen the recent performance of the *Magic Flute?*" she asked the Frenchman.

He replied he had. Mary Todd entered into the conversation on *The Magic Flute*. Elizabeth hadn't attended the opera, but of course she'd already heard about it from Mary Todd. Mary Todd had taken an immense dislike to the opera's leading evil figure, the Queen of the Night. "We've got more than one such queen in the North," she had said to Elizabeth, "and they've attempted to seduce and destroy my husband with all their wiles."

Elizabeth hoped the conversation wouldn't linger on *The Magic Flute* because of the ugly images stirred up in Mary Todd's mind. The evening was going so well. The war and wickedness and all the sins of mankind seemed so far away. It was if they were on a magic voyage. Who would wish to end the voyage?

Mary Todd showed a wise hand and steered the conversation in a new and fruitful direction. She asked the marquis what contemporary French authors he'd recommend for reading. He suggested several — Elizabeth couldn't remember their names — but added it would be a time before their most current works would be translated into English. One author in particular, he said, couldn't be translated too soon for Americans. This author would appeal to the American sense of adventure, of a taste for the new, and a love of invention. His name was Jules Verne. He'd written a novel published in 1863 about five weeks in a balloon and another just the past year about a journey to the center of the earth. He was said to be at work on a novel about a journey to the moon.

"Fantastique!" said Mary Todd. "These are the very kind of stories that might engage the interest of my Tad. Please tell us more about them."

The marquis did. The tales of the fantastic journeys added magic to the evening. But the spell, of course, came to an end. Just past eleven o'clock Mary Todd said she must retire for the evening, even though she had immensely enjoyed everyone's company. She thanked everyone for coming on the trip to City Point and said that none, she trusted, would be disappointed by this venture into Old Virginia.

The *Monahasset* arrived the following morning at City Point. Mr Abe came aboard to welcome Mary Todd and the others. A party of sailors took Mary Todd's and Elizabeth's luggage to the *River Queen*. The others who had come down from Washington would remain on the *Monahasset*. Mr Abe related that while the travelers had been steaming from Washington, Secretary of State Seward had been seriously injured in a carriage accident. He was laid up with a broken shoulder and a broken jaw. Secretary of War Stanton had asked Mr Abe to return to Washington. Mr Abe told everyone he wouldn't leave immediately but he said he'd stay in City Point only a few more days.

Mary Todd later muttered in private to Elizabeth that it almost seemed as if Secretary Seward was determined to ruin her husband's vacation from Washington. Oh, she knew the accident was an accident. Nonetheless, both Seward and Stanton had been less than enthusiastic about the President's visit to City Point. City Point was too close to the battlefront, they claimed. Mary Todd knew they were right but she also knew her Abe needed more time away from the capital and a vacation on the front was the only excuse he'd allow himself for being away. There was no denying he looked better at City Point than he'd looked in Washington. Events on the battlefront had perhaps helped his spirits. After all, Richmond was now in Union hands and General Lee was working hard against General Grant and his forces to break out and get down to North Carolina.

Mary Todd wanted to visit Richmond. She told Mr Abe, "You must show our guests the fallen city."

"They're welcome to see Richmond, you too, Molly, but I shall not return to that city."

"Why not?" she asked. Other than Elizabeth the other guests weren't present.

"I cannot go."

"Cannot, after inviting these people here? What was the point of inviting them if not to show the fruit of four years of hard fighting?" asked Mary Todd.

"The fruit of the fighting will be in the peace. Another visit to Richmond — by me — is definitely not a recipe for the goodwill that leads to peace."

"Fiddlesticks. This is the time to show who's in charge," replied Mary Todd.

"This is a time to be brotherly and allow Him who is the author of us all to guide us in our action." Mr Abe pointed to the ceiling, really, far above the ceiling. "Molly, if I returned so soon after my visit earlier this week, I think it would create more harm than good. You take them, Molly. I'll have Admiral Porter and a military escort accompany you."

Mary Todd seemed pleased with the idea. It probably helped that the evening before she'd been in charge of the visitors. The confidence that Mr Abe showed in her moved her to embrace and kiss him. The following day, Friday, April 7th, Mary Todd went to Richmond. Senator Sumner, Mr and Mrs Harlan, their daughter

Mary, the Marquis de Chambrun, and Madame Keckly accompanied her. The visitors were encapsulated in a contingent of Marines.

Although the Washington visitors excited some interest among the people of Richmond, the affection that had been showered on the President was nowhere to be seen. Richmond was still a picture of devastation. Smoke still hung over the city. More buildings were fire damaged or destroyed than had escaped the flames. The Washington visitors were told that convicts had set many of the fires. The departing Confederates had released these convicts. Why the convicts would have been impelled to set fires, as opposed to thieving and stealing, wasn't obvious to the visitors.

General Weitzel had managed to establish a courtroom in a wing of the capitol building, which continued to serve as a shelter for the homeless and vagabonds and as a magnet for plunderers and thieves. Before leaving Richmond the visitors were taken to Libby Prison. About 900 Confederate officers and soldiers captured in the recent fighting were now detained at the prison. When the Washington visitors passed through, the prisoners arose out of respect. A few resorted to catcalls and hissing. The Federal officer in charge of Libby reported the Confederates had imprisoned at any one time 3000 Federal officers and prisoners at this location. As it was, the 900 seemed crowded.

That evening with everyone back on board the *River Queen* a dinner of cabbage beef soup and bread was served the Presidential party. The simplicity of the meal seemed to befit the somber events of the day. There was no discussion of Mozart or French literature that evening. Rather, after dinner Mr Abe and Mary Todd excused themselves and Tad from their company, saying the guests were free to roam the boat or to return to the *Monahasett*. Everyone retired early for everyone wished to be up early. Mr Abe had said he expected to be up to receive early morning reports from General Grant.

Mary Todd asked Elizabeth to join the Lincolns briefly in their private saloon. Mr Abe had something to ask her.

"You're from the Petersburg area, as I recall, Madame Elizabeth?" said he.

"I am. I was born near there. I've always thought of Petersburg as my hometown."

"Would you like to see it?" he asked.

"I think I would. I think I would."

"Then we'll go there tomorrow. Just be prepared for a change from whatever you remember."

"Does it look as bad as Richmond, Mr Abe?"

"I don't think so. There's much less damage, so I'm told. Still, she was a city under siege. Buildings were damaged by artillery shells. And of course there's been a lot of people killed down there, both blue and gray. If you're up to it, we'll go to Petersburg tomorrow."

"Then let's go," replied Elizabeth. She was flattered to be asked. She scrutinized Mary Todd's face to discern her friend's view of this favor. Mary Todd wore a smile.

Elizabeth went to bed half elated at the prospect of a visit to her hometown, half troubled that Mary Todd might have taken offense at Mr Abe's generous offer. Tomorrow would tell whether her fears were worth the trouble.

CHAPTER 12

—⚂—

On the following day the venture to Petersburg did not get underway until noon. Mr Abe spent the morning visiting ashore with a congressman from Illinois. Mary Todd spent much of the morning with Tad and even arranged with the Harlans that Mary Harlan would tend Tad during the daytrip to Petersburg. "I want to see how Mary handles Tad," she told Elizabeth. "I want to see what kind of mother she might be. With all the fighting going on, Robert doesn't have any time to spend with her. So it might as well be Tad." Elizabeth could see Mary Todd was pleased she'd been able to turn the trip to Petersburg to her advantage. That was just as well so far as Elizabeth was concerned because she didn't want Mary Todd to hold the Petersburg visit against her.

Elizabeth accompanied Mary Todd to the City Point station, really nothing but a warehouse next to the tracks. Mr Abe walked ahead of the ladies, escorted by an Army general and followed by his bodyguard, Mr Crook. At the station a small locomotive stood panting, its crew waiting to pull one day coach to Petersburg. The men boarded the coach ahead of the ladies. An Army sergeant who acted as the train's conductor helped the ladies and Tad board the coach. Once they were aboard and seated he green-flagged the locomotive engineer to proceed down the tracks.

The coach was carrying more than Elizabeth had expected. To the rear of the coach sat Will Slade and several stewards and cooks from the *Monahasset* and the *River Queen*. Mary Harlan and Tad sat just forward of the crewmembers. Towards the center of the car were perhaps a dozen officers and sergeants. In the forward aisle stood Mr Abe, chatting with Mrs Harlan. Mrs Harlan was seated next to Senator Sumner, who was on the left side of the coach. As Mary Todd and Elizabeth walked forward to join the others in the Presidential party they saw Mrs Harlan rise from her seat. She locked arms with the President, who escorted her to a nearby seat next to her husband. Senator Harlan was talking to the Marquis de Chambrun. Mr Abe returned to sit down next to Senator Sumner. The President's little gallantry with Mrs Harlan seemed but a necessary maneuver to enable Mr Abe to visit with the senator.

Mary Todd didn't see it that way. She and Elizabeth had taken a seat about five rows back from the President and Senator Sumner, but on the left side of the car. Elizabeth had recommended sitting on the left. The train was heading south and now past noon the left side would be the shady side, such as could be found. Conversation wasn't easy. The windows, of course, were open and conversations required strong voices, being that the coach was right behind the locomotive. Almost shouted conversations remained almost private.

Mary Todd spouted as much steam as the locomotive. "I have to keep watch on my man, Lizzy. You know for the last few days, I've been walking on the clouds, my every thought for magnifying the triumph that's just around the bend. You saw me when we came down on the *Monahasset*, working on Senator Sumner to move a little from his Radical position of punishing the South. Didn't I do a good job?"

"You did," replied Elizabeth.

"And now what happens?" asked Mary Todd.

"Looks to me like Mr Abe is going to work on the senator himself."

"That's not what I mean."

"Oh, Mary Todd, don't get all afuss about Mrs Harlan. Mr Abe was just bein' courteous to her."

"Lizzy, I know it was innocent enough on his part. But what about her? And what about all the other little courtesies he extends? There are bound to be those who will try to take advantage of him *and me*."

"There's no taking advantage of Mr Abe. He's too wise for that kinda stuff."

"Oh, you don't know the half of it, Lizzy. Before I courted him, he was quite a skirt-chaser."

"Mary Todd, I don't doubt it. But since he married you, do you ever think he's been disloyal?"

"When I married him he was just a lawyer on the circuit in Illinois. Now he's President of the United States. I saw that in him when he was back on the circuit, long before anyone else. I got to him, Lizzy, I stood by him, I stood for him, and I'm not goin' to stand by doin' nothin' when I could lose him."

"He's yours, Mary Todd. He's yours. I don't see a thread of disloyalty in him."

"It's not disloyalty, it's his distraction that unnerves me. It tries me to see other women around him when I get so little attention from him myself."

"It's the war. He belongs to the US of A," said Elizabeth.

"So you've said and so I've thought. When the war ends, that can no longer be an excuse."

"Have you told him you want him to pay you more attention?"

"No. Nights together and a few meals are all I can expect with the war and sometimes even that don't happen. His showing up the other day at my last Saturday reception was a big surprise. I don't want to beg from him. He's not intentionally disloyal but all these courtesies to these women of no account is more bothersome than he can appreciate or I should have to tolerate. Sometimes I'd like to make him feel jealous. He needs to hurt the way I do, but I know he's got his own wagonload of hurts."

"Don't he ever. If I ever see anything suggestin' there's more to his courtesies than mere courtesy, you'll be the first to know."

Mary Todd said nothing more. Now that she'd promised something to Mary Todd she remembered her different promise to Ward Lamon. She was confident she'd never have a thing to report to Mary Todd and resolved she'd soon have something to report to Ward Lamon.

As the train approached the siege works around Petersburg, Elizabeth looked back and noticed even Tad had quieted down in his seat. He was all agog at the architecture of war: encampments, ammunition depots, breastworks with cannons, and thousands of blue-jacketed soldiers now dismantling the various engines of war. The Presidential party was all eyes. Only the officers and sergeants were talking among themselves, pointing to positions in the earth-works. These positions were presumably markers in their lives, in their stories. For the Presidential party in the front of the car and the boat crewmen in the back, the siege works around Petersburg were an unfolding story. There were no piles of corpses to be seen.

The train didn't actually enter Petersburg. The Army engineers hadn't built that far. Where the tracks ended the Army had arranged for three carriages to take the Presidential party into town. Will and the crewmen were left by the dead-end track. The carriages for the Presidential party moved away from the train along a badly rutted road cleared of debris. As the party approached the town, they could see a few smoldering buildings. But there wasn't widespread devas-tation, not like Richmond. The Confederate army had abandoned the town, but the town folk were still around. They were walking in a daze. Today was still a day of afterwards and after-words among the survivors. Where they talked they were gathered in knots, no doubt exchanging stories.

The Presidential party dismounted from the carriages in the center of town. As the President led the way through the streets he inevitably extended his hand to the citizens he encountered. Most recognized the offer for what it was and shook hands with the President.

Elizabeth struggled to recognize landmarks. The struggle was not against the war. The war had left miles of trench-works around the town, to be sure, but because Petersburg's buildings were largely unscathed Elizabeth's struggle was a struggle against time. She hadn't been in Petersburg in 18 years. The place had changed. Buildings she seemed to remember were no longer to be found where she had once thought they stood. Even buildings she thought she recog-nized were now put to purposes foreign to what she remembered. A building once a bakery was now a general store. A haberdashery had become a tallow-maker's shop. Undertakers flourished everywhere. It was all rather unsettling for one native to these parts. In town the

Presidential party never encountered anyone, black or white, that Elizabeth could claim to know.

After touring Petersburg afoot the Presidential party was taken by carriages on a roundabout way back to the waiting train, which had been moved several miles back up the line toward City Point. The President wanted everyone to see a tree he'd seen near Petersburg on a previous visit. After a ride over a rough road laid through the trench lands, they came upon a road banked by trees and fields. Mr Abe directed the driver of his carriage to a large oak tree visible at a road bend. The oak was a white oak with four major arms branching from a single point at the trunk. The arms pointed straight to the heavens and were crowned and largely enshrouded by a crop of spring-green leaves. Ordinarily, you would have expected a farmer to have long ago chopped down this tree but the oak had taken root in an outcrop of rock. The rock must have deflected the tree's destruction. To chop it down would yield no gain in cropland. Moreover, the tree was magnificent, just as it was.

Mr Abe stepped down from his carriage so that he could face everyone in the carriages. From the ground he spoke of heaven and earth, as it were, and what bound the two. "In our travail of tears," said Mr Abe, "we do well to remember the labor of God. Look at this tree and remember her. Sturdy she is in the anchorage God gave her, unimpeachable in her bastion of rocks. Heavenward her arms are pointed to her Author and Sustainer. Her being, as in all our Lord's doings, is more than mere signage. Her being is for our delight as well as for His. No one thing in nature carries the autograph of our God. Rather there are many signs and many notes and now as in this day we hear the songs of birds fluttering in the tree. The tree becomes the measure and staff of God's music. The birds and beasts become the glorious notes singing the song of our Creator and Redeemer. Here we see and hear life come again after winter's death. Let spring your hope upon this oak, for she is a beautiful handmaiden of the Author of life and life again."

God be praised, thought Elizabeth.

Mr Abe stepped back and gazed at the tree, silent for some several minutes. The others, too, were quieted, struck by the poetry of the tree and by Mr Abe's words of praise. Even Tad was quiet, but then he usually was when his father spoke. After a few minutes Mr Abe said the party best be off. He climbed aboard his carriage and off went the party down the road.

When the travelers came upon the train, they found it turned around. Moreover a dozen boxcars had been inserted between the day coach and the locomotive. After the Presidential party boarded the train it trundled a few miles northward, then stopped along a large tent encampment serving as a hospital city. The Presidential party stepped down from the day coach and spent about an hour at the camp. The boat crew and Army officers and sergeants remained behind, working to place wounded men in the boxcars and even some in the coach. As the Presidential party walked back to the train following the camp tour, the marquis remarked more than once on how everyone in the camp was so well behaved. Never a complaint was heard, nor did any soldiers make efforts to draw attention to themselves. Each man bore up his wounds with commendable dignity, said the marquis. There had been plenty enough to see, not only men with one or two amputations, but even with three. *What will these men do?* wondered Elizabeth. She wondered once again, as she often had, how George had died. Had he died on a surgery table or on a hospital cot or out in the field at Wilson's Creek? She had never learned.

After the visit to the hospital city Mary Todd sat with Mr Abe on the train ride to City Point, at least for a while. As before, the Presidential party was at one end of the coach, the boat crew at the other, and the officers and sergeants in between. Senator Sumner and the marquis sat immediately in front of the Lincolns. The Harlans sat across the aisle. Elizabeth sat with Crook immediately behind the Lincolns. Among the Army men and the boat crew sat a number of wounded men. One of them had taken up playing his harmonica. He favored Stephen Foster tunes played with ineffable melancholy, especially 'Oh! Susanna' and 'My Old Kentucky Home'. No one objected. Because the locomotive was now separated from the coach by the boxcars, the harmonica carried well. Most seemed inclined to listen. Not Mary Todd. She chattered almost without end, at least until Mr Abe spotted a turtle sunning itself next to the track.

As soon as he spotted the turtle, Mr Abe scurried to the other end of the car, where the conductor sergeant sat. Mr Abe asked him to stop the train. The sergeant readily complied, rushing to the rear platform, where he proceeded to wave a red flag. The train couldn't have been going more than five miles an hour. After the train came to a jerking halt, Mr Abe and the sergeant walked back down the track to fetch the turtle. Tad jumped down from the train to fetch some twigs and gather some beetles if he could. At least he found some twigs before Mary Harlan shooed him back aboard the train. About a quarter hour later the train was again underway. For the rest of the trip to City Point, Mr Abe and Tad played with the turtle in the coach aisle. The turtle seemed to enjoy snapping at Tad's twigs. The men aboard the car seemed to derive as much pleasure from this as did Tad. The harmonica player whooped things up with the likes of 'Camptown Races'.

Elizabeth knew Mary Todd was annoyed with the turtle when she heard Mary Todd ask the marquis if his family had any good recipes for turtle soup. The marquis replied his family did. Would Mrs Lincoln like copies of the recipes? She said she would. He promised in the next letter home he'd ask his wife to supply copies of her recipe and his mother's for turtle soup. From turtle soup, Mary Todd turned to triumph. She talked about the victory celebrations the Federal government should promote following the war's end. Perhaps even a victory arch should be erected over Pennsylvania Avenue. Senator Sumner said that that might be a good idea. No one else commented. Mary Todd went on about victory balls, victory dinners, and dedicating victory monuments across the country. Getting out to do these things would be good for the President. Those listening nodded in agreement. Meanwhile the President and Tad and the men at the back of the coach were diverted with the turtle.

Mary Todd wouldn't cater to this diversion. Truth be told, the ebb and flow of Mary Todd's moods seemed less bound by wider circumstances and more bound up in her wounded relation with Mr Abe. He was the earth, she the moon. He was brightened or darkened from day to day by the sun. The sun might shine on him, it might be cloudy, it might be night. He took his moods from what happened. He tried his best not to let the night get the better of him or the day give him undue pride. Mary Todd's mood phases weren't determined by night and day...but by other things. Elizabeth wasn't sure that Mary Todd's sun was the same as Mr Abe's. In fact it wasn't. Here's where she knew the analogy with planets broke down. But then Mary Todd and Mr Abe were people. Very different from one another, but like earth and moon, very much affecting one another.

Maybe making a quilt was a vain effort. Elizabeth wanted to cover the Lincolns with love. But could she? Should she? And was it any of her business? No, it wasn't business. It was love, and she wanted Mr Abe and Mary Todd to be able to fully appreciate one another again. They surely loved one another. They just weren't able to help one another in the way each might hope for. Mr Abe needed someone right now who would share his generosity of spirit, not only in politics but in everyday life. Mary Todd needed someone who would attend to her anxieties and aspirations, not only episodically but every day. Short of the war ending, neither could be satisfied. But even when the war ended, would the White House home front get any better?

Mary Todd, as exaggerated as her fears might be, was understandably uneasy with her role as First Lady. Mr Abe still relied on her but not in every way she would have liked. Truth be told, why should he? She'd shown herself to be unreliable. The Ord incident showed that for all the world to see. Mary Todd's inability to see the forest for the trees and then to misidentify the shrubbery as trees made Elizabeth uncomfortable. She knew she shared that discomfort with Mr Abe. She could tell just by looking at him that he was uncomfortable right then with Mary Todd. Every time he got within hearing of her she was chattering about victory arches and victory parades and victory parties. He for a certainty couldn't forget the men he'd just seen at the hospital city. Or the men he'd seen before those men.

It was a mighty wonder he'd ever gravitated toward her, much more that he got hooked up with her. But he did. It was a fact, too, that he often faced her with his back. He could only take so much of her, then he ambled away. To boot, for the last four years he was pulled away by the war. That was his other woman, no more, no less. Well, almost. When the war was over, you could see the new woman coming, call her 'Reconstruction'. The whole point of having Senator Sumner down to City Point was to politick with him about

Reconstruction. Mary Todd was riding the Reconstruction train but she wanted to be up in the locomotive with Mr Abe. That wasn't going to happen. There were too many stations along the way with Ord or some other name up there on the name board. These people on the way to victory had to be paid their due. Mr Abe was prepared to pay the dues of war. But Mary Todd seemed only interested in receiving the benefits of peace. There was no way both could have their hands at the throttle and either of them be satisfied. Anyway, the American people had elected Mr Abe President, not Mary Todd.

When the train arrived at City Point, dozens and dozens of soldiers were on hand to remove the wounded. While the wounded were unloaded from the boxcars, the Presidential party walked from the station to the dock. There the *River Queen* was being readied to get underway. She would take the Lincolns and the visitors from Washington back to the capital city. Mr Abe was anxious to see Mr Seward.

Before leaving City Point, the Lincolns and their guests sat down for dinner in the *River Queen's* aft saloon. While dining, an Army band dockside serenaded the Presidential party with various popular airs. When the meal had been finished the diners arose to go out on the weather deck to salute the bandsmen. The band director asked the President if he had any requests. Mr Abe had two. He asked in honor of his guest, the Marquis de Chambrun, that the 'Marseillaise' be played. After it was played he asked that it be repeated. The marquis was taken and amused by the honor, since under Napoleon III the French government forbade playing the 'Marseillaise'.

Mr Abe had one other request. The band should play 'Dixie', he said. He asked that 'Dixie' be played until the *River Queen* was out of sight. The band director was taken aback. But he and his men replied magnificently to the request. 'Dixie' was heard as the commanding general of City Point bid the President adieu, as the *River Queen* pulled away, and as she made way to the north. As the President put it to the marquis, 'Dixie' was no longer the property of the Confederacy. It belonged to the nation.

The following morning something else would belong to the nation, too.

CHAPTER 13

—ɯɯ—

As the *River Queen* made way on Palm Sunday morning, Elizabeth awoke just past sunup. She hadn't slept well. The motion of the paddleboat was gentle enough but Elizabeth's stateroom on this trip was much noisier than the one on the *Monahasett*. Along with the continual racket coming from below decks, she had been disturbed by a throbbing vibration, part noise part motion, which made sleep one long effort. She'd wanted to lie abed a bit longer but there was no point to it. She wouldn't be able to sleep. Anyway, there would be some pleasure in watching the boat's passage up Chesapeake Bay into the arm of the Potomac. Perhaps the *River Queen* would encounter crab boats.

Before sightseeing, Elizabeth would have breakfast. Everyone had been told the evening before that breakfast would be served on an as-ordered basis, meaning you could come when you wanted. The two tables in the dining saloon were decked in fresh white table linen. There were place settings before every chair. Not a table chair was occupied, but the *River Queen's* two cooks sat along one wall. They stood as soon as Elizabeth entered the room. She asked where she should sit. They told her anywhere. She ordered coffee, scrambled eggs, oatmeal porridge, and a slice of Virginia ham. It was delivered piping hot. Because there was no one to visit with, she didn't linger over breakfast.

At first she sauntered forward walking down stairs to the *River Queen's* bow. There was too much spray there so she decided to walk aft to the stern. As she approached the stern she noticed a man bent way over the stern rail. He seemed to be examining the water, rather than looking at it. He was hatless. He was lanky, like the President. He had his elbows on the railing and his hands clasped almost as if in prayer. Not more than 50 yards behind the stern about a half dozen seagulls swooped and dived over the boat's wake. But the man wasn't watching them. He was peering down into the water. This was the President.

Elizabeth startled him from his preoccupation when she bid, "Good mornin', Mr Abe."

"Oh, good mornin', Madame Keckly."

He looked somewhat red eyed. He probably hadn't slept well. Fact of the matter was that many a night he hardly slept. Mary Todd had told Elizabeth this had been true since their arrival at the White House. She'd had to have a separate bed from Mr Abe just to keep her health.

"See anythin' in the wake?" asked Elizabeth.

"Oh, this? No, nothin'," said Mr Abe.

"Have any breakfast?" she asked.

"Just a cuppa coffee. And you?"

She told him what she'd had. "Sounds like you're well fortified," said he. Then he looked back in the water. "Wish I could see that tree this mornin'. Sometimes you can't see the tree for the forest, for everything, for the flood of events that can carry you away."

Elizabeth could tell the President wanted to talk. She said, "What you said about that oak tree yesterday was beautiful. Thank you for your fittin' words. People have come to know they've much to learn if they'll just listen to you."

"Thank you. That's very kind of you to say, thank you. You've always been a good listener, I expect, from the time when you were on you're mama's knees."

"Listenin' like talkin' takes practice. I suppose I did get an early start," said Elizabeth.

Said the President, "You've been an immense help bein' along, because you listen, listen better than do I to Molly. You should have been along when we first went down to City Point. I'm sorry that didn't happen. Molly needs to be heard but I just don't have the time or energy for it. This war's been so awful. You've seen. You know what I mean. Richmond. Petersburg. Vicksburg. Gettysburg. Shiloh." He paused, lifted his eyebrows, then said, "Wilson's Creek."

Elizabeth felt a lump in her throat.

"Forgive me for mentioning that," said Mr Abe.

"It's an honor," said Elizabeth, "but his death still hurts."

"Forgive me," he said.

"It's bigger than all of us," she said.

Mr Abe was silent for a time, but he was now looking aft, towards the seagulls in their swooping and diving. Elizabeth looked, too.

"There are so many threads to the course of human events," said he. "So many, some made by others, others made by ourselves, and everywhere there's entangling." He said nothing more for a while. Neither did Elizabeth. They both watched the swooping gulls in the wake of the *River Queen*. Then Mr Abe spoke again. "How I love this country! It breaks my heart that the grief of slavery could only end by the grief of my country. Slavery had to end. The yoking of those griefs is the just handwork of Almighty God."

"The grief will pass, Mr Abe, and the good that God wants out of it will live on. You can be sure of that."

"That is our consolation, isn't it, Madame Elizabeth?"

"Yes, sir."

"I want to tell you somethin'. Don't tell anyone else even if you hear about it from others. I don't think you will." Mr Abe looked directly into her eyes, as if waiting for some sign of assent from Elizabeth.

"You know you can rely on me, Mr Abe," said she.

"Indeed," said he, pausing, then looking toward the horizon. He began to give vent to something she had half expected. "I recently had a dream. I was walking about the White House. The White House was empty, yet I could hear weeping and crying. I could tell the mansion was captive to some sadness. As I walked about I came into the Blue Room. There I saw a catafalque and upon it a coffin with an American flag draped over it. Around the coffin stood four Army guards, standing at attention just beyond each corner of the catafalque. I approached one of the guards and asked what had happened. He said, 'The President was assassinated.' And then I awoke. I wasn't able to go back to sleep, but I got down on my knees and prayed to God. I asked if possible that I be spared this cup of death, but that if it was His will, then I asked His favor that I see at least a glimmer of victory before I die and that no one else should have to die with me if I were to be killed.

"After that prayer, I remained on my knees. It was very quiet. And then I felt coming over me a gentle warmth and the remembrance, oddly, of my baptism, which had been cold and wet."

"You *have* been baptized," said Elizabeth.

"Yes, just before we came to Washington four years ago. But only a few German Baptists know and Mrs Vance, our old housekeeper in Springfield, and now you. But you absolutely must keep this a secret. I don't want anyone ever to use my baptism to my personal or political advantage. I've always seen baptism as a dedication to God. It's that, for sure. Our Lord showed the way. But it's also a great consolation — not against others, but as a gift from God in the labors of this life. It's not something to be used to one's own advantage but for the advantage of God.

"You'll not say a word?"

"You can rest assured," replied Elizabeth.

"Thank you. I wouldn't have said a word unless I could trust you. I needed to tell someone, not only about the dream. Everyone in my cabinet or at the White House might expect me to report on dreams." He laughed. "But not just anyone should know the consolation that followed this dream. The affairs of humankind are so tangled and not just beyond our doorsteps but right in our own homes, our own hearts."

"So true, Mr Abe. So true. May I ask…"

"A question," said Mr Abe. "Go ahead."

"Does Mary Todd…"

"She cannot," blurted Mr Abe, facing Elizabeth. "She cannot. Your question is neither unreasonable nor unexpected. But she cannot."

She cannot know. Elizabeth had expected this, but she still had felt compelled to hear it from Mr Abe himself. She was shaken by the almost unimaginable trust he had placed in her. She looked away at the gulls, as did he. The two were looking aft when Will appeared.

"Mr President, Mrs Lincoln requests your presence in the dining saloon."

"Aye, aye," said Mr Abe to Will. "You see, Madame Elizabeth, I'm learning Navy as well as Army lingo these days. I wish you a good day, madam."

Said Elizabeth, "You should be more careful, Mr Abe. I know Mr Lamon is concerned…"

"He is, he is, but there's a world to do before our appointed day. Today's Palm Sunday and I'm summoned. Good day and thank you, Madame Elizabeth," said Mr Abe, nodding toward her.

The passengers were less celebratory and more cerebral than you might have expected for a Palm Sunday morning. There was no effort to gather for prayers and hymns. Everyone was to attend to their own affairs, rather than joining in a group endeavor. They had had enough of that on the days before. Mary Todd, for one, asked Elizabeth to come to the Lincoln stateroom. She wanted to talk about the lavender dress she'd wear Easter Sunday. Elizabeth had made the dress two years previously. Mary Todd wanted it modified by the addition of lace cuffs and a lace collar. She had the lace at the White House, purchased from a Philadelphia dealer who specialized in Dutch, Belgian, and French lace. Elizabeth promised to look at it after arrival in Washington. If suitable, the lace could be applied in time for Easter.

Mr Abe came to the stateroom shortly before noon to fetch Mary Todd and Elizabeth for lunch. Mary Todd reminded him that next Sunday would be Easter. He knew. She said she would want him to attend church with Tad and her. He promised he would. He said it had just seemed they were celebrating Christmas. That mention of Christmas may have prompted Mary Todd to lead off the luncheon conversation with talk about the Christmas gifts the White House had received from various ambassadors. The Spanish ambassador had given a box of oranges from Valencia. Mary Todd said the taste for oranges was an acquired taste; Mr Abe added it was a taste easily acquired. She said the Japanese ambassador, just recently arrived, had given four fine prints, one of each season depicting a cottage with a Japanese farmer and his family. They both adored the prints. The ambassador from Bavaria had given a nutcracker, which Tad said was his favorite. Then there was the gift from the Russian ambassador, a nesting doll.

Senator Sumner asked what a nesting doll was. He'd never heard of nesting dolls. Mary Todd explained that nesting dolls were made of wood shaped somewhat like a knob on a piece of furniture, though much smoother than ordinary and painted. A nesting doll could be pulled into its two parts. Each part was snugly fitted to its mate. Inside a nesting doll another was to be found. When that second nesting doll was pulled apart yet another was to be found. You could pull apart any number of nesting dolls until a point when a small doll would be found that didn't conceal yet another.

Senator Sumner wondered whether a given nesting doll set was made from one piece of wood.

Mr Abe spoke up, "I happened to ask the ambassador that very question but he didn't have an answer. He'd never seen a nesting doll being made. He'd never been told how they were made but it raises the general question of how you go from the big to the small or from the small to the big or why you'd go in one direction or the other."

Said Senator Sumner, "I don't follow you, Mr President."

"Well," said Mr Abe, "I once heard a story about two cousins that farmed on opposite sides of the Mississippi. One lived in Missouri and one in Illinois and they both happened to be courtin' the same lady, who came from Keokuk, Iowa. She was a very pretty lady and a number of men had already paid court to her. She had told 'em all she would marry a man who was not only rich but also wise. A man without wisdom, however rich now could soon fritter it away, she said, but wisdom grew with age. She told the two cousins that if she married one of the two, one would have to prove to be wise.

"One Sunday one cousin took the lady out to his farm. They had to cross the Des Moines River by ferry because this cousin's farm was in Missouri, across the river from Iowa. The Missouri farmer showed off his farm, then took the lady back to Keokuk. The next Sunday the Illinois cousin took the lady to his farm, to show it off. Because this cousin lived in Illinois they had to cross the Mississippi by ferry. Some months later the Missouri farmer took the lady to his farm to show her a small barn he'd made. He said he'd add on to it as he cultivated more land. A month later the Illinois farmer took the lady to his farm to show a large barn he'd put up with the help of neighbors. He'd planned ahead, he said, and would only have to construct small additions to his barn, if he had to make any at all.

"Well, as it turned out those two farmers courted that lady for another three years. Both farmers prospered and each had become determined to have this lady as his wife. They passed up other ladies just because they were competin' with one another. The Missouri farmer kept addin' on to his barn. And the Illinois farmer had to make a small addition to his barn after all. By the last year of their competitive courtin' they told the lady she'd have to make a choice. Both farmers wanted to be in a family way. And you know what happened?"

Senator Sumner shook his head. The Harlans shook their heads. Madame Keckly hunched up her shoulders and wondered to herself whether the key to this story was 'another man'. She said nothing. Mary Todd said nothing. Perhaps she'd heard the tale before. Then the Marquis de Chambrun spoke up.

"She married zomeone ozer zan zee farmers."

Everyone laughed.

"Exactly," said Mr Abe. "That lady had crossed the Mississippi and the Des Moines so many times she eventually became acquainted with the young man at Keokuk who owned and ran both ferries. When she was faced with a choice, she decided to choose him. She said, 'He don't have to become big or small to impress me. All he has to do is plug along and the money comes rolling in. That's right smart enough for me.'"

Senator and Mrs Harlan laughed, perhaps because the Iowa man had gotten the Iowa lady. Mary Todd reddened, no doubt because of the vulgar overtones of the story.

But Mr Abe didn't leave it there. As he continued to talk he especially eyed the marquis and Senator Sumner, as if he were teaching the one and reminding the other. "In this story there's encapsulated the whole matter of enlargement and diminishment and what's 'fitting', if you will. In some ways that's what been at issue these last four years, in fact these last 76 years here in our country. How were we going to enlarge the country? Was it going to expand all free, or partly free and partly slave, or was the slave power going to grow, even beyond the South into the North? And what, if any of those things, would be a fitting conclusion to the constitution written in Philadelphia in 1789 and subsequently ratified by all 13 states so recently colonies of Great Britain?

"That constitution had made the Union possible and yet likewise that constitution made certain the future would have to resolve its basic contradiction, the contradiction of slavery to freedom. Now the gentlemen, most of the gentlemen, who framed the constitution hoped and thought slavery would wither away. But it didn't wither away. Instead the cotton gin was invented and cotton became a big enterprise. The Southern plantation power was of a mind that the only way cotton profits could be had was if slavery expanded. Cotton expanded and slavery expanded but not with an easy conscience. Slavery had to be justified. To forbid slavery's expansion into the new American territories would be an affront. And that became intolerable to the slave power.

"Likewise that expansion became an affront to those who saw our constitution as a promise of a just freedom. So the war came with my election, even though I was willing to pay to have the slaves freed."

The marquis spoke up, "You were willing to purchase zee slaves from zee owners to obtain zer freedom in zat way?"

"He was," said Senator Sumner, "and that would have been a grave wrong, I respectfully submit."

"We differed on that point, Senator. It was a price I would have gladly paid to avoid war. Neither North nor South could abide the idea of compensation. The North saw it wrong to buy out the slave power. The South saw it wrong to even suggest the slave power was in the wrong. So the compensation idea quickly died and even more quickly came the war.

"In this war amidst all the sacrifices made by both sides there have been enlargements and diminishments. Some men have been diminished in stature. And many men and women have been enlarged in stature, but often enough because of sacrifice. Now I ask you to think of the two regions, North and South. Have they been enlarged or diminished because of the war? I'm not asking about the size of the territories. I'm talkin' about the spirit of the people. Before anyone answers I want to read some passages from *Macbeth.*"

Will, who was standing nearby, was sent off to fetch Mr Abe's copy of Shakespeare. In a few moments he returned, handing over the Shakespeare volume to its owner. Mr Abe read several passages from *Macbeth* and a few from *Hamlet,* too. Elizabeth couldn't remember the exact passages but she remembered that Mr Abe read over twice Macbeth's tribute to the king — Duncan — whom he had just murdered. It must have been,

> *Duncan is in his grave;*
> *After life's fitful fever he sleeps well.*
> *Treason has done his worst; nor steel, nor poison,*
> *Malice domestic, foreign levy, nothing,*
> *Can touch him further.*

All this reading, enjoyed by Mr Abe for its own sake, was for a point. He hadn't forgotten his point. After he'd read several passages he asked, "Do you think the North could be diminished in some ways by the war with our Southern brothers? Do you think there are ways we of the North could envy our fallen Southern brother? Are there ways they will see *us* as treasonous?"

"Mr President," said Senator Sumner, "the notion that we of the North could in any way be treasonous is utter nonsense. It was the South that broke away from the Union. The South's leaders were treasonous. We of the North must act accordingly. Anything less than justice will make a mockery of all those who have died in this conflict."

Senator Harlan remarked, "The senator has a good point, Mr President, but I would narrowly define those who should be tried for treason."

Mr Abe spoke at once, "My hopes for trials are so narrow that however you define the treasonous leaders, I pray God grants them escape."

Senator Sumner turned livid. Mary Todd looked alarmed. The marquis appeared to wonder what would happen next. Mr Abe appeared to be savoring the moment. He asked if anyone would like some tea or coffee. The Harlans said they would like some tea and the marquis requested coffee. Everyone else except Mr Abe ordered a beverage. The President had more to say.

CHAPTER 14

—m—

"When Macbeth murdered Duncan, was he diminished or enlarged as a man?" asked Mr Abe.

"He was diminished," answered the marquis.

"And as a ruler?" asked Mr Abe.

"He didn't become ruler by killing the king," said Senator Sumner. "The others didn't know Macbeth had killed Duncan, other than Lady Macbeth. In her eyes Macbeth was more of a man than he had been before. In her eyes, Macbeth was enlarged."

Mrs Harlan spoke, "Everyone else was willing to make Macbeth king. He had been such a brave commander. He gained more responsibilities but he and his lady committed more and more murder to protect their position. You could say he became a diminishing ruler because he in fact was becoming a diminished man."

"Very well said, Mrs Harlan. Well said. And we too can diminish ourselves as people if those of us given power abuse that gift and the responsibility entrusted to us by God."

Senator Sumner spoke. "To walk away from executing justice is to walk away from the responsibility granted us by the people by God's grace."

"It could be, Senator, it could be," replied Mr Abe. "But I don't think God would have us execute justice without mercy. I do think we will diminish ourselves, perhaps even destroy ourselves, if we don't especially rely on mercy in this case. For despite everything in these last years, we are still brothers and sisters, Americans of different origins, different color, different status, yet one in our commitment to liberty under God."

Senator Harlan spoke, "The North and South have had a very different view of liberty or freedom."

"True, true, Senator. The North's has been a *freedom for*, a freedom to seek happiness, a freedom to speak, a freedom to worship God in one's own way. There's been that, too, in the South, but mangled by a *freedom from*, a freedom from the constraints of conscience when it comes to slavery, a freedom from the North, which has tried to call the South to its conscience and curb the expansion of slavery. Not that the North is free from sin.

"Now the labors of our bloody strife appear to be coming to an end. I think a sense of grace compels us to acknowledge that the South, at least, has become enlarged in this strife."

"Mr President, I beg to differ," said Senator Sumner.

"Hear me out," said Mr Abe. "We've all read accounts of recent discussions about freeing those now in slavery to serve in the Confederate army. Well, it has come to pass. Even now men of African ancestry are being recruited into the Confederate army. Indeed, for some time there have been Negro units serving in Louisiana, so I'm told."

Senator Harlan spoke. "It's a measure of their desperation. If they had done this four years ago, they might have won the war, but it's too late now."

"If they'd recognized the dignity of the slaves in their midst four years ago, if they had freed them then, there would have been no cause for war," said Mr Abe. "They wouldn't have wanted to leave the Union. By an act of grace, we would have been spared much strife.

"But the slave power in the South was untouched with this grace. And men North and South fell to arms. For our tolerating slavery, South *and* North, God would have us be taught. These years of war have been a hard lesson for North and South. And the South *has* been taught. By necessity they've learned."

"*We* have taught them," said Senator Sumner.

"No sir, I beg to differ," said Mr Abe. "In war or politics it's always better to play the student than the teacher with your opponents. Look at Hamlet. He learned many things, had many suspicions confirmed. But when he finally got his ire up and acted, he overacted, you might say. The poison he would have directed to his uncle was a poison he too supped to his fatal detriment. There is a need for justice, yes, but not if justice covers a poison that's become self-inflicting. There's a danger of that now and it could be fatal to true Union. It's not enough to win the battle of arms. We must also win the battle of hearts. If we are self-righteous we will lose that battle. As much as possible we must be merciful. After all we are brothers and sisters in this vessel called America."

Senator Harlan conceded that Mr Abe was persuasive, that *he* was persuaded, but that many others in the Congress would have to be persuaded, too. Senator Sumner conceded only that justice and mercy would have to be worked out in the details. But, yes, he wasn't deaf to mercy and not unmindful of the battle of the hearts. Mr Abe was so put at ease that he put off any more politicking that afternoon. The senators seemed happy enough to put politics aside. They encouraged Mr Abe to read more Shakespeare.

Mary Todd had had enough Shakespeare for now. She excused herself and asked Elizabeth to join her in checking up on Tad. Mrs Harlan arose from her chair to join the two ladies. Mary Todd insisted that Mrs Harlan rest easy and stay and hear some Shakespeare. Mary Todd said she'd want to hear from Mrs Harlan what she would miss.

Mary Todd went to the Lincoln stateroom, where Annie was packing away Mary's clothes in anticipation of arrival in Washington in the early evening. Mary Todd asked Annie if she knew where Tad and Mary Harlan might be found. Annie said the two were on the upper deck. She asked if she should fetch the boy. Mary Todd replied she just wanted to check on the boy and would do that herself.

Mary Todd and Elizabeth went to the upper deck. The main features of the upper deck besides the *River Queen's* two stacks were the boat's pilot house forward and an open area aft covered by a canvas awning. Under this awning Mary Harlan sat reading to Tad. Tad sat on the deck near Mary Harlan's chair, listening while eyeing nearby the very turtle spotted by Mr Abe the previous day. The turtle was contentedly chomping away on lettuce leaves.

Mary Todd gave Elizabeth a look of surprise, then marched over to Mary Harlan and Tad. Mary Harlan stopped her reading. She and the boy looked up to Mary Todd.

Pointing to the turtle, Mary Todd said, "I thought that thing had been left behind at City Point. What's it doing up here?"

Tad said, "Dad said we could bring it home."

"Home! We've got enough creatures at home."

"Oh, Ma."

"Oh, Ma, my eye," replied Mary Todd.

"I'll take care of it."

"You and a dozen others at the White House. I think it's about time to start sending some animals off the ark."

Mary Harlan laughed.

"What's so funny?" asked Mary Todd.

"We were just reading about Noah and the Ark," said Mary Harlan.

"We? Who's 'we'?" asked Mary Todd.

"Well, really me. Tad didn't want to read."

"I like the story, Ma, how Noah saves the animals like God wants."

"Well, you might have drawn the wrong conclusions, my boy."

"No, Ma, I like to hear stories about how God saves."

"Well, that's good, Tad, real good. But I want to talk to Mary for a moment. Mary, would you join me for a moment?"

Mary rose from her chair, carefully putting the Bible down where she'd sat, and then followed Mary Todd to a railing. The *River Queen* was making steady progress in open waters. Elizabeth decided to talk with Tad while his mother talked with Mary Harlan.

"Have you liked being at City Point?" she asked Tad.

"It was bejiggers," said Tad. "I'd go again any time."

"I'm sure you would. I'm sure your papa was happy to have you down there with him."

"Yes'm," said Tad looking towards his mother.

She and Mary Harlan had just strolled back from the railing. Mary Harlan pursed her lips. Elizabeth guessed that Mary Todd had chastened her.

"Let's be off, Lizzy," said Mary Todd.

Elizabeth nodded to Mary Harlan and said to Tad, "You take care of that turtle, now."

"Yes'm," replied Tad with a smile.

Before rejoining the Shakespeare reading, while the two were in the dining saloon, Mary Todd shared with Elizabeth her opinion of Mary Harlan. "Lizzy, that girl's a pretty face with little between the ears to back it up."

"What d'ya mean, Mary T?" asked Elizabeth.

"She shouldn't have been reading about Noah and the Ark to Tad. She should have shown better judgment than that."

"Well, least she was readin' from the Bible."

"True, she's to be given credit for that. But it seems to me she could have read a less gruesome story."

"Is that what you talked to her about, Mary T?"

"Exactly. I want her to know that I expect the very highest standards in every way. If she and Robert want to get married, there's probably no way I can stop it. But she should know when she's in my household, *I'm* the person in charge."

Elizabeth nodded in acknowledgment and let the matter go at that. She couldn't help but wonder whether this incident boded troubled waters between Mary Todd and her future daughter-in-law. Time would tell.

The *River Queen* arrived at the Arsenal dock just before sundown that Palm Sunday. The streets of Washington were alive with people and lit by bonfires along the gutters. The government and city had received word that General Lee had surrendered that morning to General Grant at Appomattox, Virginia. General Johnston's Confederate army was still very much at large in North Carolina but with Lee's surrender the cessation of war seemed almost certain. General Lee could not be diminished but his Army had been hammered. The blows were coming from so many quarters and his resources had been so used up that in good conscience his only course was surrender. At least that was the way Mr Abe described things as the Presidential carriage traveled from the Arsenal to the White House.

Mr Abe, Mary Todd, Tad, and Elizabeth marveled in the good cheer. Men flung hats into the air and young women blew kisses as the carriage passed. Several military bands had struck up impromptu concerts for the milling crowds to savor. If not for the celebrations following the fall of Richmond, Elizabeth would have said she'd never seen a thing like it in her life. Especially for Mr Abe the widespread cheer was a revelation. Of course he'd been at City Point when Richmond fell. Mr Abe, Mary Todd, and Tad responded to the cheers by waving at the crowds. Tad was especially exuberant.

The White House was surrounded by a large crowd, which had to be cleared away to enable the Presidential carriage to pass through. As the carriage entered the White House grounds three bands amongst the crowd struck up 'Hail to the Chief' but not in unison. Before stepping down from the carriage Mr Abe promised the crowd he'd deliver a speech the next day. Once inside, he headed to his office to review telegrams that had arrived during the day.

While Mr Abe was reviewing telegrams, Mary Todd and Elizabeth went to Mary Todd's bedroom. Before letting Elizabeth return home, Mary Todd wanted to find the lavender dress to be embellished with lace. Out of the blue Mary Todd asked Elizabeth what she thought of Mr Abe's story about the young woman of Keokuk.

"It was funny and instructive as so many of Mr Abe's stories are," said Elizabeth.

"Oh, it was instructive, *wasn't* it?" said Mary Todd.

"I *thought* you were a little upset about it," said Elizabeth.

"Not a bit, a lot, Lizzy."

"Because of the barnyard humor? Mr Abe always favors a little of that humor, Mary Todd. It gets people's attention. I think he thinks it helps people remember his stories. He's probably right."

"It was enough when that story-tellin' made us look like hicks from Illinois. I could put up with that, at least once in a while, when people here thought we were sodbusters, at least in the beginning. It's not the vulgarity per se that gets to me now. It's what it points to on my man's heart. I tell you there *is* another woman."

Responded Elizabeth, "I've told you, Mary Todd, it's the war and she'll be on her way out the door soon enough." *No point in bringing up Reconstruction.*

"The lady isn't the war, Lizzy. Whoever she is I don't think the lady's going away."

"How you figure?" asked Elizabeth.

"I can't say. I just know. Why else bring up this story featuring a young lady being courted by the men? Why a young lady?"

"That's what Mr Abe heard. You remember he said he'd heard this story. Probably heard it when you folks were livin' back in Illinois. Anyway, it's usually young ladies that get courted."

"Lizzy, you know darned well he's capable of changing stories to suit the occasion."

"Sure. He's always got a point to his story tellin'."

"His preoccupations show through, Lizzy."

"It's the war, Mary Todd."

"No, it isn't."

"If not the war, then America. That's his woman."

"That's even worse. There's someone out there. I know."

Elizabeth had found the lavender dress the two had been searching for. Mary Todd had already found the lace. "How you goin' to identify this woman? Except for goin' to City Point, Mr Abe is practically tied to this house or out there at Soldiers' Home. And when he's out now, Crook or someone like him follows. I don't think there's anyone except in your imagination. Rest easy, Mary Todd."

"I won't."

CHAPTER 15

—◊◊◊—

When Elizabeth left Mary Todd's bedroom she carried away the lavender dress and lace. She wasn't certain how she would carry these items and her luggage, too. If necessary she would take the dress and lace to her shop and then return for her luggage. No one had thought to make arrangements for her getting home, certainly not Mary Todd. And Elizabeth wasn't one to routinely ask favors of her friend other than having invoices be paid on time.

She decided to ask the White House doorkeeper for a carpetbag. He was a new man, promoted to replace the doorkeeper Mary Todd had recently fired. Elizabeth would roll up the dress and lace in the bag to protect them from dirt and loss. When she arrived at the front door the doorkeeper and others were rather preoccupied. The President was about to depart for his visit to Secretary Seward. The President's carriage was at the ready under the porte-cochere. Beyond, on the White House grounds, the crowds and bands could be heard. Fireworks crackled up in the sky.

Elizabeth introduced herself and asked that someone fetch a carpetbag 'on behalf of Mrs Lincoln's business', as she put it.

The doorkeeper replied, "Yes, yes, yes. Mrs Lincoln's business. I'll get a bag in a moment." He appeared quite anxious.

Elizabeth decided this wasn't the occasion to press her business. She could wait rather than distract and torment this agitated fellow. Moments later Mr Abe appeared, looking eager to be on his way to visit Mr Seward. When he noticed Elizabeth waiting in the foyer he came over to her.

"Ah, Madame Keckly, it looks like you've got a handful of business to take with you this evening. Once again, thank you so much for joining us at City Point."

"My pleasure, Mr Abe, thank you for having me along," replied Elizabeth.

"I trust arrangements have been made to convey you home."

"None. Anyway, the main thing is to get this dress and lace organized so I can get to my home and shop."

"Yes, I can see. Will someone see that a carriage takes Mrs Keckly to her shop and home?" asked Mr Abe.

The doorkeeper spoke, "I will see to it, sir."

Mr Abe nodded to Elizabeth, put his hat on his head, and strolled out to the waiting carriage, which took him away. Soon afterwards the doorkeeper presented Elizabeth with a large carpetbag. She folded the lace and dress into the bag. In a few minutes a carriage appeared, which the doorkeeper said was for her. This carriage was driven by a fellow in a mulberry outfit smoking a corncob pipe. The doorkeeper set the carpetbag and Elizabeth's two leather grips on the carriage floor. Then he helped Elizabeth aboard. This was the first time in her entire life that a carriage had been ordered to carry her anywhere. Elizabeth felt like a queen.

The little episode at the door of the White House brought home a signal difference between Mr Abe and Mary Todd. He was invariably thoughtful in so many different ways and towards so many different people, even people like the Secessionists, who opposed him. But if Mary Todd was thoughtful she was more akin to one of the numerous people tending the bonfires along the streets of Washington this night. She could be stirred up by events but she faced inward to her own flames, which she would hasten to tend and stoke. Elizabeth didn't want to think just now what that might portend.

Better to think of Mr Abe but it seemed impossible to think of him without contrasting him to Mary Todd. He was considerate; she much less so. He was disposed to like others; she was disposed to suspecting others. He was willing to give authority to others; she wanted to control things. He was thrifty; she was extravagant. He was humble; she expected others to be humble toward her. Maybe, maybe this course of humility had carried them as man and wife through their marriage. Mr Abe just naturally played court to Mary Todd. Mary Todd could feel enlarged and not diminished. Elizabeth chuckled to think she was thinking in the language of the nested dolls. She marveled how rapidly new ideas could take hold when they provided insight into old situations.

With new insight came a new light. With the new light came new shadows, shadows disturbing to Elizabeth. If there was one thing about Mr Abe and Mary Todd in which they were very much alike it was this: they shared secrets and thoughts with Elizabeth they weren't able to share with one another. Mr Lincoln didn't know of Mary Todd's budget-busting purchases of jewels and dresses. Elizabeth and many others did. Mr Lincoln didn't know of Mary Todd's practice of coercing or inducing government employees to funnel funds to White House refurbishments that were labeled, really mislabeled, under other accounts. The old doorkeeper had been fired at Mary Todd's insistence precisely because Mary Todd was afraid Mr Abe would hear the doorkeeper's tales. Mary Todd, at least until now, had trusted that her friend would disclose nothing intentionally or unintentionally to her husband. But you never knew. Mary Todd might someday take a fright to Elizabeth and cast her away.

Not that that would be the end of Elizabeth's world. Elizabeth's business had been on solid ground long before Mary Todd appeared and would be on solid ground so long as she, Elizabeth, could attend to it. But, and Elizabeth hated to admit it, she would be hurt to be separated from Mr Abe. Here was someone she could admire without reservation, someone, yes, that she could...love. How else could she put it? But no one could understand her love for Mr Abe unless they understood God's love for mankind. That was the kind of love she felt toward Mr Abe. She loved Mr Abe in some small measure the way God must love, or so she felt. What was that godly love? Elizabeth wasn't sure. God's love wasn't carnal, no, but it was intensely satisfying even if mysterious. Maybe it was satisfying because it was mysterious. Elizabeth's head fairly spun with thoughts. Mr Abe was as precious to her as her own child, George, had been. She had hated losing George.

The thought of *his loss* made her flinch. After all, Mr Abe was different than George or her mama or her papa. She felt guilty to have placed Mr Abe in the same category as people whose mourning she could readily justify to society. How could society ever abide or want to acknowledge that the Republic's chief magistrate was able to share knowledge with her — a former slave no less — that he couldn't and wouldn't share with his own wife? Yet such a sharing had occurred the morning of this very day. The remembrance of the President at the stern rail of the *River Queen* would never be forgotten. Elizabeth had no wish to forget it.

She was relieved nonetheless to arrive at her shop across and down the street from the Lewis home. As soon as the driver stepped down to tether the horses to the hitching post, she let herself down from the carriage. The driver retrieved a lantern sitting on the platform in front of his seat. He took a wad of paper from his pocket and lit it by dipping its edge into the bowl of his corncob pipe. With the lit paper he set the hand lantern alight.

"D'ya want me to go up with you, ma'am?" asked the driver.

"I'll go on my own, thank you," replied Elizabeth. She noticed for the first time that he might be a mulatto. Like George he had a very fair skin. That fair skin had been deadly to George. Without it he wouldn't have been admitted to the Army, not then. Only later, thanks to Mr Abe, would those of African ancestry be able to serve in the Army. She was proud that African Americans had so early brought valor to their bearing of American arms. They were proof in blood that her people could be good Americans too. Her pride faltered a bit as she thought of George. She acknowledged she'd probably never know exactly how George had died at Wilson's Creek. She couldn't believe he'd died running away. She couldn't believe he was anything other than brave. Wasn't it valorous enough that he had gone to America's colors, that he'd fought for the dignity of his race and for the American people? Surely he had done that and surely he must have done more. He had fought for home and country. Would that he could still be found at home. But enough, enough. She must get the carpetbag upstairs.

Perhaps Elizabeth should have asked the driver to accompany her. He seemed happy enough waiting outside watching fireworks sporadically light up the horizon. With the bag in one hand and a lantern in the other, she ascended the stairs. Ascent was a balancing act, hardly Elizabeth's first such act or her last. Upstairs she set the carpetbag down and unlocked the shop door. The place was deserted. Elizabeth entered the office and set the lantern on her desk, placing the carpetbag on the floor. She adjusted the valve on a gas lamp to give sufficient light for the office. She removed the lace from the bag and placed it on a table next to her desk. She removed the lavender dress, which appeared none the worse for having been rolled up in the bag. Perhaps the daylight would prove otherwise. In any event she hung the dress in the cherry wardrobe that stood nearest her desk.

Atop the wardrobe was the camel-colored hatbox full of First Lady scraps. Elizabeth pulled out a small, self-standing ladder stored between the wardrobe and an adjacent table. She climbed the ladder to reach the hatbox. There was no good reason for looking in the hatbox now but looking would take but a minute. Elizabeth removed the lid and pawed through the neatly stacked scraps of Mary Todd's dresses. The scraps were all still there. And why shouldn't they be? She replaced the lid and placed the box back on top of the wardrobe. She resolved to soon begin making the quilt. She resolved then and there that the quilt should have a patriotic theme. . She didn't have a design in mind, though. Not yet. She felt the material on hand wouldn't make a satisfying quilt, at least not satisfying to her. Something was missing, but she would have to deal with that later. The driver was waiting.

Elizabeth placed the stepladder back where it had been. She turned down the gaslight, took hold of the empty carpetbag, and lifted the lantern. She decided to leave the carpetbag at the shop. She could return it to the White House in daylight. For now it was enough to walk down with the lantern. She locked up the shop and quickly descended the stairs.

The carriage driver didn't appear upset with waiting. He had been leaning against the carriage smoking his pipe. He snuffed it out when Elizabeth appeared, placing the pipe in his front coat pocket. Elizabeth asked if he would take the lantern and walk with her across and down the street to the Lewis house, her home as she explained to him.

"I'll be happy to carry your baggage, too, Ma'am," said the driver.

That is the privilege of a queen. Best let it pass, thought Elizabeth then. She was always so independent and wanted to keep things that way. Later, thinking back, she said she should have accepted this small courtesy. Instead she said, "I'll carry my bags, thank you." And she did, allowing the driver to lead the way with the lantern.

Someone must have sent word to the Lewises that Elizabeth was at hand. As soon as the driver knocked at the Lewis door, the children bounded out and surrounded the driver and Elizabeth. Walker and Ginny Lewis followed. Elizabeth handed her luggage to Walker, who carried it inside. Mrs Lewis and Elizabeth followed. The children watched the driver unhitch the horses and then clatter off with his carriage. Never before had a White House carriage delivered someone to the Lewis household. The children would have bragging rights at school.

Ginny had fixed a meal of creamed asparagus soup and bread for Elizabeth. The asparagus came fresh from the family's kitchen garden. Walker and Ginny heard bits and pieces about the *River Queen*. Before supper was over they invited Elizabeth to join them and their children at a victory thanksgiving service at the Fifteenth Street Church starting in a half hour. Elizabeth excused herself saying she wanted to unpack and settle in for the evening.

After the Lewises had gone Elizabeth proved less industrious than she'd wanted to be. She found herself once again ruminating over the promise of a quilt. Really, there had been no promise. She hadn't even promised God or herself she would make one. But somehow making a quilt seemed a God-ordained thing. She needed to let *both the Lincolns* know how much she loved them. She assured herself she loved them both.

Elizabeth knew Mary Todd better than she did Mr Abe. After all Elizabeth spent far more time with Mary Todd and did far more with her than she ever did with Mr Abe. Elizabeth's relation to Mary Todd was a contained relationship and Mary Todd was the container. Mary Todd cared little for the rest of Elizabeth's life and wanted nothing of that life other than what she, Mary Todd, chose to partake of. Mr Abe's relation to Elizabeth was more open.

Mr Abe was more like a hat than a box. He understood Elizabeth had a life of her own, a life he honored. This evening he'd honored her by recognizing her needs. In the morning he'd honored her by sharing something of himself. Mr Abe was protective of others, particularly those he loved. His gift and his burden was that he loved so many. In some way the quilt must reflect not only Mary Todd's life as the Republic's chief hostess. It must reflect the honor and love Mr Abe brought to the office of the Republic's chief magistrate. Tangibly the quilt would incorporate Mary Todd in the material remnants from her dresses. But how incorporate Mr Abe? Elizabeth hadn't made a stitch of clothing for him. She had nothing tangible of his to work with. She turned to putting her own clothes away.

When the Lewises returned from the thanksgiving service, Elizabeth greeted them even more warmly than the first time. Her quilt quandary had made her feel alone. She was ready for company. The Lewis children on the other hand were tuckered out. It had been a big day. The news of Lee's surrender at Appomattox Court House had fired up the spirits of young and old alike. That exultation was now spent to exhaustion. The children were ready for bed and were soon asleep.

After the children were abed, Ginny remarked to Elizabeth, "I thought you might be in bed by the time we got home."

"Hard to go asleep on a day like this," replied Elizabeth.

"At least if you're not 12 or under," said Ginny. "Like some tea or coffee?"

"Tea sounds good," replied Elizabeth.

Walker joined the ladies at the kitchen table, all three at first taking tentative sips of the steaming tea. Elizabeth described the tours of Richmond and Petersburg. She talked about the others she had traveled with. Walker asked about the President. Elizabeth reported he seemed physically in better health. His spirits had been lifted by the good news they'd all received when they arrived in Washington. Neither Walker nor Ginny asked about Mary Todd. They were eager to hear about Tad. Mr Lewis remarked that the boy's tutor should have been along on the trip. Ginny said the trip was meant as a vacation.

"Didn't sound like a vacation for Mr Lincoln," replied Walker. "Like father like son. The boy should have been tendin' to his work. Sometimes people take the education of their children for granted."

"It was a vacation, Walker," said Ginny.

Elizabeth raised her eyebrows in surprise. Silently she agreed with Walker. The Lincolns *should* place more emphasis on educating Tad. Perhaps when Willie died the education emphasis died with him. No question Tad was nowhere as bright as Willie had been. Any harvest for all the effort was going to be little more than paltry. No matter. Education had to be emphasized or where would the next generation end up? If it hadn't been for all the efforts of her mama and her papa to educate her, she might still be a slave. Her education in sewing and, just as importantly, in reading and calculating had enabled her to work her way to freedom. She would never, never forget that. Ignorance was the first chain in bondage. With that thought she very much wanted to free herself from the haunting aspects of her relationship to Mr Abe and Mary Todd. She wanted the benefit of Ginny and Walker's wisdom without breaching the privacy of her relationship with the Lincolns. Rather than speak directly, she would speak in analogies.

"I want to talk about baptism," she said out of the blue.

"Baptism?" asked Ginny.

"Yes," said Elizabeth.

"Was someone baptized during this trip?" asked Ginny.

"No," replied Elizabeth, "but I got thinkin' about it and some questions baptism raised for me."

"You can talk about baptism any time," said Walker, "whatever the reason. The Holy Spirit is promptin' you. So go ahead."

"I will," said Elizabeth. "I've been wonderin' about the case of a man in business. He runs a shop, let's say. Any kind of shop for business, to make money. Let's say he's not a Christian but one day he decides to become baptized. He's heard the Gospel all his life. He's even read the Bible since he was young but he's never been baptized. Now he wants to be baptized. Where should he be baptized?"

"You're askin' me now?" said Walker.

"I am," said Elizabeth.

"Well, people become baptized among the Christians they join, you know that."

"What if this man hasn't joined any group of Christians? What if he's an outsider?"

"You can't be an outsider with God's people. If you want to be baptized you've got to make a commitment to live and worship among God's people, some particular people or 'tother. You can't baptize yourself on some island all alone."

"Granted. But what if this businessman has a wife that wants him to be baptized?"

"I don't see the problem," said Ginny. "He'd be baptized at her church."

"But might there be good reasons not to be baptized at her church, to want to be baptized, but to not want her or practically any one else to know you been baptized?"

"That's a strange kettle of fish," said Walker.

"There's all kinds of creatures in the sea," said Elizabeth.

"There is, there is," said Walker.

"You're askin' whether there's ever a good reason to keep your baptism a secret," said Ginny.

"I am," replied Elizabeth.

The three sat a few moments, taking gulps of their tea. Walker spoke first, "I guess if you lived under a Jesus-hatin' tyrant, you'd have a good excuse to keep your baptism a secret. But you'd have no excuse for not proclaiming Jesus as Lord. So keepin' a secret about your baptism wouldn't hardly do you much good."

"What if someone wanted you to announce your baptism so that your business would improve? Let's say you have a partner in business and he wants you to tell the world you've been baptized so that your business among Christians improves. Would that be right?" asked Elizabeth.

"That would be an abomination," said Walker. That's no good reason for announcin' a baptism. That's tryin' to use baptism for worldly ends. Baptism is commitment to God, as God revealed hisself in the Lord Jesus. Baptism is dedication to God, not to mammon."

"This I've known," said Elizabeth, "but you've helped my thinkin'."

"Is that all?" asked Walker.

"That's all," said Elizabeth.

Walker appeared both puzzled and gratified. Shortly thereafter all three went to bed. For Elizabeth the night was lonely, though the talk with Walker and Ginny had helped. She hadn't felt this alone since George died. There didn't seem to be a thing she could do to help Mr Abe. Not in any meaningful way. Not morning after morning as she'd been able to help him, to hear him out, at the stern rail of the *River Queen*. No, that couldn't go on. That was the sorta thing Mary Todd ought to do. Elizabeth was harrowed to think if there was another woman in Mr Abe's life *she* was that woman — but in no way that Mary Todd would be able to imagine.

Oh, that she could speak the name of God's love. But, thanks be to God, she finally went off to sleep, the sounds of fireworks still crackling in the distance.

CHAPTER 16

—ᴡᴡ—

As Elizabeth remembered, the White House and the capital city were more astir than usual in the days leading to that last night in the President's life. General Lee's surrender sustained the capital's mood of exhilaration, even though General Johnston's strong Confederate army in North Carolina had yet to surrender. As Walker Lewis had put it over breakfast, 'Victory's no longer just beyond. She's got her foot in the door.' The closer Victory came, the more feverishly Washington worked, Mr Lewis included. He had hardly spotted Victory's whereabouts when he himself was out the door — off to work.

While Washington bustled, Elizabeth lingered in her lodging that first morning back from City Point. For much of her life, work had been its own reward. Work had brought and bought things dear to Elizabeth, not least her freedom. She found herself once again thinking about what had happened just the previous morning, when she'd encountered Mr Abe at the *River Queen's* stern rail. She couldn't dislodge the dream Mr Abe had shared with her, nor that dream's secret consolation. The fingers of that secret probed for a door that would give way and give out. She knew fresh secrets are restless secrets. They had to be given an indirect airing, the better to put them to sleep. Last night's airing with Walker and Ginny had not been enough. Elizabeth hoped for another airing, the better to seal the secret away. So Elizabeth lingered to help Mrs Lewis get her household underway. As Elizabeth helped the younger Lewis children eat their porridge, Mrs Lewis could hustle the older children out the door. The two women agreed that Victory needn't shove Elizabeth out the door.

"Everyday life is busy enough as 't is," observed Ginny. "Victory can take her place with everythin' else. Neighbors are sayin' we should do this and do that as if she was a special guest. Well, I guess Victory ain't an everyday guest when you're at war. But once the war's over, it's over. There's still lots of work to do."

"And memories to live with, victory or no victory," said Elizabeth.

"Yes, and memories. You said it. Memories," said Ginny, exiting to the next room to accelerate the departure of the older children. "You know the preacher wants you in the school room by the time the 9 o'clock bell strikes. I just heard them strike quarter-to, so get on out with ya. I'll bring your lunch over at noontime. Now get on out."

They done got. The stay-at-home tots finished breakfast and went playing in the back yard before the two ladies could resume their conversation.

"Ginny, I think a lotta people may think victory is some sort of consolation for what we lost along the way."

"'Suppose you're right 'bout that," Ginny replied. "But I don't 'spose that's true for you, Lizbeth."

"No, but I'd be feelin' worse if the loss had been for nothing."

Ginny sat across the table from Elizabeth, "Hard still after almost four years, ain't it, to have to remember 'bout George and not never see him come through the door."

"There's that, Ginny, there's that," admitted Elizabeth. "There's more. Things come to an end, great or small. My dresses, my business gives me good satisfaction. But that's not enough. Anyway some things can't be concluded the way you'd want. Maybe they just can't be concluded...like my memories of George. Then you need consolation."

Ginny put her hand across the table and took Elizabeth's hand. "Thank you," said Elizabeth. "There's a whole lotta other people that have it a whole lot worse."

"That's so," said Ginny.

Elizabeth wanted to say something about her secret, about Mr Abe's secret, but she couldn't think of anything so clever as in last night's conversation. She wouldn't be able to give the secret a secret airing.

"I'd better be gone," said Elizabeth. "I've got an order for Mary Todd for Easter and given what happened down at Appomattox Court House I wouldn't be surprised if I get a rush of orders for victory dresses. I'd best be on my way, Ginny."

Said Ginny, "Good thing you're makin' dresses for Mrs Lincoln 'cause sure 'nuf you wouldn't be makin' em now for Mrs Davis." The two ladies laughed and Elizabeth went on her way. She wondered how Varina Davis might be managing at this moment, then resolved to shake off the thought.

When Elizabeth arrived at the shop, her lead 'girl', an Irish woman in her 40s, and six other 'girls' in their 20s were already at work. After looking over the work at hand and discussing work prospects with the Irish lady, Elizabeth began embellishing what by day's end would be Mary Todd's revived Easter dress.

In the afternoon Elizabeth had a surprise visitor at the shop: Ward Lamon. When he appeared he asked whether he and Elizabeth could talk immediately indoors or out. Elizabeth chose the outdoors, not wanting to be closeted with Mr Lamon. Conversations with him left her feeling a bit scummy, maybe because by profession he thought the worst of others. Lamon had questions, he said.

As the two descended to street level, Lamon advised 'Madame Lizzy' that once they were outdoors they must keep walking. At all costs they must avoid situations where they might be overheard. At street level he began peppering Elizabeth with questions. There were numerous ladies shopping and a number of soldiers. The ladies came singly or in bunches, like the flowers in their hats. The few soldiers seemed to come in pairs, like bookends walking about. Elizabeth was confident the 'flowers' and 'bookends' could hear. She surmised that Lamon saw these strangers in a similar way, albeit without the light touch she brought to her own impressions. Lamon was rather humorless. He was all astir this morning about Mary Todd's spending habits.

"What do you know about Mrs Lincoln's spending habits?" asked Lamon.

"Whatever I happen to know, I trust, is not a part of your business," said Elizabeth.

"Is that for you to say?"

"I really think that's an unnecessary question. I don't presume on your business, but then I don't think you should presume on the privacies of your employer, Mr Lincoln."

"Don't get all riled up," said Lamon.

"Look who's talkin'," said Elizabeth.

Lamon flinched, stopped walking, and shoved his hands in his pockets. "You're one tough customer, Madame Lizzy."

"No, not Madame Lizzy. You're talking to Mrs Keckly and she knows how to handle customers. Perhaps if you pull your hands out of your pockets and put on the velvet gloves, you'll find her more accommodating. We both care about the Lincolns, do we not?"

"You're one determined lady, Mrs Keckly."

"Thank you. Now we're talkin' business."

The two resumed walking side by side. Said Mr Lamon, "Have you talked to Mr Lincoln about exercising more precaution?"

"You might say I have, you might say I haven't. Would that I had said more but I'm afraid whatever I say would make no difference."

"Why didn't you say more?" asked Lamon.

"Because I think Mr Lincoln thinks his life is wholly in God's hands."

"So he'll take no responsibility..."

"He is the President, Mr Lamon," said Elizabeth.

The two walked for a time without a word said. Then Lamon said, "What if I were to tell you there are those of us who believe Mary Todd..."

"You mean Mrs Lincoln," said Elizabeth.

"Yes, Mrs Lincoln," repeated Lamon, "we believe she could be subjected to coercive tactics designed to endanger the President."

"Go on," said Elizabeth.

"You and I know the President is unaware of the huge bills she's accumulated in his name. Her White House refurbishment and the bills associated with that have only been paid because of her manip- ulations of government employees."

"That's pretty strong language," said Elizabeth. "You know or think you know about Mrs Lincoln's spending habits without talking to me. Maybe you'd better get to the point of bringing this up here and now, because right now I don't see how any of this could help protect the President."

"Mrs Lincoln has shown she can be ruthless in protecting her position. Others with an interest in hurting Mr Lincoln could be even more ruthless in blackmailing her in a way that ultimately hurts the President."

"I don't follow," said Elizabeth. "In fact I'm not even sure that Mrs Lincoln is ruthless. She's got her strong opinions, she's temper- amental, even strong-willed, decisive you could say. But ruthless?"

"We all know the White House has a new doorkeeper. Everyone who works in the White House except for the President knows the real reason the old doorkeeper was fired."

"I don't know that I know," said Elizabeth. "I hear different rumors almost every time I visit the White House."

"Indeed, as I suspected," said Lamon.

"It's not a crime to hear rumors," said Elizabeth.

"But in this case we had a White House doorkeeper who indis- creetly talked of exposing accounting irregularities at the White House. Somehow Mrs Lincoln got word of the doorkeeper's indiscre- tions and she had him immediately dismissed. Was it through you?"

"Is that a question or an accusation, Mr Lamon?"

"Don't try to dance around my question," he replied.

"I'm not dancin'. I'm tryin' to keep us on track. Mrs Lincoln's spending habits may imperil the President's reputation. That I see. How would they imperil his life?"

"Mrs Lincoln, I would think, could be readily enticed by offers of money. She may have managed to refurbish the White House by manipulating government accounts but she hasn't so far succeeded in finding a way for the government to pay for her dresses, hats, gloves, and who knows how much jewelry. By our reckoning she has incurred substantial debts at every major jewelry store in New York and Washington and in some places in between. She could be 'persuaded', if you will, to afford someone intimate access to the President, someone who might not otherwise gain access."

"The way I see it," said Elizabeth, "just about anyone with white skin and some now even with black skin can walk right in and see the President. While you're worryin' about an open window in the hayloft the barn door's wide open. Not that I think that's the part of the farmyard you're really interested in anyways. Everyone in the White House knows you and Mrs Lincoln dislike each another. Dislike can't be the basis of a government investigation, Mr Lamon."

Mr Lamon pursed his lips and squinted. Were these signs of disgust or of dismay? Elizabeth wasn't certain. She decided she'd had enough. She said, "Good day, Mr Lamon."

"We will talk again, Mrs Keckly. Really, we must."

"Good day," she repeated.

"Good day," said he, reluctantly tipping his hat.

Elizabeth returned to the shop. Once upstairs she trembled so much a half hour passed before she could resume sewing. Mary Todd, she knew, had her faults but none that warranted a political lynching party, especially since Mr Abe would be hurt. Elizabeth would have no part in that sort of thing and not least because she believed loyalty worked in two directions. Mary Todd was loyal to her. She was and would be loyal to Mary Todd whatever her faults.

Late that afternoon Elizabeth took Mary Todd's renovated Easter dress to the White House. When she arrived, as on the previous evening, the mansion was surrounded by a crowd of citizens. Among the crowd were two Army bands battling it out with patriotic airs. Elizabeth managed to thread her way through the crowd and past the guards, who were now demanding to see the pass bearing Lamon's signature. The guards, in any event, recognized Elizabeth.

She and Tad encountered one another in the foyer. He asked for her pass, looked at it, saluted her, then ran off upstairs. She wondered whether Tad's tutor, Mr Williamson, had managed any progress today. As always the state of Tad's educational progress, or lack thereof, distressed Elizabeth. Upstairs Elizabeth was invited to join the Lincolns in an early light meal. Tad ate his dinner rather rapidly, then asked to be excused. The boy *was* learning manners at least.

Later that evening a delegation of 15 men presented Mr Abe with a picture of himself in a silver frame. Earlier in the day he'd had portrait photographs taken. At dinner he told the ladies he was barely able to keep a straight face during the photographical affair. Mr Abe, though weighed down by events, always thought of himself as cutting a somewhat ridiculous figure. Perhaps he was right as far as that went but it didn't go far enough as far as Elizabeth was concerned. There was more to the man than others could so readily account for. What wasn't seen, she was sure, enlarged rather than diminished the man.

For Mary Todd enlargement was a constant affair. A simple life could never be adequate. No feast was enough. So Mary Todd and Elizabeth talked through several hours in the evening, planning a series of dresses that Mary Todd intended to wear in the various inevitable victory celebrations. Elizabeth suggested the most prudent course of action would be to modify several dresses in Mary Todd's wardrobe, just as she'd done with the Easter dress. Mary Todd was pleased with that dress's alteration. However she insisted she must have new dresses for the victory celebrations. She discussed taking the train to Philadelphia and New York to purchase suitable fabrics. Elizabeth agreed to accompany Mary Todd but on condition she be gone only four days. Mary Todd agreed.

The following evening Elizabeth returned to the White House, bringing Ginny Lewis along. The previous evening Mary Todd had told Elizabeth she could bring a friend with her the next evening, when Mr Abe would be delivering a public speech from a White House window. Ginny was delighted to be introduced to the White House and to Mary Todd. Mary Todd was welcoming to Ginny but not to Elizabeth's ideas for innovative dresses. Elizabeth had brought recent issues of *Frank Leslie's Lady's Journal* that depicted the latest dress fashions. Elizabeth wondered whether Mary Todd would want to try the new styles. Mary Todd dismissed these offerings. She would stick with styles she'd worn in the first four years at the White House, but thank you. With such words she excused herself to join Mr Abe in the room where he'd deliver his address from a window overlooking the North Lawn.

From another window Elizabeth and Ginny watched Mr Abe's delivery. Tad held a lantern aloft so his papa could read from his prepared remarks. Elizabeth would never forget the look of pride on the boy's face as his papa spoke. The crowd may have expected a speech extolling the Army's great victory. Instead, Mr Abe began by referring to an impending and necessary day of national thanksgiving to God. Then he talked about practical steps to recognizing the new government in Louisiana and so forth. Really, the speech wasn't about victory but about the hard work of reconciliation. Nonetheless, the crowd interrupted the speech often with cheers.

Mary Todd had hoped General Grant would accompany her and Mr Abe in a carriage ride through the city following the speech. Washington had become a city of lights. Every window of every home, business, and government building, it seemed, was lit at least by a candle if not by a kerosene lantern. Before the large government buildings there were signs or lamp letterings of "Grant" or "Sherman" appearing in specially constructed shelving set on the lawns. Even the great dome of the Capitol was alight with rings of kerosene lamps. Rather than ride about Washington, General Grant sent his regrets.

CHAPTER 17

—⁀ⱲⱲ⁀—

Elizabeth joined Mary Todd and Mr Abe for lunch the day following his address. Their talk was of the business of ending the war. Mary Todd was keeping abreast of events.

Said Mary Todd, "Yesterday the cabinet talked about reviving cotton. Today Abe tells me they talked about openin' Southern ports to foreign trade — while we're still fightin' a war. And then there's that darn legislature from your home state, Lizzy, trying to claim it's the legal representative of the people of Virginia."

"They're not really legal," said Mr Abe, "but they have real power to withdraw Virginia troops from the conflict. To encourage withdrawal I encouraged General Weitzel down in Richmond to afford the Virginia gentlemen the protection of the Army to meet. So far the Virginia gentlemen are acting much slower than our own generals in removing Virginia troops from the conflict."

"That General Weitzel is nothin' but a windbag, Abe, like the gentlemen from Virginia. This is one time I agree with Stanton, our *glorious* Secretary of War. Weitzel knows not when to speak unless he's told. He deserves Stanton's reprimand."

"What's this about?" asked Elizabeth.

"Oh, I don't know that there's much to say. Anyway, Molly, how'd you learn about this minor perturbance between Stanton and Weitzel?"

"Stanton told me about it when I saw him here this morning."

"I see," said Mr Abe. He resumed eating a slice of pork with a heap of mashed potatoes and peas. Elizabeth wanted to learn more about whatever was the matter between Stanton and General Weitzel. Since her first visits to the White House four years earlier she'd acquired a taste for politics. That taste was an appetite she'd acquired from Mary Todd. That shared taste helped nourish their friendship. Elizabeth had only to ask and surely Mary Todd would resume speaking of the Stanton/Weitzel spat. But Elizabeth didn't want to irk Mr Abe, not for anything in the world. She decided she could seek more information later.

Mary Todd was as tenacious as General Grant. *Hallelujah!* She said, "I think Stanton was right to reprimand General Weitzel."

"I'm surprised he'd have to be reprimanded over anything," said Elizabeth.

"I was, too," said Mr Abe. "It seems he didn't issue an order to the churches in Richmond that prayers be raised on my behalf on Palm Sunday. When Secretary Stanton learned of this, he reprimanded the general in a telegram providing me with a copy."

"You should have left it at that, Abe. They should have raised prayers on your behalf. They're a part of the Union again," said Mary Todd.

"As such they have freedom of religion. So whether they raise prayers on behalf of the President of the United States down there isn't my business as the President. Of course, I would hope that with time the people of the South will want to raise prayers for officials in government all the way to Washington. That will only come if we live and govern in a spirit of reconciliation but I wasn't about to undercut the authority of our Secretary of War. His dedication and savvy and loyalty have been immensely important in this conflict."

"He's too ambitious, Abe. He's got to be watched," said Mary Todd.

"Not so much watched as guided. That's all I can be, a guide through the thickets. So I sent a letter to General Weitzel and copied Stanton and simply told the good general I had no doubt he acted in the spirit and temper I think I showed when I visited Richmond. General Weitzel is not being heavy handed and that's as I would like it."

Said Mary Todd, "Well, I still say Stanton was right on this occasion. The singe General Weitzel received will hopefully cause him to speak up in the future when silence only comforts those arrayed against you."

Elizabeth thought Mr Abe had the better part of the argument. Nothing more was said of the Stanton/Weitzel spat. As soon as Mr Abe finished eating he excused himself. After he left the room Mary Todd launched into the topic that had prompted her to invite her friend to lunch. She wanted advice.

"As you know, General Grant did not join Abe and me on our tour of the illuminations last evening. I don't understand how he could turn down a request from his own commander-in-chief or how Abe would tolerate that kind of behavior. Abe's political naiveté cannot be allowed to stand in the way of his political best interests. General Grant has only come to the city for a few days. Abe had suggested the general take a week's rest. We are told the general and Julia will be visiting their children in New Jersey soon. Before he leaves town we've got to provide some occasion where Abe can be seen with the general."

Elizabeth replied, "I see what you're gettin' at but if you can't get him before he leaves town I don't know that it matters. There'll be victory parades soon enough."

"Those will be several weeks off. Now, while people's minds are on it, they need to associate Abe with victory. In all the illuminations about town I saw not one in which the name 'Lincoln' appears. When I asked about this I was told there aren't any. *That* is intolerable."

"Maybe Mr Abe's name isn't in lights because that's the one folks figured needn't be said. Everyone knows Mr Abe's steered us through this fight, Mary Todd. So I wouldn't make much of it. You've seen how the people have been cheering for Mr Abe ever since we arrived back from City Point. They love him."

"The crowd is fickle. This morning a messenger came over from Ford's Theatre with an invitation from the management for a performance of *Our American Cousin* Friday evening. Abe isn't eager to go. He's feeling tired again. Had a headache last night. But it would do him good. You know he loves the theatre. And the politics could be especially helpful, if we could convince General Grant to come. I can't have another invitation turned down and Abe won't make him come. You have any ideas what to do about this, Lizzy?"

Elizabeth said nothing at first. Then she spoke. "You invited General Grant for the carriage ride. Did he know the invitation came from Mr Abe?"

"I wrote him, as I told him, on behalf of the President."

"I noticed," said Elizabeth, "that you didn't mention anything about Julia Grant. Was she invited, too?"

"No, why should she be? She's not a general."

"But she's the general's wife."

"She spoke up for that horrible Mary Ord. I don't want her to ride in the same carriage with me or with Abe. The Grants are both butchers but at least the general's butchery has been in the service of the cause. If I had my choice I'd much prefer to invite the Marquis de Chambrun to join us. He was here this morning, by the way. But there would be no political gain from it. None. So we must invite the likes of General Grant."

"If Julia isn't in an invitation, you ain't goin' to get the general to come to Ford's Theatre. Even with Julia in the invitation they might not come."

Mary Todd pouted. "Well, you're right. I'll tell Abe I think both Grants should be invited. With the publicity and Abe's request from this end I don't see how General Grant can turn us down."

Before Elizabeth returned to the shop the two ladies had agreed on a departure date late the following week to acquire bolts of cloth and other 'necessities of victory', as Mary Todd called them.

The following day, Thursday, the newspapers carried advertisements and announcements about the Ford's Theatre production of *Our American Cousin,* starring Miss Laura Keene. Friday's performance was to be her closing one, a benefit performance for wounded soldiers. That day the President invited General Grant and Julia Grant to accompany the Lincolns in attending *Our American Cousin* on Friday. General Grant was hesitant about accepting the invitation, not least because he and Julia had planned to depart on Friday. Later Elizabeth learned that Secretary of War Stanton had strongly advised both Grant and Lincoln not to attend such public spectacles.

Stanton was concerned about assassination attempts. Reports were still coming into the War Department about possible attempts to kidnap or assassinate government leaders. Mr Lamon was not alone in his quest to protect the President. So far no conspirators had been identified, much less captured. Vigilance was imperative, even in the hour of victory.

CHAPTER 18

—ᴍ—

G ood Friday morning Robert Lincoln had breakfast with his
father at the White House. Mary Todd had told Elizabeth that
Robert would be coming up to report what he had seen at Appomattox.
She had said she was working on Mr Abe to have Robert discharged
from the Army. The fighting was coming to an end. Mr Abe had
said Robert would have to remain a soldier until peace was established. Mary Todd told Mr Abe she'd lost *him* to the war, lost Eddie
and Willie, and couldn't bear the thought of losing Robert through
any accident 'of the last hour'. She'd read a newspaper account of
a young soldier who'd lost his life in an exchange of gunfire near
Appomattox *after* General Lee had surrendered his forces to General
Grant. Mr Abe replied that Robert must abide by his obligations as a
man to the end. Anyway, he said, God would determine who would
live beyond this conflict. Within our limited means we each had to
try to do what was right as God gave us the ability to see the right.
Mary Todd told Elizabeth she couldn't counter that argument but
she still thought it was time for Robert to be discharged.

Good Friday morning Elizabeth joined the Lewises at a prayer
service at the Fifteenth Street Church. Walker Lewis read from
Luke's account of the arrest and crucifixion of Jesus. It never ceased
to amaze Elizabeth that the crowd before Pilate insisted that the
criminal Barabbas be released instead of Jesus. But it was always
gratifying to hear that one crucified criminal saw the light as Jesus
suffered with him. That criminal had the sense to see that Jesus was

entirely innocent. Just recognizing Jesus for who He was brought deliverance. Jesus promised the criminal he'd be with Him in paradise that very day. The criminal hadn't even been baptized! He was a sinner. In the nick of time, he acknowledged God and was saved from eternal loss.

All seemed to depend on our ability to see the truth. If we couldn't see the truth it was, said Elizabeth, like being in a closed box. We couldn't see the light. There was no promise for 'boxed' people that they would live. On the contrary, they could count on being discarded with the rest of history, lost for eternity in a forgotten state, lost beyond redemption. So much depended on the ability to see that Elizabeth wondered if it wasn't unfair. She was thankful her mama raised her in the faith that God in Christ had come to save all the world from being lost. If all the world were saved, did that mean the blind, too, were somehow enlightened in the world to come? Or that they just didn't appear there?

She so much wanted George to be there and so once again she worried about him. George as a young man hadn't shown any particular fervor for his baptized faith. He was dutiful and honest and kind. If he'd been born in another time and place he might be equally dutiful, honest, and kind. But he was also independent — just like his mama. And Elizabeth knew in her heart that independence meant you often carried secret thoughts. So perhaps he'd only been trying to please his mama and not the Lord God. Baptism aside, had he really seen and had he really acknowledged Jesus as his Lord? The fact that George sinned was not a good clue to his innermost attitude toward God. We all sin, after all, baptized and un-baptized alike. But some are righteous sinners, some aren't. The righteous sinners honor God and repent. George, she hoped, had been a righteous sinner, someone who daily repented and sought to grow in the Lord. George's sins were minor, but hopefully not so minor in his own eyes as to cause him to neglect repentance. The Lord only knew, of course, but thank God, God was merciful.

Yes, He was merciful. But God had His expectations in this world for this world. The Lord came to save the world, not just those passing through it. So the here and now was important, which was why seeing God in Jesus must be important. George had surely seen.

He was so unselfish he must have seen. Surely, his was a baptism of the Holy Spirit.

Elizabeth thought of the Lincolns. She wasn't sure about the boys, Robert and Tad. They hadn't had the best guidance from their mother. Their father was so unusual in so many ways. Perhaps Mr Abe had been a guide for the boys but no more than he'd been a guide for General Weitzel. The growth of the boys' religious faith had depended almost entirely on Mary Todd. For Mary Todd Christian faith was a garment. You could take it off whenever convenient. At least she wore it most of the time. That was a starting point. God could work from the outside in. Indeed, that seemed to be the way He worked with everyone. He had the advantage of knowing what the inside was like to start with. But if people were determined not to admit God, God surely must have a harder time being seen. Mary Todd, Elizabeth had to admit, came at everything with a set of blinders. She was partially blind — weren't we all — but partial to her blinders. All that trouble over Mrs Ord and the generals' wives came from those blinders. Mary Todd could believe the craziest things about people. Almost no one could please her, which raised an unspeakable issue for Elizabeth. How was it that Elizabeth could please Mary Todd? Elizabeth wasn't sure she knew. She wasn't even sure she wanted to know.

The prayer service didn't seem the time or place to be thinking about the Lincolns or George. She reminded herself she should be praying for others, for all the people the prayer leader was naming out loud. She would pay attention to those he named. Just then the prayer leader named the President, thanking God for Mr Lincoln's leadership, asking for God's protection for Mr Lincoln, asking for the President's health, asking that the President and nation be spared further sorrows of war. This chain of prayers led her back to the ruminations she had just tried to leave behind. Elizabeth began comparing, again, Mr Abe and Mary Todd.

Mr Abe was surely the Lord's servant, Mary Todd was less so. Mr Abe could see; Mary Todd was partial to her blinders. And so Elizabeth again came to the thought of Mary Todd's blinders. She felt a chill, sensing that someday those blinders could spell trouble. She didn't want to think of the agony she might suffer on Mary Todd's account. *Why not just walk away?* she asked herself. A sense of guilt overcame her. Mary Todd could be very kind, at least to those close to her. She wasn't perfect, but she didn't deserve to be lost. Could she, Elizabeth, be the one to save her? The nobility of that task was offset by the remembrance that if anyone was the 'other woman' in Mr Abe's life it was she. What a tangle! It would be enough to make dresses for her friend and provide guidance from time to time. Mr Abe, a wise man if there ever was one, hadn't been able to remove Mary Todd's blinders. If not him, who could? *Keep me in your path, dear Lord*, prayed Elizabeth, *and show me how to help Mary Todd.* So Elizabeth's prayer ascended that Good Friday morning mingling with millions of other prayers.

In the afternoon a White House messenger appeared at Elizabeth's shop bearing a note from Mary Todd. Mary Todd was requesting that Elizabeth come by for dinner. Tad was being given tickets to attend Grover's Theatre for a patriotic spectacle being mounted there. He would attend Grover's with a chaperone from the White House staff while Mary Todd and Mr Abe would be going to Ford's Theatre. Could Elizabeth come by for supper at six? She wrote a reply that she'd come by in time for supper.

When Elizabeth arrived at the White House she learned that Mr Abe and Mary Todd were expected at any moment to return from the Navy Yard. The two had gone out to inspect some Federal ironclad boats, or 'monitors' as they were called, that had recently arrived in Washington for battle damage repair. A delegation of Illinois politicians, including the governor of Illinois, was waiting for the President at the White House. When the Lincolns returned, Mary Todd greeted these gentlemen, then excused herself to have dinner. She told Mr Abe she expected him to come up shortly. The visiting with the Illinois delegation would have to be kept brief.

Mr Abe wasn't able to stop talking with the Illinois folks. Mary Todd must have known this would happen. Several times she sent a messenger downstairs to summon the President to dinner. She could see that Tad could hardly wait, so even before Mr Abe appeared, supper began. While Mr Abe regaled his old political associates with humorous stories downstairs, upstairs Mary Todd regaled Elizabeth and Tad with talk about the fantastic monitors at the Navy Yard. Ironclad vessels had been evident enough on the recent journey to Richmond. Federal monitors were among the ships to be seen at City Point and abandoned Confederate ironclads were seen near Richmond. Tad had seen all this. Mary Todd apparently hadn't given these vessels of war much notice until today. Now she regaled her dinner partners with ironclad details. Tad listened eagerly, perhaps to reinforce his knowledge. Just after the boy had finished eating dinner, Mr Williamson fetched him to get ready for the Grover's spectacular.

After Tad's departure, Mary Todd switched topics. Mary Todd's excitement over the monitors may have been for Tad's benefit. Now she talked about the carriage ride to and from the Navy Yard. She said she and Mr Abe had talked about returning to Springfield in four years. The conversation had been one of the most pleasant ones they'd ever had together. Mr Abe had had a special sparkle in his eye as they talked about Springfield. But he was tired and in truth he had no wish to attend Ford's Theatre this evening. He had decided to go because he had no wish to disappoint people. The press had given notice he'd be at the performance along with General Grant.

Mary Todd reported that General Grant had declined the invitation. He had said he and Julia must leave for New Jersey. Mary Todd didn't believe that was the whole story. Surely they could have departed Saturday morning. New Jersey was a flimsy excuse. Mary Todd was sure Julia Grant was behind this little maneuver out of the theatre. These Army women were nothing but battleaxes and seductive hell queens anyway. The evening would be a grand occasion to cap a grand day. That her husband would even talk about returning to Illinois was hope-filling to Mary Todd, even if she herself had no desire for Springfield. Chicago was the place to be. No matter, at least for now her husband was thinking about *their* future, not just the future of the nation. That was a good sign, a grand sign, a hope that redeemed any petty miseries of the moment.

Mr Abe appeared just as the ladies were finishing their dinner. Mary Todd excused herself and motioned to Elizabeth that she should follow. Elizabeth excused herself also, leaving the President to eat by himself. This didn't seem quite right but Mary Todd took Elizabeth by the elbow and steered her to her bedroom. There she asked, as Elizabeth expected, whether her friend would prepare Mr

Abe for his evening appearance. Mary Todd said she wouldn't need any help herself from Elizabeth. Annie would help. Elizabeth said the President looked less rumpled than usual. No matter, Mary Todd said, he must look his very best for tonight's outing. Once Elizabeth consented to helping, Mary Todd looked relieved. From a wardrobe she retrieved the Presidential Preparation Kit. Handing the Kit to Elizabeth, Mary Todd suggested she could wait in the corridor while the President finished eating.

Elizabeth did wait in the corridor but with a sense she should seek admittance to Mr Abe. After all, he hated eating alone. As it happened Will came along asking Elizabeth whether she'd been commissioned to clean up the President's appearance. She said 'Yes'. Will told her she might be able to enhance the President's outside but from the inside there was nothing man or woman could do for him. Mr Abe was in good spirits today, as everyone could see. Will speculated the President was happy because of a dream he'd had the night before.

Will told Elizabeth about the dream as he escorted her to the library. The President had shared it with Will after getting up. He'd also shared it at the cabinet meeting held later in the morning. The cabinet meeting, said Will, had been devoted to discussions about the surrender of additional Confederate troops, especially those fighting under General Johnston in North Carolina. No news had been received about the surrender of those troops. Mr Abe told General Grant not to worry. Overnight he'd had a dream he'd had just before other great events in the war. What was the dream? asked Mr Welles, Secretary of the Navy. Mr Abe said the dream always included the Navy's element: water. In the dream Mr Abe said he always was in an indescribable vessel moving rapidly toward an indefinite, dark shore. The dream was always so powerful that he would wake up and remember it. He'd had the dream before Sumter, Bull Run, Antietam, Gettysburg, Stone River, Vicksburg, and so forth. General Grant spoke up saying they were all great events but not all victories for the North. Mr Abe granted the general his point but said he remained hopeful the dream portended yet another great *and good* event for the Union.

The night would tell.

CHAPTER 19

—ww—

When Will returned to the library to fetch Elizabeth, he told her the President was awaiting her in a room overlooking Pennsylvania Avenue. Elizabeth wondered whether Will had asked Mr Abe to come to this room in order to be further away from Mary Todd. Further away from the First Lady, Will would have more time to groom the President. Will liked Elizabeth but he resented Mary Todd's interference in his work. In any event Mr Abe, sitting by a window, seemed captivated by what he saw along the avenue. Candles glowed in the windows of the buildings across Pennsylvania Avenue. Could he be faulted for delighting in this afterglow of Appomattox? For all the afterglow, Mr Abe looked humble, his hands folded and his head slightly bowed.

As Elizabeth approached, Mr Abe looked around, smiled, and stood up. "Good evening, Madame Keckly. I stand ready for inspection."

"Good evenin', Mr Abe."

He flicked something from the front of his coat then held his hands by his side like a soldier. He stepped away from the window so Elizabeth could walk about him. She did. Will stood by the door during her inspection. Mr Abe had never appeared less rumpled, nor his coat and pants so clear of the loose strings and clutter that bedeviled whatever he wore. There wasn't a tear anywhere, nor a button out of place. Only his hair needed a little taming. That was usual or perhaps Mr Abe had previously asked Will to leave it alone.

"My compliments to you, Will. You're puttin' me outta a job, except for the hair. Mr Abe, would you sit down while I give it a brush?"

"Surely," said he.

Elizabeth retrieved a brush from the Presidential Preparation Kit and asked Mr Abe to sit down again. Will had already gone to fetch water. He knew she'd want water to tame Mr Abe's hair. Before Will returned Mr Abe spoke in a manner fit for a finality.

"You know you've always been quite kind to do this for Molly. Before we came to Washington she used to do it herself. I've always been somewhat the country bumpkin, neglectful you know. It gives Molly great comfort that you've given me these goin' overs."

"Happy to be a help," said Elizabeth.

Will appeared with a small bowl of water. He held it while Elizabeth dipped in the brush and sprinkled Mr Abe's hair. After several liberal sprinklings she began brushing down the hair.

"Will, would you mind fetchin' Mr Abe's hat? You can set the bowl on the table. I think I got enough already."

"I'll get it," said Will setting the bowl down.

"Sprinkin's enough tonight, rather than full immersion, is it, Madame Elizabeth?" Mr Abe chuckled.

"I guess it is."

Mr Abe patted his right front pants pocket. "I've got a fresh clean handkerchief."

"So I can skip the sermon," said Elizabeth.

"Yes, ma'am," said Mr Abe, breaking out into a belly laugh.

Elizabeth laughed, too. Mary Todd had long ago told Elizabeth to admonish Mr Abe if he failed to produce evidence he had a clean handkerchief for an outing. Tonight he appeared ready. When Will appeared with Mr Abe's stovepipe hat, he was about to show the hat to Elizabeth.

"Don't need to see it, Will. Mr Abe's done passed inspection."

"Thank you, Madame Elizabeth. Will, my hat, please."

When Elizabeth had finished brushing, Mr Abe stood up and offered his right hand to her. "Thank you," he said.

He had that sweet, warm smile that Elizabeth would never forget. For some reason she was prompted to say, "God be with you, Mr Abe."

"And you, too, Madame Elizabeth. Well, I must be off." He left the room.

Mary Todd appeared at the door waving at Elizabeth saying, "We'll see you Sunday."

Elizabeth waved back. "All right, Sunday," she said. There hadn't been any talk of a Sunday get-together. That could be easily arranged. Her only plans for Easter Sunday were to go to church and then have a noon meal with the Lewises.

Mr Crook, Mr Abe's bodyguard, didn't accompany the Lincolns to the theatre. He had the evening off. In his place some Washington city policeman showed up — late at that — to provide protection. The Lincolns rode through a city still aglitter with candles bought on the heels of General Lee's surrender. The Lincolns were cheered in the street. They were cheered at the theatre. They would be cheered by *Our American Cousin*. And they would not be alone in the Presidential box. Clara Harris, who'd attended *The Magic Flute* with the Lincolns, was in the box, this time with a Major Rathbone. Before the evening was done the Presidential party would be joined by one other person, the uninvited actor who would bring the house down. John Wilkes Booth, the actor who seized the role of murderer, gained easy entry to the box. He knew the theatre and knew the box. He got where he wanted and got off the bullet. The fool policeman wasn't even watching out for Mr Abe. He was watching the show.

The only foil Booth encountered was Major Rathbone, who lunged for Booth when he realized what was happening. Booth slashed the major with a hunting knife, then jumped to the stage. But he'd been caught off balance. When the actor hit the stage he broke a leg. He had sufficient stage presence, you might say, to manage shouting out in Latin *Sic semper tyrannus*, or 'Thus always tyranny'. Obviously he saw himself as a hero but he didn't loiter for cheers. He got out of the theatre. He got out of town, out into Maryland. His accomplices were supposed to murder, too. The Vice President was supposed to be murdered. The man who was to do that decided to run off. The man who was supposed to murder Mr Seward almost succeeded. Poor Mr Seward was just barely recovering from the carriage accident. If not for his daughter, Fanny, his nurse, an Army sergeant, and his son, Fred, Mr Seward would have been killed. Fred almost was. But the man who bloodied the Seward home was foiled in delivering death.

Death and rumors of death would stir up all Washington by midnight. After leaving the White House Elizabeth had gone home and to bed. About 11 o'clock a neighbor lady came banging at the Lewis front door. Elizabeth was the lightest sleeper in the house so she went down and opened the door. The neighbor said the entire cabinet had been attacked but that Mr Abe was not mortally wounded. Elizabeth knew she should go to the White House. She woke up Walker and Ginny Lewis, who suggested she not go. Who knew what was really happening? Perhaps Secessionists in civilian clothes had infiltrated the city with the sole purpose of murder and mayhem. Who knew what really had happened or was happening?

Something must have happened, it seemed. People were milling in the street. How much of the news was truth, how much just fiction? No one could tell. Elizabeth was sure Mary Todd would be totally beside herself if Mr Abe had been shot at. Whatever her misgivings about Mary Todd, they were beside the point now. Elizabeth knew she must comfort Mary Todd — and Tad. When the Lewises saw Elizabeth was determined to return to the White House, they all got dressed. Walker and Ginny had decided that Elizabeth must not walk alone in this wild night.

When the three crossed Lafayette Square they passed the Seward house. Every room in the house was lit. The house was surrounded by soldiers. They carried their rifles at the ready with bayonets fixed. Armed sentries were also posted around the White House. Elizabeth showed her White House pass to several of the sentries. Not one would allow her entrance, nor would any even summon a sergeant to inspect her pass. Fear was written on their faces and not one face was any that Elizabeth recognized. These soldiers had been rousted out to fend off they knew not what. Elizabeth and the Lewises were not welcome and returned home, only able to confirm the President had been shot.

Around 11 the next morning a White House carriage pulled up in front of the Lewis home. The driver alighted, tethered the horse, and knocked on the door. He bore no news. His commission he said was to bring Elizabeth to the White House. Would she come? Of course she would.

The streets of the city were comparatively deserted. Oddly, the gas streetlamps were still lit. Ordinarily they would have been snuffed out shortly past sunrise. No one had done that this morning. Moreover black crepe had been hung in some shop windows. Most flags were at half-mast. Elizabeth guessed Mr Abe was dead. Her guess was confirmed when the carriage entered the White House grounds. There, several hundred African Americans, mostly women and children, were weeping and comforting one another.

A hush prevailed in the White House. Not a visitor was to be seen anywhere, only the staff carrying on their duties, teary eyed and somber. Elizabeth left her cloak and bonnet with the doorman and then took the liberty of going upstairs. She went to Mary Todd's bedroom but Mary Todd wasn't there. She went to Mr Abe's bedroom next door. Will was there, sitting on a stool, brushing up a pair of Mr Abe's black boots. He looked up at Elizabeth. His mouth was pursed, his eyes abrim with tears. He closed his eyes, lowered his head, and resumed brushing the boot in hand. Elizabeth asked if he knew where Mary Todd was. He shook his head No and continued brushing. The sound of that brushing would last longer than the hearing of it.

Elizabeth went out into the central corridor. Just then the butler Peter Brown came into the corridor from what was called the 'Summer Bedroom'. During the summers, when the Lincolns stayed at the Soldiers' Home, Mr Abe would sometimes stay overnight at the White House. Mary Todd had arranged the Summer Bedroom, a comparatively small bedroom, for such overnight stays. Elizabeth guessed that Mary Todd might be in the Summer Bedroom. Peter Brown confirmed she was. Mrs Dixon, wife of one of Connecticut's senators, was there as well as Mary Jane Welles. Of all the cabinet wives Mary Jane was the only one you could say had anything like a friendship with Mary Todd.

Mary Todd was lying curled around three or four pillows. She had buried her head in one. As she sobbed she would hit the mattress with her right fist. Sitting on a chair next to the bed, Mary Jane held Mary Todd's left hand. Mrs Welles was in front of Marry Todd; Mrs

Dixon stood in back. The consoling ladies looked up at Elizabeth, showing relief at her arrival.

"You've come. Thank God, you're here," said Mary Jane. "She's asked for you numerous times last night and this morning."

Mrs Dixon added, "Messengers were sent out several times in the night."

"I'm sorry they didn't find me," said Elizabeth.

Mary Todd stopped beating the mattress and took her head out of the pillow. She looked frightful, her hair matted and awry, her eyes swollen, her face red, and her cheeks glistening with tears. Elizabeth instinctively pulled a handkerchief from a skirt pocket. The remembrance of Mr Abe and his handkerchief flitted then fell away as Mary Todd swung into action.

"Why didn't you come? You must have known I needed you."

Mary Jane spoke softly, "Mary, how would she have known? The messengers never found her."

"Where were you?" asked Mary Todd.

"At home with the Lewises. When we heard news there'd been an assassination attempt, we came here to the White House. The Lewises came with me. But the soldiers wouldn't let me in, even with the pass."

Mrs Dixon added, "Everyone was panicky last night and anyway we were still across from Ford's Theatre until a few hours ago."

"I needed you," said Mary Todd speaking towards the pillow.

Mary Jane let go and Elizabeth took up Mary Todd's hand as she sat down on the bed. In an instant Mary Todd abandoned the pillow and wrapped her arms around Elizabeth. Elizabeth stroked Mary Todd's back. "Where's Tad?" she asked.

Mary Todd replied, "I don't know. Stay here with me."

"Of course," said Elizabeth. She nodded at the two ladies, who nodded in reply.

"Mary, we are going to be going now, if that's all right with you. We will be keeping you and Tad and Robert in our prayers," said Mary Jane.

"Thank you," said Mary Todd with a sob.

The two ladies left Mary Todd and Elizabeth alone. For a good while Elizabeth held Mary Todd like a mother soothing a child. As she did so, Mary Todd talked about what had happened at the theatre and what had happened afterwards. Before Mary Todd fell asleep in her arms she learned that Mr Abe's body had been laid out in a guest bedroom. She asked if she might view the body and Mary Todd had replied, 'Of course'.

When Elizabeth left Mary Todd asleep, she went out into the central corridor. She walked toward a cluster of guest bedrooms and was surprised to see that Mr Abe's body had been laid out in the same bedroom where Willie had laid in his coffin three years earlier. She would not be alone here. Sitting around the room were several officials, although she knew none by name, other than Commissioner French, who oversaw public buildings in Washington. Some of the men were openly weeping.

A white sheet had been laid over the length of Mr Abe's body. The boots had been removed. Were these the boots that Will was brushing up? Perhaps, but Elizabeth had no interest in conducting a dress inspection. If she were to look under the shroud she would want only to look on Mr Abe's face. She had learned from the doorman that Mr Abe had been shot in the head, more or less from behind. The bullet had traveled from behind the left ear and lodged behind the right eye. It hadn't come out. His face wouldn't be a bloody mess.

She stood before the bed, the men around her perhaps wondering what she would do. She put her hands together in prayer and bowed her head. What followed maybe wasn't so much a prayer as it was an 'exchange of ideas before God', as she would later term it. On the one hand, why would she not want to remember Mr Abe for that last sweet smile playing over his rugged face? On the other, how could she not bid him the honor of looking on his face? Would she look upon him and not live? Or would a failure to look be a failure of life? Mr Abe was not God. But Elizabeth was sure Mr Abe was God-given to America and especially to the people out of Africa, now freed thanks to the Moses God sent them. To not look would be to dishonor the martyr of God. To not look would be to dishonor the Living God who had sent him. She would look.

She stepped up to the bed and slowly, reverently pulled back the portion of the sheet enshrouding Mr Abe's face. Some of the men approached, to see whatever Elizabeth might see. Mr Abe's countenance was in ashen repose, even the bulge around the right side of his face, where the bullet had lodged. The absence of the living man would be felt far beyond those who now gazed at the rock-hewn face. Here, now Mr Abe seemed but a monument. And indeed the husk of his body was but a memorial to the living man. Oddly, that thought comforted Elizabeth. There was something merely monumental, merely dead about death. Death was real, as real as life, but it was real like a counterfeit bill. Real money had real backing — a saying Elizabeth remembered from the living Mr Abe. Counterfeit had no backing. And death had no backing from the Living God. It hurts to have but a counterfeit. But she would place her hands and her hope in the Living God. Thanks be to Him for His American Moses! Elizabeth gently replaced the sheet over Mr Abe's face.

As Elizabeth entered the central corridor she could hear shrieks from down the hall. Mary Todd was no longer asleep, nor her anger. There seemed to be as much venom as victim in Mary Todd's shrieking. Elizabeth dreaded the scene she would encounter in the Summer Bedroom. She heard "Mother, calm down. Calm down, Mother," repeated again and again by Robert.

Mary Todd was sitting on the edge of the bed rocking back and forth. Robert's left arm was enchained with her right. With his right hand Robert was attempting to capture her flailing left arm.

"They've killed my Abe. Killed him. Killed him. I hate them, hate them all. They killed, they killed. I HATE THEM! Don't try to stop me."

Robert tried to grab her left arm. Mary Todd slapped him across the face. Mary Todd was making such a fuss Elizabeth hadn't noticed that Tad was at his mother's feet. He had clasped himself around her legs bawling for all the world.

"Please, Mama, please. We love you. Please, Mama."

"They killed my Abe. Killed him. MURDERERS! I HATE THEM!"

"Mother, please calm yourself down. Please."

"Don't try to tell me what to do! I am your MOTHER! I hate them!"

"Please, Mother."

"Shut up, I HATE THEM! May they burn in Hell forever! Damnation on them forever!"

"Mother."

Mary Todd screamed.

"Mama, Mama, please don't scream," sobbed Tad, trying to subdue his convulsions.

When Elizabeth placed her hands around Tad's shoulders, the boy looked up at her, then released his mother. This allowed Elizabeth to pull him up from the floor. He hugged Elizabeth, pressing his head into her bosom. Heaves of sobbing shuddered the boy as Elizabeth used her right hand to rub his back.

Mary Todd took notice of this. She stopped flailing her left arm. Robert looked around, taking note of what had happened.

"Thank heavens," he said, "you're here, Elizabeth."

"I hate them, Lizzy. Bobby's stupid. I HATE THEM!" Mary Todd shouted.

"We understand you, Mother. But you must calm down."

"Hate can only take you so far, Mary Todd," said Elizabeth, "and even that far's not good to go. Hate will only poison the sting, I can tell you that. Have a good cry now with Lizzy."

"Please, Mama, just cry," said Tad. "Come cry with us."

"I hate them," said Mary Todd. "Tad, forgive your mama, forgive your mama."

"I'm not angry at you, Mama."

"But you're afraid."

"Yes'm."

"Bobby, let your little brother come to me. Come here, Tad."

Robert let his mother go and stood up, patting down his Army jacket. Tad sat on his mother's lap, and nuzzled his head beneath her chin. He continued to cry. And now so did Mary Todd. Elizabeth used her handkerchief to wipe the tears staining Mary Todd's and Tad's faces as she sat next to them. Robert walked to one of the windows, facing away while he wiped a hand over his face.

Robert remained standing at that window as his mother's and brother's crying subsided to be replaced by occasional sobs. Mary Todd clasped Tad ever more tightly. Elizabeth stood up wiping tears from her own eyes.

"I do not want to see anyone, anyone. Just you three. That includes the White House staff. Give Annie the next several days off. I'm not goin' anywhere. Tell her to report back on Wednesday. If I eat, one of you three can bring food to me here. Right now I think I'd rather die than eat."

"Mother, please don't talk that way," said Robert.

"Hush," she replied.

"Mama, we love you," said Tad.

She squeezed the boy and kissed him on the cheek. Elizabeth couldn't remember a time when Mary Todd so clung to Tad since Willie's death. Little did she appreciate that the Lincoln tableau she saw before her would come to represent the relationship among them in the years following Mr Abe's death: Tad so close to his mother, Robert far, and Elizabeth trying to make sense of it all. It was enough now, in any event, to make it through the coming days. The trial of sorrows would not be brief.

CHAPTER 20

—◊◊◊—

Easter morning Elizabeth joined the Lewises at church. She had come home the evening before exhausted from being with Mary Todd. She wanted to be able to attend church this morning with a family she knew. The Lincolns wouldn't be attending church. Mary Todd was too distraught. The jubilation that would otherwise be so evident on Easter morning was subdued this day. The tears would have been enough to fill two collection plates. But this was Easter and shouts of joy were heard despite the tears. The shouts were offered, it seemed, more from a sense of duty and truth than from passion. As far as Elizabeth was concerned, motivation by duty was more to be admired, in any event, than motivation by passion, which was as fickle as a child. She felt good to be among the people of praise at Fifteenth Street Presbyterian, and was gratified to hear the sermon, which put her to thinking what she must do now that an earthquake had shaken up so many lives, hers included.

The Easter sermon began with a reminder that the Lord God redeems and renews all things through His Son. The resurrection of His Son is the sign and promise of that. His Son had claimed all life by taking on death, atoning for all sin as the sinless one. The Lord Jesus calls all the baptized renewed in life imperishable to spread the gospel and witness of His Father's mercy. The nation, said the preacher, had traversed a baptism by fire unto death, atoning for its sins — especially the sin of slavery, so hated by God — and in His mercy God had sent a Moses to lead black Americans out of slavery and all Americans out of the sin of being wed to slavery. We could all hope the baptism by fire was coming to an end. Our Moses had been taken away. Who would be the Joshua to lead the people over the Jordan into the Promised Land?

Each and every disciple of Christ is the Joshua in each and every day, said the preacher, because those who are baptized are baptized into the name of Jesus, which is just the Greek way of saying 'Joshua'. The disciples of Jesus, baptized in His name, are to make themselves available to the Holy Spirit to be little Joshuas for the sake of others. Now was a time of testing, after the baptism of fire, when those who bore the name of Jesus must open themselves daily to the baptism of the Holy Spirit so that they could live His name. If the people who were called by the name of Jesus lived by His name, then life would be redeemed and death would come to nothing. If the people of God gave only lip service to the name of Jesus, while selfishness and revenge and anger governed their hearts, then no good would come and much evil would be sown. Every Christian had a choice, but God showed the good choice, the right choice. The choice for life was to be a Joshua, to be less oneself and more like Jesus, serving others in their need, helping deliver others from their bondage, showing by example and courage the better way, the better life, to the Promised Land of God's salvation.

Elizabeth couldn't help but take to heart this sermon. It addressed the turmoil in her own heart. More than anything, passion, a felt sympathy for Mary Todd, had called her out the night of Mr Abe's assassination. Passion — compassion — had compelled her to heed Mary Todd's summons, had guided her through the dark hours of yesterday to comfort Mary Todd and Tad. But at some point the passion would wear out, would dribble away. She knew that. Then what? Mary Todd wasn't the easiest person to abide. For the past four years Elizabeth had abided her. Indeed, they had become friends. And in part that friendship grew because Mary Todd could be sympathetic. She helped Elizabeth in introducing various African Americans into the White House. She had helped support Elizabeth's efforts in the contraband associations (to help the freed black people). She could be witty. She could be suave. But she also could be petty and vindictive and incredibly suspicious. And she had a low tolerance for correction, except ever so slightly from Elizabeth or Mr Abe, now gone.

That tolerance was both good and bad. The good was that Elizabeth had some ability, however limited, to influence her friend. The bad was that her influence with Mary Todd stemmed from the fact she wasn't a white woman. Elizabeth knew that. It was good that Mary Todd could be comfortable with Elizabeth, comfortable as she had been with the mammy who'd raised her back in Kentucky. It was bad that Mary Todd couldn't see Elizabeth as being an equal to her. To be sure, what woman could be equal to the First Lady of the Land? No one. But Mary Todd saw white women as competitors. Some she saw as competitors to become First Lady or at least the first lady of society in Washington. Others, too many others, were seen as competitors for the affection of Mr Abe. Now Mr Abe was gone. In this world he was alive only in memory. Where would that leave Mary Todd? Elizabeth wasn't eager to find out, or rather, she was sure she already knew the days ahead would be a trial. Mary Todd's sun had been Mr Abe. Now the light had gone out. Mary Todd's flailing for the light could become exhausting, hopeless, life-ending, because she saw only by human light, or so it seemed, and then with her blinders on.

So there wasn't the greatest eagerness to return to the White House this Easter Sunday. But the preacher had said what needed to be said. If she was to live up to the name of Christ, into which she'd been baptized, she must show Christ's love to Mary Todd. That duty and her friendship seemed compelling. She must return to the White House. Nothing had been said of her returning when she'd left the evening before. Mary Todd, she knew, assumed her friend would return. Well, yes, she would return. She'd be guided by the renewing word she'd heard this morning. That word was a comfort, a consolation, a compass heading in the passage through rough waters. She would have time enough to decide what to do beyond the near morrows. For the time, Christian duty and compassion called her to bring comfort and hope to her friend. So after breakfast with the Lewises Mrs Keckly went to the White House.

Mary Todd and Tad were still in bed, sleeping in the Summer Bedroom, she on the bed and he on a sofa brought into the room.

Indeed, in the roughly 40 days that followed, before Mary Todd departed Washington, she and the boy would most nights sleep in the same room, just as had happened following Willie's death. Right outside the bedroom lay Elizabeth Blair Lee, a woman who, like Mary Jane Welles, was connected to Mary Todd by politics and by a spirit of compliance that could make tolerable an otherwise threatening white woman. Mrs Lee, related by marriage to Robert E. Lee, had come an hour before Elizabeth left on Saturday, offering to stay the night in the White House. Elizabeth thought it best to allow the sleepers their due rest this morning. She had no doubt they'd been awake late as Mary Todd refused the rest that could provide respite from her sorrows. Elizabeth headed back downstairs to the kitchen.

About an hour past noon the kitchen staff received a summons to serve breakfast in the Presidential quarters. Elizabeth, who'd been visiting downstairs, headed upstairs. She expected to find a sober if weepy Mary Todd. Rather, that's what she hoped for. After she'd received word George had been killed, that's how *she* had reacted. Her friend was not subdued. Mary Todd had amazing reserves of energy that would be used, but not used up, in displays of passionate grief. This afternoon she was in passion. She would often be in such passions in her remaining days in Washington. Elizabeth had heard that in some countries professional mourners could be hired. These mourners, women, were prone to hysterical displays of grief, albeit grief-for-hire. Elizabeth thought Mary Todd could be such a hireling. Sometimes, though, Mary Todd could play the corpse. These were times when Mary Todd would be utterly listless, unable to arise from her bed, shackled to grief. There seemed to be no intermediate stage that afforded the possibility of grieving and living at the same time, except for the last days of Mary Todd's stay at the White House.

Mary Todd was able to converse with Elizabeth this Easter Sunday. Her grieving was punctuated with talk about arrangements in the coming days. She asked her friend whether she'd be willing to stay overnights. They agreed that Elizabeth would stay every other night, starting that evening. Mary Jane Welles or Elizabeth Lee or Annie, Mary Todd's maid, would stay with her on the other nights, sleeping on the sofa just outside the Summer Bedroom. Mary Todd refused to use her own bedroom. It was too close to Mr Abe's.

At day's end on Easter after Tad had fallen asleep on his sofa Elizabeth asked Mary Todd, "Would you like me to read somethin' from the Bible? I shoulda offered before Tad went to sleep."

"Don't apologize, Lizzy. I haven't the faintest interest in hearing anything our Lord might have to say to me now." Tears welled up in Mary Todd's eyes. "It's just two nights ago but the shot's still ringing in my ears. If the Lord didn't want that to happen He could have stopped it. I don't want to hear any consolation from *Him* just now. It would be nothin' but an excuse for His doin' nothin'. First Eddie, then Willie, now Abe."

"Death takes us all, Mary Todd, at least for the time of this world."

"Then I guess this world isn't totally His," replied Mary Todd.

"Mary Todd, you know God is reclaiming the world for Himself through His Son."

"Well, God is getting the short end of the bargain. Jesus died but sin and death are still around."

"Sin and death aren't the last words, Mary Todd. God's kingdom was planted, it's growing and one day it'll be full-blown."

"This ain't that day, Lizzy, and for all the growing, I can't live on promises. Abe's been taken away from me."

"From you, from everyone, Mary Todd. Likewise was Jesus, yet Jesus lives."

"Like how?"

"Like I probably wouldn't stay around, wouldn't be here now, if it weren't for Jesus. I think He's helped me through my life, helped me to better myself, helped me to overcome the sin I've managed to overcome. I'm still a slave to some sin. But I'm no longer a slave. I worked hard to get outta that but I know the kindness of others helped too. Without their love of Christ, those ladies back in St Louis probably woulda never given me the money I turned into a loan to purchase my freedom. I'm thankful."

"You have as much cause to be bitter as me. Slavery, then losing your only child in the war. Lizzy, you're so clear headed. Can't you see I've got a right to be angry at God. You, too."

"We all got a right to be angry at God, I suppose," said Elizabeth, "but we all have an obligation to be thankful. If God hadn't made us, there'd be none of us to be angry in the first place. He didn't have to make anyone. And He didn't have to love anyone. Any anger's got to be a short-lived thing when you consider how puny we are to God, Mary Todd. God is almost beyond comprehendin'. I'm thankful He sent Jesus so we could all see His face and know His heart in our own flesh."

"That flesh was crucified. I feel like I've been crucified, Lizzy. Where's God? He's forsaken me and sends only words. God's words are no comfort to me now because he's taken too much from me."

"Don't talk that way, Mary Todd. Pray that God will show you a way to receive His love and love Him again."

"I can't pray, not these days. Maybe again someday, but not now. Oh, don't worry, I believe in God. But I'm not going to pray to Him any time soon."

"Belief ain't faith, Mary Todd. You must place trust in God."

"After He allowed Abe's murder!"

"Shssh, Mary Todd."

"You know it's the truth."

"Jesus Christ is the truth. Everything else takes its measure from Him," said Elizabeth.

"My only measure now is my suffering."

"Jesus knows that, Mary Todd. He suffers when every man, woman, or child is murdered. But those murders aren't the last word on the people murdered or on the murderers. You got to remember that."

"Right now I don't believe that. My hope now is to have a word from Beyond — from Abe."

"What are you talkin' about? Are you thinking of going to spiritualists?"

"Exactly. To hear from Abe is better than hearing mere Bible words."

"One thing about you, Mary Todd, you've always been blunt. You're even blunt with God. He probably appreciates your honesty, but don't stretch His mercy."

"You've gone to a spiritualist, Lizzy. Don't try to diminish the value of spiritualists, not now."

"Well, maybe not now, but they can't substitute for God or the word of God. It may be more foolish than evil to go to séances. After George died Ginny Lewis and her husband, Walker, convinced me God provides the only real consolation. They were part of God's antidote to death's sting. Reject God's antidote and death will only poison you in every which way. Don't let that happen to you, Mary Todd. The Good Book and people like the Walkers show the way."

"If they're right and you're right, God will teach me. He'll redeem me."

"I'll pray that's so," said Elizabeth.

Mary Todd went to her bed and Elizabeth bedded down on the sofa, which had been equipped with fresh pillows and a blanket. Everyone slept through the night.

The following morning Mary Todd didn't want to get up. That was just as well, for Elizabeth could more easily leave for the shop. Mary Todd asked Elizabeth to attend to Tad before leaving. Elizabeth, of course, consented. Tad was easily roused. After he and his mama kissed, Elizabeth delivered the boy to Annie, who knew where all the boy's outfits were stored. Elizabeth was surprised to learn Annie knew something else. She knew how to dress the boy.

On his bed Annie had laid out a white shirt and a black jacket and knickers. "Here," she said, "you gonna take off the night shirt or will I?"

"I will," said the boy, "and I'll dress myself once you both leave."

Annie's jaw dropped. "You're gonna dress yourself?"

"I am. Now that my pa is dead, things will be different. I'll change myself from now on."

Said Annie, "Well, better late than never. You're a good lad, there now." She gave the boy and Elizabeth a big smile. Then she left. As Elizabeth was about to follow, the boy spoke again.

"I can see for breakfast myself, Mrs Lizbeth. I'll eat down by the kitchen."

"You're sure?"

"I'm sure."

"God bless you, Tad," said Elizabeth. Then she left. She was pleased about the boy. Mr Abe would have been pleased, too. Why had he tolerated so long the mis-education of his youngest son? Was it to placate Mary Todd? Sad, she thought, that Mr Abe had had to die for the boy to throw off the fetters of mis-education. She hoped the boy would take a new interest in reading, writing, and arithmetic.

In the following days arrangements were made to terminate the services of Mr Williamson, Tad's tutor. Slowly, very slowly, arrangements were made for the Lincolns to depart the White House. To his credit Andrew Johnson, sworn in to succeed Mr Abe, never once asked Mary Todd to hasten her departure. To Mr Johnson's dishonor, he never once called on her, never once sent a message of condolence. Never once. But no matter, said Mary Todd, the man was nothing but a drunk. As for the rest, Mary Todd wasn't interested in pretending to conform to the expectations of the powerful. She didn't attend the funeral service for Mr Abe held in the White House. She didn't accompany the return of Mr Abe's body to Springfield. She stayed put and went about packing. Indolent industry was allowed to interrupt her regimen of grief, but grief for 40 days would be the White House's mainstay and the wellspring of Mary Todd's diminished living.

So Mary Todd gave herself over to mourning virtually without letup. Elizabeth had no desire to remember every incident but she could recall an instance in almost any day if asked. Early in the first week following Mr Abe's assassination Elizabeth found herself having to compromise her integrity just to get Mary Todd through the night. Tad had already been put to bed. The blessed boy had put on his own nightclothes without help. If only he could teach his mother, thought Elizabeth. Elizabeth tucked him in for the night, then paged through the Brothers Grimm with him. As she turned down the lights in the room, the boy asked her to say a prayer. She did.

In the library Mary Todd was waiting, reading a newspaper. Elizabeth had suggested that Mary Todd read something, hoping the distraction might quiet any tears. That was not to be. Mary Todd picked up a newspaper that brought the latest news about the massive manhunt for John Wilkes Booth and his accomplices. This was the first newspaper Mary Todd had read since the assassination. By the time Elizabeth arrived, Mary Todd held one hand over her mouth while tears dampened the paper.

Elizabeth hadn't realized that fresh newspapers were still being delivered to the White House library. When she saw Mary Todd's distress, she grabbed the newspaper, wadded it up, and discarded it in a wicker basket.

"They are monsters!" sobbed Mary Todd.

"Yes," said Elizabeth, "but they are also men and they'll be caught."

"They have made me SUFFER so!" shouted Mary Todd.

"You are not alone," said Elizabeth, hoping to temper the flare-up.

"I am alone. I am alone. I am alone. God has made me be alone. God hates me and I HATE Him! He hated Eddie. He hated Willie. He hated my dearly beloved husband. I HATE HIM!" she screamed.

Robert came into the library. "What's all this shouting for, Mother?" He addressed his mother but looked to Elizabeth for an answer.

"She's been reading the newspaper."

"There shouldn't be newspapers in here," said Robert.

"Well, I guess someone better say somethin' or they'll keep showing up in this room. Should I say something?" asked Elizabeth.

"No, I'll attend to it."

"Then do something about it right NOW!" shouted Mary Todd.

"No one meant any harm," said Elizabeth taking Mary Todd into her arms.

Robert glared. "It's been hard on all of us, Mother. Hysterics aren't going to bring Father back."

"I want him back," she sobbed. "He shouldn't have been taken."

"I know, I know," said Robert. "But don't blame me or anyone else for what's happened except for the men who did it. Justice will be their due. I'm not to be blamed for your aggravation."

"Aggravation? This was more than aggravation, this was murder," said Mary Todd. "Now go away, Bobby. You only make things worse." She looked away from Robert, over the shoulder of Elizabeth. "Go."

"Mother, please."

"You heard me, go."

"Yes, ma'am."

Robert turned, walked out, and closed the library door softly behind him. Elizabeth secretly admired Robert's ability to walk away without a favorable resolution of his relationship with his mother. She also pitied him and Mary Todd for all the rancor. And again she feared she might get caught up in that someday, sooner or later.

CHAPTER 21

—ɯ—

Robert again and again told his mother she was packing 'too much too little', meaning she was taking too much and spending too little time sorting through what could and should be taken. Not that she didn't give things away. She gave away Lincoln mementoes to White House staff: a cane to a messenger, Mr Abe's last suit — the one he wore at the Ford — to a guard, this and that souvenir to people on staff, especially the ones she liked. Beyond the White House she gave out a few things: another cane to Senator Sumner, a cane to Mr Frederick Douglass, Mr Abe's last hat to Reverend Dr Gurley, who presided at Mr Abe's funeral and at Willie's. Offsetting the giving was the taking — at least some people saw it that way. Mary Todd was later accused of stealing things that belonged to the White House. The one thing that surely belonged was a small, marble-topped table she and Mr Abe had admired. Commissioner French, who oversaw the maintenance of the White House, gave her permission to take the table.

Mary Todd received few visitors during her last days in the White House. Not one relative came to offer condolences. Her sister Elizabeth, who lived in Springfield, probably didn't come because Mr Abe had relieved Elizabeth's husband from his position with the Army commissary office. As for the wives of her half-brothers, well, they were south of the Mason-Dixon line one way or another, and the half-brothers had died fighting for the Confederacy. So it was no surprise that no family showed up to comfort Mary Todd. As for the rest, who knew? Maybe they knew Mary Todd well enough to know they wouldn't be welcome. Mary Todd wanted to be alone or perhaps she wanted to be seen to be alone. Hard to say because when she wasn't weeping she walked about the White House in a daze. Robert found her difficult to communicate with even on the best of days. She didn't give attention to packing the way he thought it deserved. Other than giving away mementoes she wasn't prepared to give energy to selective packing. So more and more trunks were packed with this and that and all too much too much.

Mary Todd did get fired up about one thing in those last days. The citizens of Springfield wanted to erect a tomb for Mr Abe right in the center of town. Mary Todd would have none of that. She figured she'd end up being buried somewhere else. She wanted to be buried beside Mr Abe. She insisted that Mr Abe's body had to be buried in the big cemetery on the north side of Springfield. Mary Todd got her way. Eddie's body and Willie's would be buried next to Mr Abe's. Elizabeth was sure Mary Todd had been right to insist on these things. She wasn't so sure how she'd respond to Mary Todd's request that she accompany Mary Todd to Illinois. Truth be told, Mary Todd seemed to want something more permanent than mere accompaniment.

A few days after the assassination while the two ladies were in the library, Mary Todd began complaining to Elizabeth about Robert. "Bobby was away at college for four years and then he went into the Army. He's got no appreciation for what I've had to endure here in the White House. He's no understandin' how his father was taken up with the war. He's no idea what a harsh mistress she's been. You would think he could see. Bobby will never understand. He never will."

"I think he does," said Elizabeth.

"If he did, he would be cryin' a whole lot more than he is," said Mary Todd.

"Everyone has a different way of steering through troubled waters," replied Elizabeth. "I see him cryin' off alone."

"Why can't he cry a whole lot more with me? Is he too good for me?"

"He's tryin' to be good to you, Mary Todd. I think he figures if he cries too much with you he won't be able to help you all navigate through these troubles. He's trying to keep a level head."

"Lizzy, you're the one with the level head. I'd be lost if not for you bein' here with me. Don't ever leave me, Lizzy."

"I'll do what I can, Mary Todd."

"Never leave me, never never leave me, Lizzy. You're the only one that understands me."

Maybe more than I should for my own good, thought Elizabeth. Said she, "Let's sit down."

The two sat on a sofa while Elizabeth retrieved a handkerchief to wipe the tear stains from Mary Todd's cheeks. Elizabeth said, "No one's got perfect understandin', not in this life, Mary Todd. So don't be too hard on your Robert. He's sufferin' too. He wants to put the pieces together again of what's been broken. You're not ready to do that just yet and I think that frustrates you both."

Mary Todd broke a small smile, "You can always see things so well, Lizzy."

"Sometimes."

"But the pieces will never be put together, Lizzy. One day I'm Mrs President and the next day I'm nobody. Nobody." Mary Todd began weeping again, 'fixin' to get in a state', as Elizabeth would say.

"Well, we're always somebody..." said Elizabeth, *somebody to God* she had wanted to say, but she was afraid to say anything like that just now, knowing how angry Mary Todd was with God. As it was, Mary Todd supplied the word.

"You didn't finish, Lizzy. You didn't finish."

"Whaddya mean, Mary Todd?"

"Oh, I know you, Lizzy. You were goin' to say I'm somebody to God. I know. And I know I'm just about nobody to God or I'm a somebody He hates. I had the gumption to marry Abe because I saw he could become President. I pushed him, I combed and brushed him, I cleaned him up, tried to kill those backcountry ways, I advised him...and he became the man I thought he could be. He became the man I wanted him to be, well almost, and now God is punishing me. He's a jealous God. He's jealous and pitiless. As if Abraham hadn't made a world of difference for the better for this country. If it had been up to God Abe would have still been back there on the circuits, chewing the fat with the lawyers and two-bit hicks 'round Springfield."

"I wouldn't be so sure," said Elizabeth. *Mr Abe was the Moses God sent America.*

"I'm sure I'm the one that made the difference, at least until we got to the White House."

"Well, I don't know that that excludes God from the picture, Mary Todd."

"I'd say it does. Abe would see it different than me, I know that. He opened his Bible almost every day of the week and often more than once when we got here. You know I'm just a Sunday kind of Christian, Lizzy."

"You're being hard on yourself, too hard I think. When I think of how you helped with the contrabands and with other ways black folk have tried to better themselves here, I think you were being more than a Sunday Christian."

"Those were the right things to do. I wasn't thinkin' about Jesus. I certainly wasn't when I pushed Abe along. No, I certainly wasn't."

"I thank God Mr Abe became President," said Elizabeth.

"And not me?"

"Well, now that you say it, thank you, too, Mary Todd, for doin' what needed doin' to do what God wanted done."

"I get little thanks. Perhaps that's right just now." Mary Todd started to whimper. "If he hadn't become President, Abe would still be alive now. Still alive."

While just seconds before she'd been almost dry-eyed, now it was if a dam had burst. She shook, she bent over, she placed her head in Elizabeth's lap, and rocked back and forth crying. "They killed the man I made. If I'd only left him alone, he'd be alive. Killed 'im. Killed 'im."

Will Slade happened to come into the library about a half hour later. Elizabeth asked him to bring a bowl of water and a terry-cloth towel. Before he had returned, Elizabeth had gotten out from under Mary Todd, who was now propped up with pillows on the sofa. Propped though she was, Mary Todd seemed to have entered a kind of delirium. Elizabeth dampened the towel then wiped it across Mary Todd's brow and temples. She did this repeatedly.

Will asked whether he should fetch Dr Henry. The doctor had been in City Point but was now back in Washington. Elizabeth didn't think the good doctor was needed just yet. She asked that Will or someone else check back once an hour through the night. She thanked him for his help and said he could be on his way. Will left.

After perhaps another hour of massaging Mary Todd's face with a wet towel, the delirium ended. Mary Todd was asleep. Elizabeth went to the Summer Bedroom. Tad was asleep. Elizabeth took pillows and a blanket with her back to the library. She made up a bed for herself on a sofa near Mary Todd. She chose to remain in her day clothes. When she turned down the gas lamps along the library wall she must have made a noise that roused Mary Todd.

"Lizzy, don't turn 'em down too low. I want light in here."

"You awake, Mary Todd? I'm sorry if I woke you. I'll just turn 'em down a bit for sleepin' sake."

"How can you talk that way? Why should I sleep? I need to be comforted."

"You need your health, Mary Todd. That's why you should sleep."

"I need Abe. I need Abe. Willie, too."

Mary Todd began rocking on the sofa. She put a fist to her mouth and wailed, "I need Abe! I need Abe!"

Here we go again, thought Elizabeth. Mary Todd might discount her sleep, but Elizabeth was more than ready for bed.

"Mary Todd, calm down now. You need your sleep. Me, too. Think about…"

"I NEED ABE!"

Will poked his head through the doorway. "Is everything all right?"

"It could be better," said Elizabeth.

"I want my President," shouted Mary Todd, who began sobbing.

Will looked befuddled.

"Thank you for looking in. I'm afraid you can't provide the impossible. You can go, thank you."

Will left.

While Mary Todd sobbed, Elizabeth continued to turn off some gas jets and turn down others. Mary Todd for some reason decided to unlace and remove her shoes. She said, "You know it's not impossible. Abe could be summoned. Willie, too."

"What about Eddie?" asked Elizabeth, hoping sarcasm wasn't evident in the question.

"I don't want to see Eddie. The angels are takin' care of him, have been a long time and let 'em. I want Abe and Willie."

"There's a time for holding and a time for lettin' go. But in the end lettin' go's gotta happen."

"Never! I will never let go! Love never lets go."

"In God that's the God's truth, Mary Todd," said Elizabeth removing her shoes. "But take comfort and rest in that. You — and I — need our rest. How else we gonna live?"

"I don't want to live."

"Don't talk that way now."

"Then bring me Abe and Willie."

"I'm not a spiritualist, Mary Todd."

"You've gone."

"Just for a while after George…"

"But you've gone and you believe that they live on."

"Course I do, but I decided it's not a good idea to linger around the tomb. That's unhealthy. God don't like that. You know that."

"God is just about the last person I want to consult right now. I want some consolation from people I love."

"And what do you want me to do?" asked Elizabeth, as she lay back on the pillow and covered herself with the blanket. *We've gone over this territory before. There's nothin' here to live on.*

"You've got that special sense, Lizzy, I'm sure. You got that from your mama growing up."

"I never told you anything like that."

"No, but black mamas are that way. They're alive to the spirits."

"So that's how you see it?" said Elizabeth. Prejudices work every which way, she thought, but one thing was certain, she was tired. She might as well use a prejudice to her advantage now.

"Mary Todd, we've got to be very quiet. Some people may be able to bring up spirits as easy as I can make dresses. I'm not one of those people. But if we're quiet enough and close our eyes, who knows what we may see."

"Lizzy, you're so kind."

"Right now, I'm exhausted. Let's just close our eyes and listen to the night."

Elizabeth prayed a silent prayer for relief. With Mary Todd quiet the sounds of a city could be heard. A wagon clattered on some nearby street. Elizabeth wondered whether it might be a milk wagon. A train whistle let off in the distance, then an owl hooted. After a while a Whip-poor-will began its song, there in the very city.

"Did you hear that, Lizzy?"

"I did."

"What do you think it means?"

"I remember how Mr Abe loved that song, 'Listen to the Whip-poor-will'. Maybe, just maybe…"

"Abe is present," said Mary Todd.

"That's one way to think of it, yes," said Elizabeth.

"He *is* present. I know he's present. What's he sayin', Lizzy?"

"Remember the song in your heart and rest. That's what the bird was sent to say."

"I think you're right, Lizzy. Can you remember the words?"

"I can't. But I bet you can, Mary Todd. So remember 'em just now."

"Yes, I'll remember 'em. Thank you, my dear Abe."

Elizabeth thought, *Thank you, my dear God.*

At last sleep came. But every other night for Elizabeth some variation of that night made for largely sleepless stays at the White House. She never inquired from the other ladies how their nights went. Surely, they weren't expected to be mediums of the dead. No doubt in other ways Mary Todd taxed their energies and patience. She was a master at such things. Within the first week of her Easter attendance on Mary Todd, Elizabeth had resolved she would give herself a two-day holiday once Mary Todd left town.

Mary Todd had other ideas. She had resolved that Elizabeth must accompany her to Chicago, where she intended to take up residence. Elizabeth told her friend that that would be impossible, indeed, it would seriously harm her business. Orders were coming in, big orders even. She had a huge order from Mrs Stephen Douglas for a spring trousseau. The orders were piling up. Her own production had gone down since Good Friday and her ability to oversee and guide the work of her girls had been compromised by her stays at the White House. She depended on her shop's sterling reputation for quality and timely work and she simply couldn't allow that to be compromised by staying on with Mary Todd back in Illinois.

Mary Todd would have none of this. As for Mrs Douglas and her likes, other dressmakers could do the job. As for the money, Mary Todd would have a talk with Commissioner French. There was no doubt Elizabeth had put in an extraordinary amount of time helping Mary Todd in her sorrow. The least the government could do was pay Elizabeth for her services. Mr French was readily convinced of the merits of paying Elizabeth for her time from Easter through up to two weeks of stay back in Illinois. Under this arrangement Elizabeth consented to travel with Mary Todd to Chicago. There seemed no other way to close out the last four years.

When Mary Todd left Washington the baggage car was loaded with many, many crates from the White House and several score pieces of Lincoln family luggage. Trailing the train's end was the special car that Mary Todd had used in her wartime, incognito shopping trips between Washington and New York City. The departure from the White House was without fanfare or fuss. Commissioner French was there to bid his goodbye. No other representatives of the executive, legislative, or judicial branches of the government were present. Washington was astir with preparations for the two victory parades that would take place on the morrow and the day after. Mary Todd wouldn't stoop to asking to review these parades. And no one seemed prepared to stoop or rise to asking the former First Lady to review them.

Traveling with Mary Todd, besides Elizabeth, were Tad and Robert and two bodyguards including Mr Crook. Two nights were spent on the train. For Elizabeth these were somewhat restless nights, as were the nights of the two following weeks at the Chicago hotel where the Lincolns initially settled in. When Elizabeth departed for Washington in mid June, Mary Todd hugged her for dear life, saying again and again how much she appreciated Elizabeth's help. Elizabeth, she said, was her truest, dearest friend. That was gratifying to hear but Elizabeth found the parting easier than Mary Todd would have liked. She had her business to return to and her own community of friends in Washington. She had done her duty and now looked forward to having a long distance friendship with Mary Todd, one sustained by correspondence, shared memories, and the quilt she hadn't forgotten.

This would not be an easy quilt nor the friendship unending.

CHAPTER 22

—∽∽—

In the two years following Elizabeth's return to Washington she and Mary Todd corresponded regularly. Mary Todd did most of the writing but Elizabeth paid another visit to Chicago during Christmas 1865. Otherwise she occupied herself with managing her prospering dressmaking business. Mary Todd occupied herself with importuning Congress to provide her a pension and the remainder of the four years' salary her husband would have earned had he not been assassinated. Short of the money from the national government, Mary Todd scraped by on paltry sums divvied out by Judge Davis, the executor Mr Abe had long ago named to oversee the Lincoln estate. Neither the divvied amounts nor the prospect of her share of the estate could keep Mary Todd's creditors at bay, much less pay them off. Mary Todd had undertaken where possible to return purchases, especially of jewelry. That aside she needed to raise more money. The one treasure trove she had was her trousseau of dresses, bonnets, shawls, and non-returnable jewels.

Mary Todd kept Elizabeth apprised of her various, futile efforts to raise money. In the summer of 1867 she wrote Elizabeth that she intended to come to New York City and oversee directly the disposition of her 'excess attire'. Mary Todd asked her friend to join her there in September to help her dispose of this attire. Elizabeth assumed the disposition might take anywhere from two to four weeks. Could she afford to be absent from her Washington business that long? More importantly, might there be even more that Mary

Todd wanted from Elizabeth, more of the motherly kind of support that proved so taxing following the assassination?

Elizabeth told the Lewises of Mary Todd's request one Sunday afternoon when she and the family were picnicking along the Chesapeake & Ohio canal, west of Washington. Following lunch the children were playing hide-and-seek among the trees and shrubs. Ginny Lewis was the first to note Elizabeth's misgivings about rendezvousing with Mary Todd.

"You're not sure whether to go, Liz. I can guess why," said Ginny.

"You're right. I'm afraid of being asked to provide more help than I can provide. It can be a heap o' trouble with Mary Todd, you know."

"Still an'all you want to help if you can, right?" replied Ginny.

"If I can. She deserves help — from all of us — for what Mr Abe done. She shouldn't have to go beggin' to survive. She isn't gettin' help from others. She's put off too many people, you know."

"Puts to mind this mornin's sermon on the Good Samaritan'," said Walker. "That set-upon Jew in the road put off his betters, who kept themselves holy by not helpin' the man. Or so they thought. But I 'spect God is lookin' to you, Liz, to be the Good Samaritan."

"I suppose you're right Brother Walker, but what if you came upon a man laying in the middle of the road 'cause he squandered his money and now hoped to attract some attention by beggin' but got beat up?"

"Could happen and that sounds more like the story of the Prodigal Son. Love don't always ask a lot of questions. Love just does," said Walker.

"Love can get little payment for the effort," said Elizabeth.

"Love's its own payment," replied Walker.

"My bank of it probably ain't as big as it ought to be," said Elizabeth.

"God does the replenishing," said Walker.

"It's one thing to say that," said Ginny, "and another to live it with someone who's taxin' your love away."

"True, true," said Walker. "What'cha goin' do, Liz?"

"I know what she'll do," said Ginny. "She's goin' up north to help Mrs Lincoln. But don't you forget, Liz, to ask the rest of us to help, too. You can't help that woman all alone and for what her husband did you shouldn't have to."

"Thank you," said Elizabeth. "I'll keep that in mind."

A few days later she wrote Mary Todd to tell her she'd be pleased to meet her in New York. In subsequent correspondence she learned that Tad would stay in Chicago with his brother and that Robert opposed his mother's efforts to raise money by selling off 'old clothes', as he called them. But many of the dresses had only been worn once or twice. Elizabeth wrote that 'judicious placements' could yield a good profit. She encouraged her friend to clear out the clutter of her wardrobe. She said she would wait word of when and where to meet Mary Todd in New York. She would speed up her work for her clients so she could afford to leave Washington for several weeks in September.

On September 17th Elizabeth received a letter from Mary Todd, dated 13 September, mailed just before Mary Todd boarded a New York-bound train. Mary Todd said she expected Elizabeth to meet her at the St Denis Hotel. Mary Todd would be staying in a room there reserved under the name 'Mrs Clarke', a name she had used during the Civil War when traveling incognito. When Elizabeth found Mary Todd's letter awaiting her at the Lewises she knew Mary Todd was probably already in New York, unless she had changed her mind. Elizabeth left Washington on the 18th, arriving in New York that evening. She went straight to the St Denis Hotel.

The St Denis would subject Elizabeth to a number of humiliations. She wouldn't be permitted in the large dining room reserved for guests, even though she was a guest. Instead she would have to eat in a room reserved for the servants of guests. Further, when she had arrived Mary Todd, to her credit, had attempted to secure a room for her friend a few doors down from her own room. The desk clerk had refused to allow Elizabeth to stay on the same floor as 'Mrs Clarke', whose luggage had already identified her to the hotel management as one Mrs A. Lincoln, Springfield, Illinois. Elizabeth would have to stay in a cramped room on the 5th floor, a floor reserved for servants. It was inconceivable to the hotel management that Elizabeth could be a friend of the former First Lady. To Mary Todd's credit, once she learned her friend must stay on the 5th she insisted she would remove herself to the 5th floor also. As Elizabeth would often say, Mary Todd could be wrong headed about many people and many things, but one thing she always was right about was her utter disdain for the conventions on how white people were supposed to treat black people.

Mary Todd and Elizabeth would leave the St Denis and stay at three other hotels. While the effrontery of the St Denis may have been the primary reason for decamping there, the subsequent moves were motivated by Mary Todd's insistence on keeping secret her presence in New York. The luggage gave the lie to that insistence. Once Elizabeth discovered that Mary Todd wished to conduct business in a covert fashion, she counseled her friend on several occasions to disclose her identity.

"After all," said Elizabeth, "you have nothing to hide. Having others recognize you as Mary Todd Lincoln will be to your advantage."

"You mean recognize me as Mrs Abraham Lincoln, but Robert doesn't know I'm in New York to sell clothes and I don't want it in the papers. Anyway, the clothes I'm offering are mine, not Abe's. They're worth a lot but not worth pity's sake. I've found a dealer who will handle the sale, W. H. Brady & Co., on Broadway. They're diamond brokers."

"Diamond brokers?" asked Elizabeth. "How're they going to sell your clothes?"

"They're shrewd businessmen," replied Mary Todd. "They have asked me to prepare a handful of letters dated last month, as if written from Chicago. I am to write these letters with a tone of urgency, indicating I desperately need funds. Then the brokers will take these letters around the city to the offices of various politicians who received appointments under Abraham's administration. The Brady people will cleverly suggest that if these politicians aren't forthcoming with support and purchases of my clothes, then the newspapers will be shown the letters to their embarrassment. I think they've discovered a way to milk some money out of New York."

"Mary Todd, I don't think you want to do that. Plain dealing is best in business. I wouldn't do anything like what you call milkin'. It will do no good and could bring much harm."

"Lizzy, my husband almost totally surrounded himself with no-goods, appointed no-goods. He was so naïve."

"That is harsh, Mr Abe…"

"It's true. I know these men and no one can expect any favors from them. I need money, so I must be bold."

After two weeks in New York and before Brady & Co. put Mary Todd's attire up for sale, Mary Todd left for Chicago. Bold she might be, but not so bold as to be around for the sale of her clothes. Before leaving town she authorized Mr Brady to place her wardrobe on exhibit and if necessary to publish her letters in the *New York World*, a Democratic newspaper. She insisted that Lizzy remain behind to oversee her interests in New York. Once the money was in from the sale of the clothing, Lizzy would get a commission for her labors. Elizabeth told Mary Todd she was happy to help as a friend but that staying in New York was out of the question. She must return to Washington.

"You can't abandon me. You can't. Everyone but you and Tad have abandoned me," said Mary Todd, beginning to sob.

"Mary Todd, you have Mr Brady and his people representing you here. What more can I do?"

"Abandon me if you will."

"I'm not goin' to abandon you. I'm just askin' you to tell me what I could possibly do if I stay here."

"Isn't it obvious?" asked Mary Todd, sobbing. "I trust you. I don't trust the Bradys."

Elizabeth was about to ask why Mary Todd engaged the Bradys if she didn't trust them. Given her choice, perhaps Mary Todd would have entrusted the sale to Elizabeth. But, alas, neither New York nor Washington was ready for the likes of Elizabeth to be a broker at a socially conspicuous event. As at the St Denis, she must be invisible. The thought rankled and saddened her. Mary Todd was indeed in a bind, partly of her making and partly beyond her ability to correct.

"All right, I'll stay in town, at least for a while."

"Oh, Lizzy, I knew you would!" said Mary Todd, showing a smile. She threw her arms around Elizabeth and kissed her. She asked, "Where will you stay?"

At least she asks, thought Elizabeth. As it happened Elizabeth would stay with friends and she would take in sewing work, although nowhere on the scale of her Washington enterprise. That enterprise she'd manage through Mr Oliver. Little did she know that when she saw Mary Todd off at the station she would never see her again.

In the ride to the station the two were blessedly relieved of reviewing the tactics of the impending sales through Brady & Co. The city was astir with commerce and traffic, but the minds of those on the cusp of travel would fly to times immediately future and to those long past.

As the cabman slammed shut the carriage door, Lizzy asked Mary Todd whether she had her tickets ready for presentation at the station.

"Of course, I've got them in an envelope. Right here in my purse," said Mary Todd. But her purse wasn't at hand.

Elizabeth thrust her head out the carriage window and got the cabman's attention just as he was about to take his seat.

"Driver, hold the horses. Don't go to the station just yet," she said.

The driver nodded and took his seat.

Elizabeth dreaded the thought of having to search for the purse. Mary Todd was beginning to panic as she realized the purse wasn't evident on the seat. Elizabeth began moving luggage to see if the purse lay hidden behind a bag. She heard a boy shout from the curbside, "I've got your purse, ma'am."

By this time Mary Todd was looking for the purse on the floor. Had she heard the boy?

Elizabeth said, "The purse's been found."

"Good," said Mary Todd with relief. She straightened up and sat back down, appearing exhausted. "Would you, Lizzy?" meaning *Would you attend to receiving it, to passing it along?*

What will become of Mary Todd if she doesn't have her Lizzy for a friend? thought Elizabeth.

Elizabeth opened the carriage door so that the boy could easily hand up the purse. He was a bellhop from the hotel. He looked to be about 12 or 13 years old and could easily have passed as a cousin of Tad and Willie.

As the boy handed up the purse, he saluted with his free hand and said, "With the hotel's compliments to Mrs Lincoln, I mean Mrs Clarke."

"Thank you," said Elizabeth, passing the purse back over her shoulder to Mary Todd. As the bellhop shut the door Elizabeth looked around at Mary Todd. Mary Todd was pawing through the purse by way of making a rapid inventory.

"It's all still here," she said with joy, shaking an envelope that contained the railway tickets. "Here, here. Let's give the bellhop a gratuity."

She pulled out two silver dollars from her purse, stood up, and steadied herself at the carriage window as the driver flicked his horse into motion.

"Here, my lad. Thank you," she said, flinging the coins towards the bellhop. They amounted to a good week's pay for the boy.

Elizabeth could hear the coins ring against the sidewalk. She was delighted at her friend's generosity, the first such showing to strangers in what otherwise had been such a pinched New York stay.

After Mary Todd sat down, she again inventoried her purse. When she completed the second inventory she said, "Past times it was a joy to arrive in New York. Now, leavin's the real joy."

"Times have changed," said Elizabeth, "and I guess we change with 'em."

"Don't we," said Mary Todd. "But we're still friends, Lizzy."

Mary Todd took Elizabeth's hand and wouldn't let go until they arrived at the train station. Along the way they reminisced about days at the White House and summer times at the Soldiers' Home. Despite all the anxieties of the Civil War years, Mary Todd's remembrances now had a golden glow about them. Elizabeth was happy they did. She would say, 'Happy memories are like honey. They are the sweetness after the sting is gone and well worth the savoring.'

Once the carriage was at the station, two porters helped the ladies carry Mary Todd's baggage to her coach on the waiting train. Elizabeth came aboard to see Mary Todd seated and to see that all Mary Todd's luggage was placed around her. Mary Todd gave a dollar tip to each porter. The conductor said he would see to placing the luggage on the overhead racks for the trip. He didn't want visitors lingering on the train. Not much could be said in this parting moment. The ladies hugged and kissed. Elizabeth reminded Mary Todd to enjoy the golden foliage in her journey up the Hudson Valley and beyond. Mary Todd said she would. She hoped Elizabeth would soon see a harvest in New York. The two ladies squeezed hands, then parted.

When Elizabeth alighted from the train she walked along the railway coach to the window where Mary Todd sat. Rather than sit right next to the window, Mary Todd was seated next to the center aisle. The otherwise empty seat next to the window was jammed with luggage. The inside of the car wasn't well lit so Elizabeth didn't have a clear, lasting last image of her friend's face. Moreover light from elsewhere reflected off the window, further obscuring Mary Todd from view. Thus even before pulling away, Mary Todd seemed cut off but, said Elizabeth, 'So it was with Mary Todd and so it was to be.'

As the train began to pull away the future was yet unknown. Elizabeth waved and Mary Todd briefly waved back. In the waving Elizabeth recalled some of her own journeys and wished she, too, could now be leaving for home. Instead, before the train was out of sight Elizabeth was on her way to resume her labor of love.

CHAPTER 23

—◈—

Elizabeth of course would be diligent on her friend's behalf. In its own way Brady & Co would be diligent too. The politicians, however, would refuse to yield to the coercions implicit in the letters from Mary Todd. The *World* was all too happy to print these letters, which raised a storm of indignation in New York and a domestic ruckus in Chicago. Robert was furious with his mother for putting her wardrobe up for sale. He was even angrier with the published letters. However much she might try to distance herself from New York, from the sale, from the letters, Robert was certain his mother's hand, mind, and mindlessness were deep, deep into creating an embarrassment for the Lincoln name. When Mary Todd relayed her son's reaction to Elizabeth, her friend was convinced she'd be ever guilty in Robert's eyes. She was guilty by virtue of her work on his mother's behalf.

The work was neither easy nor rewarding. The wardrobe was put up for display at Brady & Co. Thousands trekked through. The display was the talk of the town. The askings were too rich for the masses and too offensive for those who could afford them. The sale was a disaster. Brady & Co. said it would have to recoup its expenses by holding back some items, the remainder being returned to Chicago. While the show was on at Brady & Co. the newspapers had a field day, savoring every extra paper they could sell by reporting about what they labeled 'Mrs. Lincoln's Old Clothes Scandal'. Mary Todd was the object of almost unending vituperation. She was labeled an 'intensely vulgar woman', 'unprincipled and avaricious', 'a woman who had gone outside the womanly bounds of gentleness and obedience'. The Old Clothes Scandal opened up the issue of Mary Todd's exodus from the White House, laden with who knew how many crates full of government property. The clothes sale became a convenient entry point for a political battle.

Mary Todd hadn't lost her ability to assess a political situation but she had lost the heavy artillery to repel assaults. She instructed Lizzy to give an interview to the sympathetic *New York Herald*. The *Herald* ran a number of favorable articles, but in sum they were small cargo carried away by the stream of invective gathering all around. Elizabeth asked Mr Frederick Douglass and other leaders in the black community to help extricate Mary Todd from the penuriousness that had given ground to the Old Clothes fiasco. These leaders were prepared to help Mary Todd. Mary Todd waffled in accepting their help. Eventually, the offers of help withered away, felled by time and by the settlement of the Lincoln estate. The settlement of just under $100,000 to be divided equally among Mary Todd, Robert, and Tad gave the world the impression that Mary Todd would have the means to live comfortably in the years ahead.

Just before the settlement of the estate, Elizabeth had given permission to Brady & Co. to take Mary Todd's wardrobe to Providence, Rhode Island, where it would be displayed to all willing to pay a price of admission. If the Providence show proved profitable, the wardrobe would be sent elsewhere on exhibition. When Mary Todd learned of this initiative in a letter from her friend, she telegrammed a reply forbidding that anything be taken to Providence and demanding that Elizabeth request a bill from Brady & Co. for their services. It took some time to close up matters with the brokers, who meanwhile managed to sell one diamond ring and two clothing items. It was agreed the money grossed from these sales would be retained by the brokers to cover their expenses. In March 1868 Elizabeth packed up Mary Todd's clothing and jewels and shipped them back to Chicago. Then Elizabeth returned to Washington.

She returned not entirely empty-handed. Obviously, Elizabeth left New York City without a commission. Moreover, she had bills to pay and her own dignity to recover. The Old Clothes Scandal not only disgraced the Lincoln name, it had tarnished Elizabeth. Or so she thought. Somehow, some way, some good must be brought from this tawdry affair. A memoir seemed the very ticket. Civil War memoirs were flooding the bookstalls and people were buying them. Elizabeth left New York with the knowledge her memoirs would soon be published by Carleton & Co, a respectable New York publisher. Shortly after Mary Todd had returned to Chicago and sensing a profitable stay in New York was unlikely, Elizabeth had sought out advice on how to publish memoirs. Without Mary Todd's knowledge she began working with a Scotsman, one James Redpath, who had helped Frederick Douglass publish his memoirs. Redpath avidly supported Elizabeth in her project. He believed a memoir from her hand would provide an insider's look at the White House and would provide Elizabeth's perspective on the Old Clothes tumult. Elizabeth believed her perspective might at least partly vindicate Mary Todd Lincoln.

Elizabeth had written the book in part as a defense of the dignity and integrity of Mary Todd and of herself. But the book wasn't sold under such sentiments. Instead, it was sold as an exposé, as a series of revelations. As such the book bombed. From all sides, at least the ones wielding power of pen and press, Elizabeth's memoirs were condemned. The reviewers accused the author of transgressing the accepted social codes governing friends, women, and people of lower social status. Should the nation stoop to read the gossip of 'Negro servant girls'? No. Could the nation afford to encourage every servant — white or black — to betray the confidences of the families they purported to serve? Absolutely not. Indeed, the book was held up as an example of the dangers of educating 'the black and Irish working drudges', especially their women. Bitter was the cup of rejection offered by newspapers otherwise so delighted to pile invective on Mary Todd. They were offended that a woman of dark skin tone and former slave status should presume to offer her own views on Mary Todd and the Lincolns.

Elizabeth's book and the rage surrounding it soon disappeared beneath waves of Civil War memoirs. Her Washington dress business was largely unaffected by the tumult. The one lasting effect of the book was to sever the relations between Elizabeth and the

Lincoln family. That Robert was offended by Elizabeth's publication was little surprise. He'd always seemed put off by his mother's closest, dearest friend. Anyway, he just tended to keep his distance from others. 'If he'd only kept his distance', Elizabeth would say. She was sure he'd worked with Redpath to suppress sales of her book. She had no firm evidence of this.

Mary Todd was utterly mortified. She stopped replying to Elizabeth's letters. Letters and telegrams stopped arriving from Mary Todd. It was as if Elizabeth had ceased to exist. To be sure, Mary Todd had never been the sunshine of Elizabeth's life. Yet Elizabeth grieved the loss. The two ladies had traversed so much together. Elizabeth was saddened by their estrangement. She thought about how she and her friend could be reconciled. She prayed about it. She kept at her business, of course. And then one day she thought of what she must do to repair the breach.

CHAPTER 24

—∿—

The breach might be healed, thought Elizabeth, if she were to resume the long laid-away quilt project. After Mr Abe had been assassinated she'd set aside the project. After all, she'd intended the quilt as her affirmation of Mr Abe and Mary Todd's marriage. Death had nullified that affirmation. Yet Elizabeth had never discarded the hatbox of scraps at her office. She had decided to keep the box as a remembrance, but not as a constant remembrance. When she had returned from Chicago, Elizabeth had moved the box to a storeroom where she kept bolts of cloth and other hatboxes full of odds and ends. The box would sit there until a summer morning in 1868, when she removed it and placed it above the cherry wardrobe where it had been in 'active service' during the years she was making dresses for Mary Todd.

Each summer evening thereafter, after her girls had gone home, she'd stay another hour planning her quilt and cutting up old remnants to fit into it. She now thought of the quilt as partly an embroidery on the lives of Mary Todd and Mr Abe and partly as an embroidery of reconciliation between Mary Todd and herself. The quilt would be designed as a series of frames around a centerpiece. The centerpiece would be adorned with a spread eagle, beneath whose claws would dangle the word 'LIBERTY'. Aside from golden spread eagles on each of the four edges, the frames would incorporate embroidered florets or cloth flowers. These florets would honor Mary Todd's love of flowers. The center would honor Mr Abe's love of his countrymen.

While the borderlands might exceed in size the area devoted to the 'temple of liberty', as she saw it, both the Lincolns would be enlarged by this remembrance and reconciliation quilt. Elizabeth hoped Mary Todd would see it that way back to their old friendship.

There was only one problem: Elizabeth was running out of blue cloth. She had thought she'd had enough from the blue remnants at hand to make the outermost portions of the sixteen florets, four to a side, that would figure prominently in the quilt. The inner petals of these florets were composed of remnants of all sorts and all hues. But she was determined the outmost petals of all the florets be made of one cloth that would serve to unify the frame of florets.

Rather than compromise on using a unifying color, Elizabeth decided she would have to purchase a bolt of blue cloth having nothing to do with Mary Todd. She would pick a blue of tone and texture close to the blue cloth she had intended to use. A few days before committing to purchasing the substitute cloth a girl about 12 years old and a boy about 8 came into the shop. A visit by children was almost unheard of except as messengers. The girl was carrying a folded dark blue Army jacket. The boy was carrying sky blue trousers, also neatly folded. When Elizabeth saw the children, she at first thought they might have been sent out to get the uniform repaired. She wondered what their story would be because she could tell their papa must have served in an African-American unit. Before Elizabeth could ask any questions, the girl blurted out that her papa had sent them to see what money they could get for his jacket and trousers.

"So your papa served in the War."

"Yes, ma'am," said the girl.

"Have you gone anywhere else with this?"

"Yes'm," said the boy.

"Your papa musta served in one of those African units?"

"Yes, ma'am," said the boy and girl.

"What's your names?"

"Vera." "Hatcher."

"Vera, that's a pretty name. Hatcher, I've never heard of a Hatcher before."

"Everybody calls him 'Hatch'," said the girl.

"Hatcher's where my papa grew up," said the boy.

"Musta had fond memories of that place. I have fond memories of where I grew up. I think your papa might want to hold on to this uniform. Are you sure he wants you to sell it off?"

"We're supposed to find the best place for a price, then he'll come in for the sale," said Vera.

"So he wants to sell it, you say," said Elizabeth, shaking her head. "I'm surprised."

"Our mama passed away from the fever. We need the money for the buryin' expense," said the girl.

Elizabeth noticed tears in her eyes and the boy's, too. She said, "I'm sorry to hear about your mama." The three stood quiet for a moment and then the children looked as if they would leave. But Elizabeth spoke to the boy, "Let me see those trousers, please."

Hatcher passed them to her. She took them by the waist and shook them out. She could see that the right leg had been rolled and pinned up at one time. There were creases across the right leg and prominent pinholes.

Elizabeth said, "Looks like this right trouser leg was rolled up for a long time. Your papa missing part of his right leg?"

"Yes'm," said the boy.

"Did he ever explain how that came to be?"

Vera said, "He got hit with some metal from an explosion. Some metal came in but didn't come out, except the doctor took off that part of the leg."

"It was at the Battle of Spotsylvania Court House," said Hatcher with pride and careful pronunciation.

"Your papa named Caleb?"

"Yes, ma'am," said Vera. "How'd you know?"

"I guessed. I recall meeting him once. What's he doing now?"

"He's a watchmaker's apprentice," said Vera.

"Good for him. Real good. I'll pay $10 for the trousers. Keep the jacket."

The children looked astonished.

"That's a lot o' money," said the girl.

"Your papa was a soldier and I need cloth from a soldier. If your papa will take $10, send him on up here and I'll pay him. Or I'll pay you."

"He said to take $5 for the whole outfit if we could get it," said Hatcher.

Vera said, "You shouldn't a said that. But he's right, ma'am. If you will pay that much, our papa will be very happy."

"Good to hear," said Elizabeth.

She went to a metal box and opened it. It was full of coins and a few greenbacks. She counted out 10 silver dollars into the hands of Vera and Hatcher. The two loaded Hatcher's pockets with the coins.

"So your papa's a watchmaker's apprentice?"

"He's a watchmaker's apprentice," said the boy crisply. He looked proud to say the words and proud of his papa.

"Good to hear. You tell him Mrs Keckly sends her regards."

"Yes'm," said the boy. Said the girl, "Yes, ma'am. Thank you, ma'am."

Vera picked up the jacket she'd set aside, clasped it to her chest, and followed Hatcher out and down the stairs. They were all smiles now. Their joyous chatter as they clattered down the stairs lingered in Elizabeth's memory. As for Elizabeth there were tears in her eyes. To her last days she saw that purchase as a kind of redemption whatever happened to the quilt. She now had the outermost blue she needed for the florets, a patriotic undertone appropriate for her quilt. It was fitting that an American of African ancestry had worn that blue.

The reconciliation quilt never restored the broken friendship between Elizabeth and Mary Todd. Elizabeth wrote Robert telling him she wished to make amends, to visit his mother, and to present her with a quilt she'd especially made for her. She sent her warm regards to him, his mother, his family. Robert's reply by post was 'I can do nothing' — at least in this matter. As it happened Mary Todd and Tad left for Frankfurt, Germany in 1868. They lived there about two years before returning to the States. Shortly after their return Tad died, aged 18. A few years later Robert *did* do something, committing his mother to an insane asylum in Batavia, Illinois after an ugly hearing. About a half-year later Mary Todd managed to get out with the help of two crusading lawyers, a husband and wife team appalled by the high-handed confinement of an admittedly eccentric but sane lady.

Mary Todd took her trunks and crates to Springfield. For the remainder of her life she lived there with her sister Elizabeth and Elizabeth's husband. In Springfield she kept herself apart from neighbors and from the town-folk, who meant so much to Mr Lincoln. Whatever infirmities she suffered were as nothing to the diminishment she endured by shutting herself off from really most everyone, including those who loved her most. She died in July 1882.

In 1892 Elizabeth left Washington to accept a position in Ohio as head of Wilberforce University's department of sewing and domestic sciences. In the late 1890s she returned to Washington after suffering a slight stroke that impaired her ability to sew. When Elizabeth returned to Washington she joined the Fifteenth Street Presbyterian Church. Her 'family' grew beyond just the Lewises. She was regularly visited by friends from the Fifteenth Street and Union Bethel communities but was otherwise forgotten by the larger community. She would occasionally talk about designing and making the reconciliation quilt. A number had seen it. Elizabeth had no wish to talk of its disposition. She much preferred to talk about the Lincolns, their elevation, and their descent. In her room she had a portrait photo of Mary Todd. She was certain God's hand had accomplished a great thing by Mr Abe's elevation. She was thankful to be a part of God's story in the world, thankful, too, that it would end as all good mysteries do in the triumph of truth and goodness and beauty. 'The Lord provides' — those were her last parting words just before she died in 1907 under the very roof of an institution she helped found, the National Home for Destitute Colored Women and Children. She died feeble and forgotten, yes, but a saint undiminished.

□□□

A CHRONOLOGY

—ᴍ—

This chronology highlights the lives of Abraham and Mary Todd Lincoln, their family, and Elizabeth Keckly. Data are drawn from various sources, primarily Brown University Scholarly Technology Group and National Park Service web sites and Jennifer Fleischner's *Mrs. Lincoln and Mrs. Keckly* (See 'Further Reading', following).

1809 Feb 12	Abraham Lincoln (LINCOLN) is born near present-day Hodgenville, Kentucky.
1816 Dec	LINCOLN's family moves to Indiana, near present-day Gentryville.
1818 Feb	Elizabeth Hobbs (ELIZABETH) is born southwest of Petersburg, Virginia.
1818 Oct 5	LINCOLN's mother, Nancy Hanks Lincoln, dies of milk sickness.
1818 Dec 13	Mary Ann Todd (MARY) is born in Lexington, Kentucky.
1819 Dec 2	Thomas Lincoln, LINCOLN's father, remarries in Elizabethtown, Kentucky, to Sarah Bush Johnston.
1825 Jul 5	MARY's mother, Eliza Parker Todd, dies.
1826 Nov 1	MARY's father, Robert Smith Todd, marries Elizabeth Humphreys.

1830 Mar	Lincoln family moves to Illinois, settling near present-day Decatur.
1831 Jul	LINCOLN leaves his family and settles in New Salem, Illinois.
1834 Aug 4	LINCOLN elected as a member of the Whig Party to the Illinois General Assembly, representing Sangamon County. He is re-elected in 1836, 1838, and 1840.
1836 Sep 9	LINCOLN receives from the Illinois Supreme Court a license to practice law in Illinois.
1837 Apr 15	LINCOLN arrives in Springfield, Illinois, becoming a resident and a junior law partner of John Todd Stuart, MARY's cousin.
1839	MARY moves to Springfield, living with Ninian and Elizabeth Edwards, Elizabeth being MARY's older sister.
1839 Sep 23	LINCOLN begins traveling the 8th Judicial Circuit, which he continues to do with few interruptions until elected President.
1840	LINCOLN and MARY begin courting, until 1 January 1841, when their engagement is broken off probably because of the disapproval of the Edwards.
1841 Apr 14	LINCOLN ends partnership with John Todd Stuart and begins one with Stephen T. Logan.
1842	LINCOLN and MARY in secret resume courting.
1842 Jan	George Hobbs (GEORGE) is born to Elizabeth, who names him after George Pleasant Hobbs, a friend also in bondage.
1842 Nov 4	LINCOLN and MARY are married by Rev. Charles Dresser in the Edwards' home.
1843 Aug 1	Robert Todd Lincoln (ROBERT) is born in rooms the Lincoln family occupies over the Globe Tavern, Springfield.
1844 Jan 16	LINCOLN purchases his one and only home from Rev. Dresser.

1844 May 1	Lincoln family moves into their Springfield home.
1844	LINCOLN establishes his own law practice with William H. Herndon.
1846 Mar 10	Edward Baker Lincoln (EDDIE) born at home.
1846 Aug 3	LINCOLN elected to the US House of Representatives (30th Congress) as a Whig. The Lincoln family moves to Washington, DC, in 1847.
1847	ELIZABETH moves to St Louis, Missouri, with the Hugh and Anne Garland family, to whom she and GEORGE are in bondage.
1847	Missouri passes a law forbidding the teaching of reading and writing to Negroes.
1848	MARY, ROBERT, and EDDIE leave Washington.
1850 Feb 1	EDDIE dies at home, Springfield.
1850 Dec 21	William Wallace Lincoln (WILLIE) is born at home.
1852	ELIZABETH marries James Keckly (also spelled 'Keckley').
1852 Oct 13	MARY joins First Presbyterian Church, Springfield.
1853 Apr 4	Thomas Lincoln (TAD) is born at home.
1854 Nov 7	LINCOLN elected to the Illinois legislature, but withdraws from office 20 days later to run for the US Senate, a race LINCOLN will drop out of, directing support to Lyman Trumbull, a Republican.
1855 Nov 13	ELIZABETH and GEORGE are emancipated upon payment of $1200 to Anne Garland, a sum provided by ELIZABETH's customers, who she repays in full before leaving St Louis in 1860.
1857	GEORGE enrolls in Wilberforce University, near Xenia, Ohio.

1858	LINCOLN makes another run for US Senate, now running against Stephen Douglas, who he debates 7 times in August, September, and October at Ottawa, Freeport, Jonesboro, Charleston, Galesburg, Quincy, and Alton, Illinois. 2 November voting leads to Douglas being sent by the Illinois legislature to the US Senate.
1860 Nov 6	LINCOLN elected 16th President.
1860 Dec 20	South Caroline becomes the first state to secede from the Union.
1861 Feb 4	The Confederate States of America (CSA) established with Jefferson Davis selected CSA President.
1861 Mar 4	LINCOLN inaugurated as President.
1861 Apr 12	CSA forces attack Fort Sumter, South Carolina, marking the beginning of the Civil War. Fort Sumter surrenders 14 April.
1861 Jul 21	Battle of First Manassas (or Bull Run), near Washington, a CSA victory that shocks the Union.
1861 Aug 10	GEORGE dies at the battle of Wilson's Creek, in southwest Missouri, a CSA victory.
1862 Feb 20	WILLIE dies at the White House, perhaps from typhoid fever.
1862	ELIZABETH with 40 ladies at Union Bethel forms the Contraband Relief Association to help escaped slaves.
1862 Aug 30	Battle of Second Manassas (or Bull Run), a CSA victory.
1862 Sep 17	Battle of Antietam, effectively a Union victory.
1862 Sep 22	LINCOLN issues preliminary Emancipation Proclamation, the final version being issued 1 January 1863.
1863 Jul	Battles of Gettysburg (1-3 July) and Vicksburg (4 July), Union victories.

1864 Sep 1	Fall of Atlanta to Union forces.
1864 Nov 8	LINCOLN re-elected, defeating General George B. McClellan.
1865 Mar 4	LINCOLN inaugurated for his second Presidential term.
1865 Apr 14	LINCOLN shot at Ford's Theatre, dying at 7:22 AM on 15 April.
1865 Apr 19	Funeral service for LINCOLN at the White House.
1865 May 4	Body of LINCOLN interred at Oak Ridge Cemetery, Springfield.
1865 May 22	MARY departs the White House.
1867 Feb 25	ROBERT admitted to the Illinois State Bar.
1868 Sep 24	ROBERT and Mary Harlan marry in Washington (MARY and TAD are in Frankfurt, Germany).
1871	MARY and TAD return to the US.
1871 Jul 15	TAD dies in Chicago.
1875	MARY's insanity trial takes place. She is committed to a Batavia, Illinois asylum, then released some months later to the Edwards.
1881	President James A. Garfield appoints ROBERT as Secretary of War, a post in which ROBERT serves until 1885.
1882 Jul 16	MARY dies at the Edwards home.
1889	President Benjamin Harrison appoints ROBERT as ambassador to the United Kingdom, where Robert serves until 1893.
1893	ELIZABETH represents Wilberforce University at the World's Columbian Exposition in Chicago.
1907	ELIZABETH dies in Washington, DC.
1926 Jul 26	ROBERT dies at his home near Manchester, Vermont.

FURTHER READING

—ᗰ—

B ooks, articles, and websites about the Civil War and Lincoln
are numerous; many are good. The listing below contains
non-fiction books selected from a universe meeting two criteria:
the books (1) were in print when *Mrs Keckly Sends Her Regards*
came to press and (2) were deemed insightful to people, events, and
themes in the novel.

The Holy Bible King James Version.
>Widely published and the Bible that Abraham Lincoln read.

(Benson, Godfrey Rathbone) Lord Charnwood. *Abraham Lincoln.*
Dodo, 2007.
>First published in 1916 and again in print thanks to Dodo
Press, this is a classic biography of Lincoln written from a
foreigner's perspective.

Catton, Bruce. *A Stillness At Appomattox.* Garden City: Doubleday,
1953.
>Now reissued by Anchor, this Pulitzer prizewinner supplies
a haunting read of the final days of the Civil War.

Donald, David Herbert. *Lincoln.* New York: Simon & Schuster,
1996.

A superb biography that draws on the Abraham Lincoln papers conveyed to the Library of Congress by Robert Lincoln and made public in 1947.

Fleischner, Jennifer. *Mrs. Lincoln and Mrs. Keckly: The Remarkable Story of the Friendship Between a First Lady and a Former Slave*. New York: Random House, 2003.
Portrays the separate and eventually interwoven stories of Mary Todd Lincoln and Elizabeth Keckly as drawn from primary sources; a must-read for those interested in Mrs Keckly's biography.

Foote, Shelby. *The Civil War: A Narrative* (3 volumes: *Fort Sumter to Perryville; Fredericksburg to Meridian; Red River to Appomattox*). New York: Vintage, 1986.
A fine history of the American Civil War told from a Southerner's perspective.

Goodwin, Doris Kearns. *Team of Rivals: The Political Genius of Abraham Lincoln*. New York: Simon & Schuster, c. 2005.
A refreshing look at Lincoln and his cabinet, including political rivals Lincoln brought into his government.

Guelzo, Allen C. *Abraham Lincoln: Redeemer President*. Grand Rapids: Eerdmans, 2003.
An intellectual biography of Lincoln showing the significance of Lincoln's religious faith on his life, words, and actions.

Keckly, Elizabeth. *Behind the Scenes, Or, Thirty Years a Slave and Four Years in the White House*. New York: Oxford University Press, 1988.
Originally published in 1868 and again in print (thanks to Oxford); a must-read for Keckly and Lincoln White House aficionados.

Leech, Margaret. *Reveille in Washington, 1860-1865*. New York: Harper & Brothers, c. 1941.

The winner of the 1942 Pulitzer Prize in history, this very readable insight into Civil War Washington is now available as a paperback reprint from Simon Publications.

Ostendorf, Lloyd and Walter Oleksy (ed.). *Lincoln's Unknown Private Life: An Oral History by his Black Housekeeper Mariah Vance 1850-1860.* Mamaroneck, New York: Hastings House Book Publishing, c. 1995.

In *Mrs Keckly Sends Her Regards* the notion that Abraham Lincoln was baptized relies on Mrs Vance's oral history, which in any event provides fascinating insights into the Lincoln household in Springfield, Illinois.

Wagner, Margaret E., Gary W. Gallagher, and Paul Finkelman (eds.). *The Library of Congress Civil War Desk Reference.* New York: A Grand Central Press Book/Simon & Schuster, c. 2002.

An invaluable compendium of chronologies, maps, statistics, and articles covering all aspects of the Civil War (including its cultural legacy), organized topically with indexing.

White, Ronald C. Jr. *Lincoln's Greatest Speech: The Second Inaugural.* New York: Simon & Schuster, 2003.

An explication of Lincoln's March 4, 1865 inaugural address seen in the context of the events and politics of the final days of the Civil War.

LaVergne, TN USA
23 August 2010
194400LV00003B/140/A